SELECTED STORIES
OF NIKOLAI GOGOL

First Warbler Press Edition 2022

"The Fair at Sorochintsï" first published in *Evenings on a Farm Near Dikanka*, vol. 1 (1831). Translated by Constance Garnett in *Evenings on a Farm Near Dikanka*, vol. 1. London: Chatto & Windus and New York: Alfred A. Knopf (1926). | "The Viy" first published in *Mirgorod* (1835). Translated by Claud Field in *The Mantle and Other Stories*, New York: Frederick A. Stokes (1916). | "The Tale of How Ivan Ivanovich Quarreled with Ivan Nikiforovich" first published in *Mirgorod* (1835). Translated by Isabel F. Hapgood in *St. John's Eve and Other Stories*, New York: Thomas Y. Crowell & Co. (1886). | "The Diary of a Madman" first published in *Arabesques* (1835). Translated by Constance Garnett as "A Madman's Diary" in *The Overcoat and Other Stories*, London: Chatto & Windus and New York: Alfred A. Knopf (1923). | "The Nose" first published in 1835–6. Translated by Constance Garnett in *The Overcoat and Other Stories*, London: Chatto & Windus and New York: Alfred A. Knopf (1923). | "The Overcoat" first published in 1842. Translated by Constance Garnett in *The Overcoat and Other Stories*, London: Chatto & Windus and New York: Alfred A. Knopf (1923).

Afterword © 2022 Patrick Maxwell

Biographical Timeline © 2022 Warbler Press

ISBN 978-1-9572404-0-4 (paperback)
ISBN 978-1-957240-41-1 (e-book)

warblerpress.com

SELECTED STORIES OF NIKOLAI GOGOL

UKRAINIAN AND ST. PETERSBURG TALES

NIKOLAI GOGOL

SELECTED AND WITH AN AFTERWORD BY PATRICK MAXWELL

TRANSLATED BY CLAUD FIELD, CONSTANCE GARNETT, AND ISABEL F. HAPGOOD

CONTENTS

THE FAIR AT SOROCHINTSÏ

I

I am weary of the hut,
Aie, take me from my home,
To where there's noise and bustle,
To where the girls are dancing gaily,
Where the boys are making merry!

From an old ballad

How intoxicating, how magnificent is a summer day in Little Russia! How luxuriously warm the hours when midday glitters in stillness and sultry heat and the blue fathomless ocean covering the plain like a dome seems to be slumbering, bathed in languor, clasping the fair earth and holding it close in its ethereal embrace! Upon it, not a cloud; in the plain, not a sound. Everything might be dead; only above in the heavenly depths a lark is trilling, and from the airy heights the silvery notes drop down upon adoring earth, and from time to time the cry of a gull or the ringing note of a quail sounds in the steppe. The towering oaks stand, idle and apathetic, like aimless wayfarers, and the dazzling gleams of sunshine light up picturesque masses of leaves, casting onto others a shadow black as night, only flecked with gold when the wind blows. The insects of the air flit like sparks of emerald, topaz, and ruby about the gay vegetable gardens, topped by stately sunflowers. Gray haystacks and golden sheaves of wheat, like tents, stray over the plain. The broad branches of cherries, of plums, apples, and pears bent under their load of fruit, the sky with its pure mirror, the river in its green, proudly erect frame—how full of delight is the Little Russian summer!

Such was the splendor of a day in the hot August of eighteen hundred...

eighteen hundred... yes, it will be about thirty years ago, when the road eight miles beyond the village of Sorochintsy bustled with people hurrying to the fair from all the farms, far and near. From early morning, wagons full of fish and salt had trailed in an endless chain along the road. Mountains of pots wrapped in hay moved along slowly, as though weary of being shut up in the dark; only here and there a brightly painted tureen or crock boastfully peeped out from behind the hurdle that held the high pile on the wagon, and attracted wishful glances from the devotees of such luxury. Many of the passers-by looked enviously at the tall potter, the owner of these treasures, who walked slowly behind his goods, carefully wrapping his proud crocks in the alien hay that would engulf them.

On one side of the road, apart from all the rest, a team of weary oxen dragged a wagon piled up with sacks, hemp, linen, and various household goods and followed by their owner, in a clean linen shirt and dirty linen trousers. With a lazy hand he wiped from his swarthy face the streaming perspiration that even trickled from his long mustaches, powdered by the relentless barber who, uninvited, visits fair and foul alike and has for countless years forcibly sprinkled all mankind with dust. Beside him, tied to the wagon, walked a mare, whose meek air betrayed her advancing years.

Many of the passers-by, especially the young men, took off their caps as they met our peasant. But it was not his gray mustaches or his dignified step that led them to do so; one had but to raise one's eyes a little discover the reason for this deference: on the wagon was sitting his pretty daughter, with a round face, black eyebrows arching evenly above her clear brown eyes, carelessly smiling rosy lips, and with red and blue ribbons twisted in the long braids which, with a bunch of wild flowers, crowned her charming head. Everything seemed to interest her; everything was new and wonderful... and her pretty eyes were racing all the time from one object to another. She might well be diverted! It was her first visit to a fair! A girl of eighteen for the first time at a fair!... But none of the passers-by knew what it had cost her to persuade her father to bring her, though he would have been ready enough but for her spiteful stepmother, who had learned to manage him as cleverly as he drove his old mare, now as a reward for long years of service being taken to be sold. The irrepressible woman... But we are forgetting that she, too, was sitting on the top of the load dressed in a smart green woolen pelisse, adorned with little tails to imitate ermine, though they were red in color, in a gorgeous *plakhta* checked like a chessboard, and a flowered chintz cap that gave a particularly majestic air to her fat red face, the expression of which betrayed something so unpleasant and savage that everyone hastened in alarm to turn from her to the bright face of her daughter.

The river Psiol gradually came into our travelers' view; already in the distance they felt its cool freshness, the more welcome after the exhausting, wearisome heat. Through the dark and light green foliage of the birches and poplars, carelessly scattered over the plain, there were glimpses of the cold glitter of the water, and the lovely river unveiled her shining silvery bosom, over which the green tresses of the trees drooped luxuriantly. Willful as a beauty in those enchanting hours when her faithful mirror so jealously frames her brow full of pride and dazzling splendor, her lily shoulders, and her marble neck, shrouded by the dark waves of her hair, when with disdain she flings aside one ornament to replace it by another and there is no end to her whims—the river almost every year changes her course, picks out a new channel, and surrounds herself with new and varied scenes. Rows of watermills tossed up great waves with their heavy wheels and flung them violently down again, churning them into foam, scattering froth and making a great clatter. At that moment the wagon with the persons we have described reached the bridge, and the river lay before them in all her beauty and grandeur like a sheet of glass. Sky, green and dark blue forest, men, wagons of pots, watermills—all were standing or walking upside down, and not sinking into the lovely blue depths.

Our fair maiden mused, gazing at the glorious view, and even forgot to crack the sunflower seeds with which she had been busily engaged all the way, when all at once the words, "What a girl!" caught her ear. Looking around, she saw a group of young villagers standing on the bridge, of whom one, dressed rather more smartly than the others in a white jacket and gray astrakhan cap, was jauntily looking at the passers-by with his arms akimbo. The girl could not but notice his sunburnt but pleasant face and fiery eyes, which seemed to look right through her, and she lowered her eyes at the thought that he might have uttered those words.

"A fine girl!" the young man in the white jacket went on, keeping his eyes fixed on her. "I'd give all I have to kiss her. And there's a devil sitting in front!"

There were peals of laughter all around; but the slow-moving peasant's gaily dressed wife was not pleased at such a greeting: her red cheeks blazed and a torrent of choice language fell like rain on the head of the unruly youth.

"I wish you'd choke, you worthless bum! May your father crack his head on a pot! May he slip down on the ice, the damned antichrist! May the devil singe his beard in the next world!"

"Isn't she swearing!" said the young man, staring at her as though puzzled at such a sharp volley of unexpected greetings. "And she can bring her tongue to utter words like that, the witch! She's a hundred if she's a day!"

"A hundred!" the elderly charmer interrupted. "You infidel! go and wash your face! You worthless rake! I've never seen your mother, but I know she's trash. And your father is trash, and your aunt is trash! A hundred, indeed! Why, the milk is scarcely dry on his..."

At that moment the wagon began to descend from the bridge and the last words could not be heard; but, without stopping to think, he picked up a handful of mud and threw it at her. The throw achieved more than he could have hoped: the new chintz cap was spattered all over, and the laughter of the rowdy pranksters was louder than ever. The buxom charmer was boiling with rage; but by this time the wagon was far away, and she wreaked her vengeance on her innocent stepdaughter and her torpid husband, who, long since accustomed to such onslaughts, preserved a determined silence and received the stormy language of his angry spouse with indifference. In spite of all that, her tireless tongue went on clacking until they reached the house of their old friend and crony, the Cossack Tsibulya, on the outskirts of the village. The meeting of the old friends, who had not seen each other for a long time, put this unpleasant incident out of their minds for a while, as our travelers talked of the fair and rested after their long journey.

II

Good heavens! what isn't there at that fair! Wheels, window-panes, tar, tobacco, straps, onions, all sorts of haberdashery... so that even if you had thirty rubles in your purse you could not buy everything at the fair.

From a Little Russian comedy

YOU HAVE NO doubt heard a rushing waterfall when everything is quivering and filled with uproar, and a chaos of strange vague sounds floats like a whirlwind around you. Are you not instantly overcome by the same feelings in the turmoil of the village fair, when all the people become one huge monster that moves its massive body through the square and the narrow streets, with shouting, laughing, and clatter? Noise, swearing, bellowing, bleating, roaring—all blend into one jarring uproar. Oxen, sacks, hay, gypsies, pots, peasant women, cakes, caps—everything is bright, gaudy, discordant, flitting in groups, shifting to and fro before your eyes. The different voices drown one another, and not a single word can be caught, can be saved from the deluge; not one cry is distinct. Only the clapping of hands after each bargain is heard on all sides. A wagon breaks down, there is the clank of iron, the thud of boards thrown onto the ground, and one's head is so dizzy one does not know which way to turn.

The peasant whose acquaintance we have already made had been for some time elbowing his way through the crowd with his black-browed daughter; he went up to one wagonload, fingered another, inquired the prices; and meanwhile his thoughts kept revolving around his ten sacks of wheat and the old mare he had brought to sell. From his daughter's face it could be seen that she was not especially pleased to be wasting time by the wagons of flour and wheat. She longed to be where red ribbons, earrings, crosses made of copper and pewter, and coins were smartly displayed under linen awnings. But even where she was she found many objects worthy of notice: she was amused at the sight of a gypsy and a peasant, who clapped hands so that they both cried out with pain; of a drunken Jew kneeing a woman on the rump; of women hucksters quarreling with abusive words and gestures of contempt; of a Great Russian with one hand stroking his goat's beard, with another... But at that moment she felt someone pull her by the embroidered sleeve of her blouse. She looked around—and the bright-eyed young man in the white jacket stood before her. She started and her heart throbbed, as it had never done before at any joy or grief; it seemed strange and delightful, and she could not make out what had happened to her.

"Don't be frightened, dear heart, don't be frightened!" he said to her in a low voice, taking her hand. "I'll say nothing to hurt you!"

"Perhaps it is true that you will say nothing to hurt me," the girl thought to herself; "only it is strange... it might be the Evil One! One knows that it is not right... but I haven't the strength to take away my hand."

The peasant looked around and was about to say something to his daughter, but on the other side he heard the word "wheat." That magic word instantly made him join two dealers who were talking loudly, and riveted his attention upon them so that nothing could have distracted it. This is what the dealers were saying.

III

Do you see what a sort of a fellow he is?
Not many like him in the world.
Tosses off vodka like beer!

KOTLYAREVSKY, *The Aeneid*

"So YOU THINK, neighbor, that our wheat won't sell well?" said a man, who looked like an artisan of some big village, in dirty tar-stained trousers of coarse homespun material, to another, with a big bump on his forehead, wearing a dark blue jacket patched in different parts.

"It's not a matter of thinking: I am ready to put a halter around my neck and hang from that tree like a sausage in the hut before Christmas, if we sell a single bushel."

"What nonsense are you talking, neighbor? No wheat has been brought except ours," answered the man in the homespun trousers.

"Yes, you may say what you like," thought the father of our beauty, who had not missed a single word of the dealer's conversation. "I have ten sacks here in reserve."

"Well, you see, it's like this: if there is any devilry mixed up in a thing, you will get no more profit from it than a hungry Muscovite," the man with the bump on his forehead said significantly.

"What do you mean by devilry?" retorted the man in the homespun trousers.

"Did you hear what people are saying?" went on he of the bumpy forehead, giving him a sidelong look out of his gloomy eyes.

"Well?"

"Ah, you may say, well! The assessor, may he never wipe his lips again after the gentry's plum brandy, has set aside an evil spot for the fair, where you may burst before you get rid of a single grain. Do you see that old dilapidated barn which stands there, see, under the hill?" (At this point the inquisitive peasant went closer and was all attention.) "All manner of devilish tricks go on in that barn, and not a single fair has taken place in this spot without trouble. The district clerk passed it late last night and all of a sudden a pig's snout looked out from the window of the loft, and grunted so that it sent a shiver down his back. You may be sure that the *red jacket* will be seen again!"

"What's that about a red jacket?"

Our attentive listener's hair stood up on his head at these words. He looked around in alarm and saw that his daughter and the young man were calmly standing in each other's arms, murmuring soft nothings to each other and oblivious of every colored jacket in the world. This dispelled his terror and restored his equanimity.

"Aha-ha-ha, neighbor! You know how to hug a girl, it seems! I had been married three days before I learned to hug my late Khveska, and I owed that to a friend who was my best man: he gave me a hint."

The youth saw at once that his fair one's father was not very bright, and began making a plan for disposing him in his favor.

"I believe you don't know me, good friend, but I recognized you at once."

"Maybe you did."

"If you like I'll tell you your name and your surname and everything about you: your name is Solopy Cherevik."

"Yes, Solopy Cherevik."

"Well, have a good look: don't you know me?"

"No, I don't know you. No offense meant: I've seen so many faces of all sorts in my day, how the hell can one remember them all?"

"I am sorry you don't remember Golopupenko's son!"

"Why, is Okhrim your father?"

"Who else? Maybe he's the devil if he's not!"

At this the friends took off their caps and proceeded to kiss each other; our Golopupenko's son made up his mind, however, to attack his new acquaintance without loss of time.

"Well, Solopy, you see, your daughter and I have so taken to each other that we are ready to spend our lives together."

"Well, Paraska," said Cherevik, laughing and turning to his daughter; "maybe you really might, as they say... you and he... graze on the same grass! Come, shall we shake hands on it? And now, my new son-in-law, buy me a glass!"

And all three found themselves in the famous refreshment bar of the fair—a Jewess's booth, decorated with a huge assortment of jars, bottles, and flasks of every kind and description.

"Well, you are a smart fellow! I like you for that," said Cherevik, a little exhilarated, seeing how his intended son-in-law filled a pint mug and, without winking an eyelash, tossed it off at a gulp, flinging down the mug afterward and smashing it to bits. "What do you say, Paraska? Haven't I found you a fine husband? Look, look how he downs his drink!"

And laughing and staggering he went with her toward his wagon; while our young man made his way to the booths where fancy goods were displayed, where there were even dealers from Gadyach and Mirgorod, the two famous towns of the province of Poltava, to pick out the best wooden pipe in a smart copper setting, a flowered red kerchief and cap, for wedding presents to his father-in-law and everyone else who must have one.

IV

> If it's a man, it doesn't matter,
> But if there's a woman, you see
> There is need to please her.
>
> KOTLYAREVSKY

"WELL, WIFE, I have found a husband for my daughter!"

"This is a moment to look for husbands, I must say! You are a fool—a fool! It must have been ordained at your birth that you should remain one! Whoever has seen, whoever has heard of such a thing as a decent man running after husbands at a time like this? You had much better be thinking how to get your wheat off your hands. A nice young man he must be, too! I'm certain he is the shabbiest scarecrow in the place!"

"Oh, he's not anything like that! You should see what a young man he is! His jacket alone is worth more than your pelisse and red boots. And how he downs his vodka! The devil confound me and you too if ever I have seen a fellow before toss off a pint without winking!"

"To be sure, if he is a drunkard and a vagabond he is a man after your own heart. I wouldn't mind betting it's the very same rascal who pestered us on the bridge. I am sorry I haven't come across him yet: I'd let him know."

"Well, Khivrya, what if it were the same: why is he a rascal?"

"Eh! Why is he a rascal? Ah, you birdbrain! Do you hear? Why is he a rascal? Where were your stupid eyes when we were driving past the mills? They might insult his wife here, right before his snuff-clogged nose, and he would not care a damn!"

"I see no harm in him, anyway: he is a fine fellow! Except that he plastered your mug with dung for an instant."

"Aha! I see you won't let me say a word! What's the meaning of it? It's not like you! You must have managed to get a drop before you have sold anything."

Here Cherevik himself realized that he had said too much and instantly put his hands over his head, doubtless expecting that his wrathful wife would promptly seize his hair in her wifely claws.

"Go to the devil! So much for our wedding!" he thought to himself, retreating before his wife's attack. "I shall have to refuse a good fellow for no rhyme or reason. Merciful God! Why didst Thou send such a plague on us poor sinners? With so many trashy things in the world, Thou must needs go and create wives!"

V

> Droop not, plane tree,
> Still art thou green.
> Fret not, little Cossack,
> Still art thou young.
>
> *Little Russian song*

THE FELLOW IN the white jacket sitting by his wagon gazed absent-mindedly at the crowd that moved noisily about him. The weary sun, after blazing through morning and noon, was tranquilly with-drawing from the earth, and the daylight was going out in a bright lovely glow. The tops of the white booths and tents stood out with dazzling brightness, suffused in a faint rosy tint of fiery light. The panes in the window frames piled up for sale glittered; the green goblets and bottles on the tables in the drinking booths flashed like fire; the heaps of melons and pumpkins looked as though they were cast in gold and dark copper. There was less talk, and the weary tongues of merchants, peasants, and gypsies moved more slowly and deliberately. Here and there lights began gleaming, and savory steam from cooking dumplings floated over the hushed streets. "What are you grieving over, Grytsko?" a tall swarthy gypsy cried, slapping our young friend on the shoulder. "Come, let me have your oxen for twenty rubles!"

"It's nothing but oxen and oxen with you. All that you gypsies care for is profit; cheating and deceiving honest folk!"

"Tfoo, the devil! You do seem to be in trouble! You are angered at having tied yourself up with a girl, maybe?"

"No, that's not my way: I keep my word; what I have once done stands forever. But it seems that old grumbler Cherevik has not a half pint of conscience: he gave his word, but he has taken it back.... Well, it is no good blaming him: he is a blockhead and that's the fact. It's all the doing of that old witch whom we jeered at on the bridge today! Ah, if I were the Czar or some great lord I would first hang all the fools who let themselves be saddled by women...."

"Well, will you let the oxen go for twenty, if we make Cherevik give you Paraska?"

Grytsko stared at him in surprise. There was a look spiteful, malicious, ignoble, and at the same time haughty in the gypsy's swarthy face: any man looking at him would have recognized that there were great qualities in that strange soul, though their only reward on earth would be the gallows. The mouth, completely sunken between the nose and the pointed chin and forever curved in a mocking smile, the little eyes that gleamed like fire, and the lightning flashes of intrigue and enterprise forever flitting over his face—all this seemed in keeping with the strange costume he wore. The dark brown full coat which looked as though it would drop into dust at a touch; the long black hair that fell in tangled tresses on his shoulders; the shoes on his bare sunburnt feet, all seemed to be in character and part of him.

"I'll let you have them for fifteen, not twenty, if only you don't deceive me!" the young man answered, keeping his searching gaze fixed on the gypsy.

"Fifteen? Done! Mind you don't forget; fifteen! Here is a blue note as a pledge!"

"But if you deceive me?"

"If I do, the pledge is yours!"

"Right! Well, let's shake hands on the bargain!"

"Let's!"

VI

What a misfortune! Roman is coming; here he is, he'll give me a drubbing in a minute; and you, too, master Khomo, will not get off without trouble.

From a Little Russian comedy

"This way, Afanasy Ivanovich! The fence is lower here, put your foot up and don't be afraid: my idiot has gone off for the night with his crony to the wagons to see that the Muscovites don't steal anything but ill-luck."

So Cherevik's menacing spouse fondly encouraged the priest's son, who was faintheartedly clinging to the fence. He soon climbed onto the top and stood there for some time in hesitation, like a long terrible phantom, looking where he could best jump and at last coming down with a crash among the rank weeds.

"How dreadful! I hope you have not hurt yourself? Please God, you've not broken your neck!" Khivrya faltered anxiously.

"Sh! It's all right, it's all right, dear Khavronya Nikiforovna," the priest's son brought out in a painful whisper, getting onto his feet, "except for being afflicted by the nettles, that serpentlike weed, to use the words of our late head priest."

"Let us go into the house; there is nobody there. I was beginning to think you were ill or asleep, Afanasy Ivanovich: you did not come and did not come. How are you? I hear that your honored father has had a run of good luck!"

"Nothing to speak of, Khavronya Nikiforovna: during the whole fast Father has received nothing but fifteen sacks of spring wheat, four sacks of millet, a hundred buns; and as for fowls they don't amount to fifty, and the eggs were mostly rotten. But the truly sweet offerings, so to say, can only come from you, Khavronya Nikiforovna!" the priest's son continued, with a tender glance at her as he edged nearer.

"Here is an offering for you, Afanasy Ivanovich!" she said, setting some bowls on the table and coyly fastening the buttons of her jacket as though they had not been undone on purpose, "curd doughnuts, wheaten dumplings, buns, and cakes!"

"I bet they have been made by the cleverest hands of any daughter of Eve!" said the priest's son, setting to work upon the cakes and with the other hand drawing the curd doughnuts toward him.

"Though indeed, Khavronya Nikiforovna, my heart thirsts for a gift from you sweeter than any buns or dumplings!"

"Well, I don't know what dainty you will ask for next, Afanasy Ivanovich!" answered the buxom beauty, pretending not to understand.

"Your love, of course, incomparable Khavronya Nikiforovna!" the priest's son whispered, holding a doughnut in one hand and encircling her ample waist with his arm.

"Goodness knows what you are thinking about, Afanasy Ivanovich!" said Khivrya, bashfully casting down her eyes. "Why, I wouldn't be surprised if you tried to kiss me next!"

"As for that, I must tell you," the young man went on. "When I was still at the seminary, I remember as though it were today..."

At that moment there was a sound of barking and a knock at the gate. Khivrya ran out quickly and came back looking pale.

"Afanasy Ivanovich, we are caught: there are a lot of people knocking, and I think I heard Tsibulya's voice..."

A dumpling stuck in the young man's throat.... His eyes almost popped out of his head, as though someone had just come from the other world to visit him.

"Climb up here!" cried the panic-stricken Khivrya, pointing to some boards that lay across the rafters just below the ceiling, loaded with all sorts of domestic odds and ends.

Danger gave our hero courage. Recovering a little, he clambered on the stove and from there climbed cautiously onto the boards, while Khivrya ran headlong to the gate, as the knocking was getting louder and more insistent.

VII

But here are miracles, gentlemen!

From a Little Russian comedy

A STRANGE INCIDENT had taken place at the fair: there were rumors all over the place that the *red jacket* had been seen somewhere among the wares. The old woman who sold pretzels thought she saw the devil in the shape of a pig, bending over the wagons as though looking for something. The news soon flew to every corner of the now resting camp, and everyone would have thought it a crime to disbelieve it, in spite of the fact that the pretzel seller, whose stall was next to the drinking booth, had been staggering about all day and could not walk straight. To this was added the story—by now greatly exaggerated—of the wonder seen by the district clerk in the dilapidated barn; so toward night people were all huddling together; their peace of mind was destroyed, and everyone was too terrified to close an eye; while those who were not cast in a heroic mold, and had secured a night's lodging in a hut, made their way homeward. Among the latter were Cherevik with his daughter and his friend Tsibulya, and they, together with the friends who had offered to keep them company, were responsible for the loud knocking that had so alarmed Khivrya. Tsibulya was already a little exhilarated. This could be seen from his twice driving around the yard with his wagon before he could find the hut. His guests, too, were all rather merry, and they unceremoniously pushed into the hut before their host. Our Cherevik's wife sat as though on thorns, when they began rummaging in every corner of the hut.

"Well, gossip," cried Tsibulya as he entered, "you are still shaking with fever?"

"Yes, I am not well," answered Khivrya, looking uneasily toward the boards on the rafters.

"Come, wife, get the bottle out of the wagon!" said Tsibulya to his wife, who had come in with him, "we will empty it with these good folk, for the damned women have given us such a scare that one is ashamed to admit it. Yes, friends, there was really no sense in our coming here!" he went on, taking a pull out of an earthenware jug. "I don't mind betting a new cap that the women thought they would have a laugh at us. Why, if it were Satan— who's Satan? Spit on him! If he stood here before me this very minute, I'll be a son of a bitch if I wouldn't make a fig at him!"

"Why did you turn so pale, then?" cried one of the visitors, who was a head taller than any of the rest and tried on every occasion to display his valor.

"I?... Bless you! Are you dreaming?"

The visitors laughed; the boastful hero smiled complacently.

"As though he could turn pale now!" put in another; "his cheeks are as red as a poppy; he is not a Tsibulya now, but a beet—or, rather, the *red jacket* itself that frightened us all so."

The bottle went the round of the table, and made the visitors more exhilarated than ever. At this point Cherevik, greatly disturbed about the *red jacket*, which would not let his inquisitive mind rest, appealed to his friend:

"Come, friend, kindly tell me! I keep asking about this damned *jacket* and can get no answer from anyone!"

"Eh, friend, it's not a thing to talk about at night; however, to satisfy you and these good friends" (saying this he turned toward his guests) "who want, I see, to know about these strange doings as much as you do. Well, so be it. Listen!"

Here he scratched his shoulder, mopped his face with the skirt of his coat, leaned both arms on the table, and began:

"Once upon a time a devil was kicked out of hell, what for I cannot say..."

"How so, friend?" Cherevik interrupted. "How could it be that a devil was turned out of hell?"

"I can't help it, crony, if he was turned out, he was—as a peasant turns a dog out of his hut. Perhaps a whim came over him to do a good deed—and so they showed him the door. And the poor devil was so homesick, so homesick for hell that he was ready to hang himself. Well, what could he do about it? In his trouble he took to drink. He settled in the broken-down barn which you have seen at the bottom of the hill and which no good man will pass now without making the sign of the cross as a safeguard; and the devil became such a rake you would not find another like him among the fellows: he sat day and night in the tavern!"

At this point Cherevik interrupted again:

"Goodness knows what you are saying, friend! How could anyone let a devil into a tavern? Why, thank God, he has claws on his paws and horns on his head."

"Ah, that was just it—he had a cap and gloves on. Who could recognize him? Well, he kept it up till he had drunk away all he had with him. They gave him credit for a long time, but at last they would give no more. The devil had to pawn his red jacket for less than a third of its value to the Jew who sold vodka in those days at Sorochintsy. He pawned it and said to him: "Mind now, Jew, I shall come to you for my jacket in a year's time; take care of it!" And he disappeared and no more was seen of him. The Jew examined the coat thoroughly: the cloth was better than anything you could get in Mirgorod, and the red of it glowed like fire, so that one could not take one's eyes off it! And it seemed to the Jew a long time to wait till the end of the year. He scratched his earlocks and got nearly five gold pieces for it from a gentleman who was passing by. The Jew forgot all about the date set. But all of a sudden one evening a man turns up: "Come, Jew, hand me over my jacket!" At first the Jew did not know him, but afterward when he had had a good look at him, he pretended he had never seen him before. "What jacket? I have no jacket. I know nothing about your jacket!" The other walked away; only, when the Jew locked himself up in his room and, after counting over the money in his chests, flung a sheet around his shoulders and began saying his prayers in Jewish fashion, all at once he heard a rustle... and there were pigs' snouts looking in at every window."

At that moment an indistinct sound not unlike the grunt of a pig was audible; everyone turned pale. Drops of sweat stood out on Tsibulya's face.

"What was it?" cried the panic-stricken Cherevik.

"Nothing," answered Tsibulya, trembling all over.

"Eh?" responded one of the guests.

"Did you speak?"

"No!"

"Who was it grunted?"

"God knows why we are so flustered! It's nothing!"

They all turned about fearfully and began rummaging in the corners. Khivrya was more dead than alive.

"Oh, you are a bunch of women!" she shouted. "You are not fit to be Cossacks and men! You ought to sit spinning yarn! Maybe someone misbehaved, God forgive him, or someone's bench creaked, and you are all in a fluster as though you were out of your heads!"

This put our heroes to shame and made them pull themselves together. Tsibulya took a pull at the jug and went on with his story.

"The Jew fainted from terror; but the pigs with legs as long as stilts climbed in at the windows and so revived him in an instant with a three-thonged whip, making him skip higher than this ceiling. The Jew fell at their feet and confessed everything.... Only the jacket could not be restored in a hurry. The gentleman had been robbed of it on the road by a gypsy who sold it to a peddler woman, and she brought it back again to the fair at Sorochintsy; but no one would buy anything from her after that. The woman wondered and wondered and at last saw what it was: there was no doubt the red jacket was at the bottom of it; it was not for nothing that she had felt stifled when she put it on. Without stopping to think she flung it in the fire—the devilish thing would not burn!... "Ah, that's a gift from the devil!" she thought. The woman managed to thrust it into the wagon of a peasant who had come to the fair to sell his butter. The silly fellow was delighted; but no one would ask for his butter. "Ah, it's an evil hand foisted that red jacket on me!" He took his ax and chopped it into bits; he looked at it—and each bit joined up to the next till it was whole again! Crossing himself, he went at it with the ax again; he flung the bits all over the place and went away. But ever since then, just at the time of the fair, the devil walks all over the market place with the face of a pig, grunting and collecting the pieces of his jacket. Now they say there is only the left sleeve missing. People have been shy of the place ever since, and it is ten years since the fair has been held on it. But in an evil hour the assessor..."

The rest of the sentence died away on the speaker's lips: there was a loud rattle at the window, the panes fell tinkling on the floor, and a frightening pig's snout peered in through the window, rolling its eyes as though asking, "What are you doing here, folks?"

VIII

His tail between his legs like a dog,
Like Cain, trembling all over;
The snuff dropped from his nose.

KOTLYAREVSKY, *The Aeneid*

EVERYONE IN THE room was numb with horror. Tsibulya sat petrified with his mouth open; his eyes were bulging as if he wanted to shoot with them; his outspread fingers were frozen in the air. The tall hero, in overwhelming terror, leaped up and struck his head against the rafter; the boards shifted, and with a thud and a crash the priest's son fell to the floor.

"Aie, aie, aie!" one of the party screamed desperately, flopping on the locker in alarm, and waving his arms and legs.

"Save me!" wailed another, hiding his head under a sheepskin.

Tsibulya, roused from his numbness by this second horror, crept shuddering under his wife's skirts. The valiant hero crawled into the oven in spite of the narrowness of the opening, and closed the oven door on himself. And Cherevik, clapping a basin on his head instead of a cap, dashed to the door as though he had been scalded, and ran through the streets like a lunatic, not knowing where he was going; only weariness caused him to slacken his pace. His heart was thumping like an oil press; streams of perspiration rolled down him. He was on the point of sinking to the ground in exhaustion when all at once he heard someone running after him.... His breath failed him.

"The devil! The devil!" came a shout behind him, and all he felt was something falling with a thud on the top of him. Then his senses deserted him and, like the dread inmate of a narrow coffin, he remained lying dumb and motionless in the middle of the road.

IX

In front, like anyone else;
Behind, I swear, like a devil!

From a folk tale

"Do you hear, Vlas?" one of the crowd asleep in the street said, sitting up; "someone spoke of the devil near us!"

"What is it to me?" the gypsy near him grumbled, stretching. "They may talk of all their kindred for all I care!"

"But he bawled, you know, as though he were being strangled!"

"A man will cry out anything in his sleep!"

"Say what you like, we must have a look. Strike a light!"

The other gypsy, grumbling to himself, rose to his feet, sent a shower of sparks flying like lightning flashes, blew the tinder with his lips, and with a *kaganets* in his hands—the usual Little Russian lamp consisting of a broken pot full of mutton fat—set off, lighting the way before him.

"Stop! There is something lying here! Show a light this way!"

Here they were joined by several others.

"What's lying there, Vlas?"

"Why, it looks like two men: one on top, the other under. Which of them is the devil I can't make out yet!"

"Why, who is on top?"

"A woman!"

"Oh, well, then that's the devil!"

A general shout of laughter roused almost the whole street.

"A woman straddling a man! I suppose she knows how to ride!" one of the bystanders exclaimed.

"Look, boys!" said another, picking up a broken piece of the basin of which only one half still remained on Cherevik's head, "what a cap this fine fellow put on!"

The growing noise and laughter brought our corpses to life, and Cherevik and his spouse, full of the panic they had known, gazed with bulging eyes in terror at the swarthy faces of the gypsies; in the dim and flickering light they looked like a wild horde of dark subterranean creatures, reeking of hell.

X

Fie upon you, away with you, image of the Devil!
From a Little Russian comedy

THE FRESHNESS OF morning breathed over the awakening folk of Sorochintsy. Clouds of smoke from all the chimneys floated to meet the rising sun. The fair began to hum with life. Sheep were bleating, horses neighing; the cackle of geese and peddler women sounded all over the encampment again—and terrible tales of the *red jacket*, which had roused such alarm in the mysterious hours of darkness, vanished with the return of morning.

Stretching and yawning, Cherevik lay drowsily under his friend Tsibulya's thatched barn among oxen and sacks of flour and wheat. And apparently he had no desire to part with his dreams, when all at once he heard a voice, familiar as his own stove, the blessed refuge of his lazy hours, or as the tavern kept by his cousin not ten paces from his own door.

"Get up, get up!" his tender wife squeaked in his ear, tugging at his arm with all her might.

Cherevik, instead of answering, blew out his cheeks and began waving his hands, as though beating a drum.

"Idiot!" she shouted, retreating out of reach of his arms, which almost struck her in the face.

Cherevik sat up, rubbed his eyes, and looked about him.

"The devil take me, my dear, if I didn't imagine that your face was a drum on which I was forced to beat an alarm, like a soldier, by those pig-faces that Tsibulya was telling us about...."

"Stop talking nonsense! Go, make haste and take the mare to market! We are a laughingstock, upon my word: we've come to the fair and not sold a handful of hemp...."

"Of course, wife," Cherevik agreed, "they will laugh at us now, to be sure."

"Go along, go along! They are laughing at you as it is!"

"You see, I haven't washed yet," Cherevik went on, yawning, scratching his back, and trying to gain time.

"What a moment to be fussy about cleanliness! When have you cared about that? Here's the towel, wipe your ugly face."

Here she snatched up something that lay crumpled up—and darted back in horror: it was the cuff of a red jacket!

"Go along and get to work," she repeated, recovering herself, on seeing that her husband was motionless with terror and his teeth were chattering.

"A fine sale there will be now!" he muttered to himself as he untied the mare and led her to the market place. "It was not for nothing that, while I was getting ready for this cursed fair, my heart was as heavy as though someone had put a dead cow on my back, and twice the oxen turned homeward of their own accord. And now that I come to think of it, I do believe it was Monday when we started. And so everything has gone wrong! And the damned devil can never be satisfied: he might have worn his jacket without one sleeve—but no, he can't let honest folk rest in peace. Now if I were the devil—God forbid—do you suppose I'd go hanging around at night after a lot of damned rags?"

Here our Cherevik's meditations were interrupted by a thick harsh voice. Before him stood a tall gypsy.

"What have you for sale, good man?"

Cherevik was silent for a moment; he looked at the gypsy from head to foot and said with unruffled composure, neither stopping nor letting go the bridle:

"You can see for yourself what I am selling."

"Harness?" said the gypsy, looking at the bridle which the other had in his hand.

"Yes, harness, if a mare is the same thing as harness."

"But damn it, neighbor, one would think you had fed her on straw!"

"Straw?"

Here Cherevik would have pulled at the bridle to lead his mare forward and convict the shameless slanderer of his lie; but his hand slipped and struck his own chin. He looked—in it was a severed bridle, and tied to the bridle—oh horror! his hair stood up on his head—a piece of a red sleeve!... Spitting, crossing himself, and brandishing his arms, he ran away from the unexpected gift and, running faster than a boy, vanished in the crowd.

XI

For my own corn I have been beaten.

Proverb

"CATCH HIM! CATCH him!" cried several young men at a narrow street corner, and Cherevik felt himself suddenly seized by strong hands.

"Tie him up! That's the fellow who stole an honest man's mare."

"Damn it! What are you tieing me up for?"

"Imagine his asking! Why did you want to steal a mare from a peasant at the fair, Cherevik?"

"You're out of your minds, fellows! Who has ever heard of a man stealing from himself?"

"That's an old trick! An old trick! Why were you running your hardest, as though the devil were on your heels?"

"Anyone would run when the devil's garment..."

"Aie, my good soul, try that on others! You'll catch it yet from the court assessor, to teach you to go scaring people with tales of the devil."

"Catch him! catch him!" came a shout from the other end of the street. "There he is, there is the runaway!"

And Cherevik beheld his friend Tsibulya in the most pitiful plight with his hands tied behind him, led along by several young men.

"Strange things are happening!" said one of them. "You should hear what this scoundrel says! You have only to look at his face to see he is a thief. When we began asking him why he was running like one possessed, he says he put his hand in his pocket and instead of his snuff pulled out a bit of the devil's jacket and it burst into a red flame—and he took to his heels!"

"Aha! why, these two are birds of a feather! We had better tie them together!"

XII

"In what am I to blame, good folks?
Why are you beating me?" said our poor wretch.
"Why are you falling upon me?
What for, what for?" he said, bursting into tears,
Streams of bitter tears, and clutching at his sides.
                    ARTEMOVSKY-GULAK, *Master and Dog*

"MAYBE YOU REALLY have picked up something, friend?" Cherevik asked, as he lay bound beside Tsibulya in a thatched shanty.

"You too, friend! May my arms and legs wither if ever I stole anything in my life, except maybe buns and cream from my mother, and that only before I was ten years old."

"Why has this trouble come upon us? It's not so bad for you: you are charged, anyway, with stealing from somebody else; but what have I, unlucky wretch, done to deserve such a foul slander, as stealing my mare from myself? It seems it was written at our birth that we should have no luck!"

"Woe to us, forlorn and forsaken!"

At this point the two friends fell to weeping violently.

"What's the matter with you, Cherevik?" said Grytsko, entering at that moment. "Who tied you up like that?"

"Ah, Golopupenko, Golopupenko!" cried Cherevik, delighted. "Here, this is the fellow I was telling you about. Ah, he is a smart one! God strike me dead on the spot if he did not toss off a whole jug, almost as big as your head, and never turned a hair!"

"What made you ignore such a fine fellow, then, friend?"

"Here, you see," Cherevik went on, addressing Grytsko, "God has punished me, it seems, for having wronged you. Forgive me, good lad! I swear I'd be glad to do anything for you.... But what would you have me do? There's the devil in my old woman!"

"I am not one to hold a grudge, Cherevik! If you like, I'll set you free!"

Here he made a sign to the other fellows and the same ones who were guarding them ran to untie them.

"Then you must do your part, too: a wedding! And let us keep it up so that our legs ache with dancing for a year afterwards!"

"Good, good!" said Cherevik, striking his hands together. "I feel as pleased as though the soldiers had carried off my old woman! Why give it another thought? Whether she likes it or not, the wedding shall be today—and that's all there is to it!"

"Mind now, Solopy: in an hour's time I will be with you; but now go home—there you will find purchasers for your mare and your wheat."

"What! has the mare been found?"

"Yes."

Cherevik was struck dumb with joy and stood still, gazing after Grytsko.

"Well, Grytsko, have we mishandled the job?" said the tall gypsy to the hurrying young man. "The oxen are mine now, aren't they?"

"Yours! yours!"

XIII

Fear not, fear not, little mother,
Put on your red boots
Trample your foes
Under foot
So that your ironshod
Heels may clang,
So that your foes
May be hushed and still.

A wedding song

PARASKA MUSED, SITTING alone in the hut with her pretty chin propped on her hand. Many dreams hovered about her little head. At times a faint smile stirred her crimson lips and some joyful feeling lifted her dark brows, while at times a cloud of pensiveness set them frowning above her clear brown eyes.

"But what if it does not come true as he said?" she whispered with an expression of doubt. "What if they don't let me marry him? If... No, no; that will not be! My stepmother does just as she likes; why mayn't I do as I like? I've plenty of obstinacy too. How handsome he is! How wonderfully his black eyes glow! How delightfully he says, "Paraska darling!" How his white jacket suits him! But his belt ought to be a bit brighter!... I will weave him one when we settle in a new hut. I can't help being pleased when I think," she went on, taking from her bosom a little red-paper-framed mirror bought at the fair and gazing into it, "how I shall meet her one day somewhere and she may burst before I bow to her, nothing will induce me. No, stepmother, you've kicked me for the last time. The sand will rise up on the rocks and the oak bend down to the water like a willow before I bow down before you. But I was forgetting... let me try on a cap, even if it has to be my stepmother's, and see how it suits me to look like a wife?"

Then she got up, holding the mirror in her hand and bending her head down to it, walked in excitement about the room, as though in dread of falling, seeing below her, instead of the floor, the ceiling with the boards laid on the rafters from which the priest's son had so lately dropped, and the shelves set with pots.

"Why, I am like a child," she cried, "afraid to take a step!"

And she began tapping with her feet, growing bolder as she went on;

at last she laid her left hand on her hip and went off into a dance, clinking with her metaled heels, holding the mirror before her, and singing her favorite song:

> Little green periwinkle,
>   Twine lower to me!
> And you, black-browed dear one,
>   Come nearer to me!
> Little green periwinkle,
>   Twine lower to me!
> And you, black-browed dear one,
>   Come nearer to me!

At that moment Cherevik peeped in at the door, and seeing his daughter dancing before the mirror, he stood still. For a long time he watched, laughing at the innocent prank of his daughter, who was apparently so absorbed that she noticed nothing; but when he heard the familiar notes of the song, his muscles began working: he stepped forward, his arms jauntily akimbo, and forgetting all he had to do, began dancing. A loud shout of laughter from his friend Tsibulya startled both of them.

"Here is a pretty thing! The dad and his daughter getting up a wedding on their own account! Make haste and come along: the bridegroom has arrived!"

At the last words Paraska flushed a deeper crimson than the ribbon which bound her head, and her lighthearted parent remembered his errand.

"Well, daughter, let us make haste! Khivrya is so pleased that I have sold the mare," he went on, looking timorously about him, "that she has run off to buy herself aprons and all sorts of rags, so we must get it all over before she is back."

Paraska had no sooner stepped over the threshold than she felt herself caught in the arms of the young man in the white jacket who with a crowd of people was waiting for her in the street.

"God bless you!" said Cherevik, joining their hands. "May their lives together cleave as the wreaths of flowers they weave."

At this point a hubbub was heard in the crowd.

"I'd burst before I'd allow it!" screamed Cherevik's helpmate, who was being shoved back by the laughing crowd.

"Don't excite yourself, wife!" Cherevik said coolly, seeing that two sturdy gypsies held her hands, "what is done can't be undone: I don't like going back on a bargain!"

"No, no, that shall never be!" screamed Khivrya, but no one heeded her; several couples surrounded the happy pair and formed an impenetrable dancing wall around them.

A strange feeling, hard to put into words, would have overcome anyone watching how the whole crowd was transformed into a scene of unity and harmony, at one stroke of the bow of the fiddler, who had long twisted mustaches and wore a homespun jacket. Men whose sullen faces seemed to have known no gleam of a smile for years were tapping with their feet and wriggling their shoulders; everything was heaving, everything was dancing. But an even stranger and more disturbing feeling would have been stirred in the heart at the sight of old women, whose ancient faces breathed the indifference of the tomb, shoving their way between the young, laughing, living human beings. Caring for nothing, indifferent, long removed from the joy of childhood, wanting only drink, it was as if a puppeteer were tugging the strings that held his wooden puppets, making them do things that seemed human; yet they slowly wagged their drunken heads, dancing after the rejoicing crowd, not casting one glance at the young couple.

The sounds of laughter, song, and uproar grew fainter and fainter. The strains of the fiddle were lost in vague and feeble notes, and died away in the wind. In the distance there was still the sound of dancing feet, something like the faraway murmur of the sea, and soon all was stillness and emptiness again.

Is it not thus that joy, lovely and fleeting guest, flies from us? In vain the last solitary note tries to express gaiety. In its own echo it hears melancholy and emptiness and listens to it, bewildered. Is it not thus that those who have been playful friends in free and stormy youth, one by one stray, lost, about the world and leave their old comrade lonely and forlorn at last? Sad is the lot of one left behind! Heavy and sorrowful is his heart and nothing can help him!

THE VIY

The "Viy" is a monstrous creation of popular fancy. It is the name which the inhabitants of Little Russia give to the king of the gnomes, whose eyelashes reach to the ground. The following story is a specimen of such folk-lore. I have made no alterations, but reproduce it in the same simple form in which I heard it.—Author's Note.

I

As soon as the clear seminary bell began sounding in Kiev in the morning, the pupils would come flocking from all parts of the town. The students of grammar, rhetoric, philosophy, and theology hastened with their books under their arms over the streets.

The "grammarians" were still mere boys. On the way they pushed against each other and quarreled with shrill voices. Nearly all of them wore torn or dirty clothes, and their pockets were always crammed with all kinds of things—push-bones, pipes made out of pens, remains of confectionery, and sometimes even young sparrows. The latter would sometimes begin to chirp in the midst of deep silence in the school, and bring down on their possessors severe canings and thrashings.

The "rhetoricians" walked in a more orderly way. Their clothes were generally untorn, but on the other hand their faces were often strangely decorated; one had a black eye, and the lips of another resembled a single blister, etc. These spoke to each other in tenor voices.

The "philosophers" talked in a tone an octave lower; in their pockets they only had fragments of tobacco, never whole cakes of it; for what they could get hold of, they used at once. They smelt so strongly of tobacco and brandy, that a workman passing by them would often remain standing and sniffing with his nose in the air, like a hound.

About this time of day the marketplace was generally full of bustle, and the market women, selling rolls, cakes, and honey-tarts, plucked the sleeves of those who wore coats of fine cloth or cotton.

"Young sir! Young sir! Here! Here!" they cried from all sides. "Rolls and cakes and tasty tarts, very delicious! I have baked them myself!"

Another drew something long and crooked out of her basket and cried, "Here is a sausage, young sir! Buy a sausage!"

"Don't buy anything from her!" cried a rival. "See how greasy she is, and what a dirty nose and hands she has!"

But the market women carefully avoided appealing to the philosophers and theologians, for these only took handfuls of eatables merely to taste them.

Arrived at the seminary, the whole crowd of students dispersed into the low, large classrooms with small windows, broad doors, and blackened benches. Suddenly they were filled with a many-toned murmur. The teachers heard the pupils' lessons repeated, some in shrill and others in deep voices which sounded like a distant booming. While the lessons were being said, the teachers kept a sharp eye open to see whether pieces of cake or other dainties were protruding from their pupils' pockets; if so, they were promptly confiscated.

When this learned crowd arrived somewhat earlier than usual, or when it was known that the teachers would come somewhat late, a battle would ensue, as though planned by general agreement. In this battle all had to take part, even the monitors who were appointed to look after the order and morality of the whole school. Two theologians generally arranged the conditions of the battle: whether each class should split into two sides, or whether all the pupils should divide themselves into two halves.

In each case the grammarians began the battle, and after the rhetoricians had joined in, the former retired and stood on the benches, in order to watch the fortunes of the fray. Then came the philosophers with long black moustaches, and finally the thick-necked theologians. The battle generally ended in a victory for the latter, and the philosophers retired to the different classrooms rubbing their aching limbs, and throwing themselves on the benches to take breath.

When the teacher, who in his own time had taken part in such contests, entered the classroom he saw by the heated faces of his pupils that the battle had been very severe, and while he caned the hands of the rhetoricians, in another room another teacher did the same for the philosophers.

On Sundays and Festival Days the seminarists took puppet-theatres to the citizens' houses. Sometimes they acted a comedy, and in that case it was always a theologian who took the part of the hero or heroine—Potiphar or Herodias, etc. As a reward for their exertions, they received a piece of linen, a sack of maize, half a roast goose, or something similar. All the students, lay and clerical, were very poorly provided with means for procuring themselves necessary subsistence, but at the same time very fond of eating; so that, however much food was given to them, they were never satisfied, and the gifts bestowed by rich landowners were never adequate for their needs.

Therefore the Commissariat Committee, consisting of philosophers and theologians, sometimes dispatched the grammarians and rhetoricians under the leadership of a philosopher—themselves sometimes joining in the expedition—with sacks on their shoulders, into the town, in order to levy a contribution on the fleshpots of the citizens, and then there was a feast in the seminary.

The most important event in the seminary year was the arrival of the holidays; these began in July, and then generally all the students went home. At that time all the roads were thronged with grammarians, rhetoricians, philosophers, and theologians. He who had no home of his own, would take up his quarters with some fellow-student's family; the philosophers and theologians looked out for tutors' posts, taught the children of rich farmers, and received for doing so a pair of new boots and sometimes also a new coat.

A whole troop of them would go off in close ranks like a regiment; they cooked their porridge in common, and encamped under the open sky. Each had a bag with him containing a shirt and a pair of socks. The theologians were especially economical; in order not to wear out their boots too quickly, they took them off and carried them on a stick over their shoulders, especially when the road was very muddy. Then they tucked up their breeches over their knees and waded bravely through the pools and puddles. Whenever they spied a village near the highway, they at once left it, approached the house which seemed the most considerable, and began with loud voices to sing a psalm. The master of the house, an old Cossack engaged in agriculture, would listen for a long time with his head propped in his hands, then with tears on his cheeks say to his wife, "What the students are singing sounds very devout; bring out some lard and anything else of the kind we have in the house."

After thus replenishing their stores, the students would continue their way. The farther they went, the smaller grew their numbers, as they dispersed to their various houses, and left those whose homes were still farther on.

On one occasion, during such a march, three students left the main-road in order to get provisions in some village, since their stock had long been exhausted. This party consisted of the theologian Khalava, the philosopher Thomas Brutus, and the rhetorician Tiberius Gorobetz.

The first was a tall youth with broad shoulders and of a peculiar character; everything which came within reach of his fingers he felt obliged to appropriate. Moreover, he was of a very melancholy disposition, and when he had got intoxicated he hid himself in the most tangled thickets so that the seminary officials had the greatest trouble in finding him.

The philosopher Thomas Brutus was a more cheerful character. He liked to lie for a long time on the same spot and smoke his pipe; and when he was merry with wine, he hired a fiddler and danced the *tropak*. Often he got a whole quantity of "beans," i.e. thrashings; but these he endured with complete philosophic calm, saying that a man cannot escape his destiny.

The rhetorician Tiberius Gorobetz had not yet the right to wear a moustache, to drink brandy, or to smoke tobacco. He only wore a small crop of hair, as though his character was at present too little developed. To judge by the great bumps on his forehead, with which he often appeared in the classroom, it might be expected that some day he would be a valiant fighter. Khalava and Thomas often pulled his hair as a mark of their special favour, and sent him on their errands.

Evening had already come when they left the highroad; the sun had just gone down, and the air was still heavy with the heat of the day. The theologian and the philosopher strolled along, smoking in silence, while the rhetorician struck off the heads of the thistles by the wayside with his stick. The way wound on through thick woods of oak and walnut; green hills alternated here and there with meadows. Twice already they had seen cornfields, from which they concluded that they were near some village; but an hour had already passed, and no human habitation appeared. The sky was already quite dark, and only a red gleam lingered on the western horizon.

"The deuce!" said the philosopher Thomas Brutus. "I was almost certain we would soon reach a village."

The theologian still remained silent, looked round him, then put his pipe again between his teeth, and all three continued their way.

"Good heavens!" exclaimed the philosopher, and stood still. "Now the road itself is disappearing."

"Perhaps we shall find a farm farther on," answered the theologian, without taking his pipe out of his mouth.

Meanwhile the night had descended; clouds increased the darkness, and according to all appearance there was no chance of moon or stars appearing. The seminarists found that they had lost the way altogether.

After the philosopher had vainly sought for a footpath, he exclaimed, "Where have we got to?"

The theologian thought for a while, and said, "Yes, it is really dark."

The rhetorician went on one side, lay on the ground, and groped for a path; but his hands encountered only foxholes. All around lay a huge steppe over which no one seemed to have passed. The wanderers made several efforts to get forward, but the landscape grew wilder and more inhospitable.

The philosopher tried to shout, but his voice was lost in vacancy, no one answered; only, some moments later, they heard a faint groaning sound, like the whimpering of a wolf.

"Curse it all! What shall we do?" said the philosopher.

"Why, just stop here, and spend the night in the open air," answered the theologian. So saying, he felt in his pocket, brought out his timber and steel, and lit his pipe.

But the philosopher could not agree with this proposal; he was not accustomed to sleep till he had first eaten five pounds of bread and five of dripping, and so he now felt an intolerable emptiness in his stomach. Besides, in spite of his cheerful temperament, he was a little afraid of the wolves.

"No, Khalava," he said, "that won't do. To lie down like a dog and without any supper! Let us try once more; perhaps we shall find a house, and the consolation of having a glass of brandy to drink before going to sleep."

At the word "brandy," the theologian spat on one side and said, "Yes, of course, we cannot remain all night in the open air."

The students went on and on, and to their great joy they heard the barking of dogs in the distance. After listening a while to see from which direction the barking came, they went on their way with new courage, and soon espied a light.

"A village, by heavens, a village!" exclaimed the philosopher.

His supposition proved correct; they soon saw two or three houses built round a courtyard. Lights glimmered in the windows, and before the fence stood a number of trees. The students looked through the crevices of the gates and saw a courtyard in which stood a large number of roving trades- men's carts. In the sky there were now fewer clouds, and here and there a star was visible.

"See, brother!" one of them said, "we must now cry 'halt!' Cost what it may, we must find entrance and a night's lodging."

The three students knocked together at the gate, and cried "Open!"

The door of one of the houses creaked on its hinges, and an old woman wrapped in a sheepskin appeared. "Who is there?" she exclaimed, coughing loudly.

"Let us spend the night here, mother; we have lost our way, our stom- achs are empty, and we do not want to spend the night out of doors."

"But what sort of people are you?"

"Quite harmless people; the theologian Khalava, the philosopher Brutus, and the rhetorician Gorobetz."

"It is impossible," answered the old woman. "The whole house is full of people, and every corner occupied. Where can I put you up? You are big and heavy enough to break the house down. I know these philosophers and theologians; when once one takes them in, they eat one out of house and home. Go farther on! There is no room here for you!"

"Have pity on us, mother! How can you be so heartless? Don't let Christians perish. Put us up where you like, and if we eat up your provisions, or do any other damage, may our hands wither up, and all the punishment of heaven light on us!"

The old woman seemed a little touched. "Well," she said after a few moments' consideration, "I will let you in; but I must put you in different rooms, for I should have no quiet if you were all together at night."

"Do just as you like; we won't say any more about it," answered the students.

The gates moved heavily on their hinges, and they entered the courtyard.

"Well now, mother," said the philosopher, following the old woman, "if you had a little scrap of something! By heavens! my stomach is as empty as a drum. I have not had a bit of bread in my mouth since early this morning!"

"Didn't I say so?" replied the old woman. "There you go begging at once. But I have no food in the house, nor any fire."

"But we will pay for everything," continued the philosopher.

"We will pay early tomorrow in cash."

"Go on and be content with what you get. You are fine fellows whom the devil has brought here!"

Her reply greatly depressed the philosopher Thomas; but suddenly his nose caught the odour of dried fish; he looked at the breeches of the theologian, who walked by his side, and saw a huge fish's tail sticking out of his pocket. The latter had already seized the opportunity to steal a whole fish from one of the carts standing in the courtyard. He had not done this from hunger so much as from the force of habit. He had quite forgotten the fish, and was looking about to see whether he could not find something else to appropriate. Then the philosopher put his hand in the theologian's pocket as though it were his own, and laid hold of his prize.

The old woman found a special resting-place for each student; the rhetorician she put in a shed, the theologian in an empty storeroom, and the philosopher in a sheep's stall.

As soon as the philosopher was alone, he devoured the fish in a twinkling, examined the fence which enclosed the stall, kicked away a pig from a neighbouring stall, which had inquiringly inserted its nose through a crevice, and lay down on his right side to sleep like a corpse.

Then the low door opened, and the old woman came crouching into the stall.

"Well, mother, what do you want here?" asked the philosopher.

She made no answer, but came with outstretched arms towards him.

The philosopher shrank back; but she still approached, as though she wished to lay hold of him. A terrible fright seized him, for he saw the old hag's eyes sparkle in an extraordinary way. "Away with you, old witch, away with you!" he shouted. But she still stretched her hands after him.

He jumped up in order to rush out, but she placed herself before the door, fixed her glowing eyes upon him, and again approached him. The philosopher tried to push her away with his hands, but to his astonishment he found that he could neither lift his hands nor move his legs, nor utter an audible word. He only heard his heart beating, and saw the old woman approach him, place his hands crosswise on his breast, and bend his head down. Then with the agility of a cat she sprang on his shoulders, struck him on the side with a broom, and he began to run like a racehorse, carrying her on his shoulders.

All this happened with such swiftness, that the philosopher could scarcely collect his thoughts. He laid hold of his knees with both hands in order to stop his legs from running; but to his great astonishment they kept moving forward against his will, making rapid springs like a Caucasian horse.

Not till the house had been left behind them and a wide plain stretched before them, bordered on one side by a black gloomy wood, did he say to himself, "Ah! it is a witch!"

The half-moon shone pale and high in the sky. Its mild light, still more subdued by intervening clouds, fell like a transparent veil on the earth. Woods, meadows, hills, and valleys—all seemed to be sleeping with open eyes; nowhere was a breath of air stirring. The atmosphere was moist and warm; the shadows of the trees and bushes fell sharply defined on the sloping plain. Such was the night through which the philosopher Thomas Brutus sped with his strange rider.

A strange, oppressive, and yet sweet sensation took possession of his heart. He looked down and saw how the grass beneath his feet seemed to be quite deep and far away; over it there flowed a flood of crystal-clear water, and the grassy plain looked like the bottom of a transparent sea. He saw his own image, and that of the old woman whom he carried on his back, clearly reflected in it. Then he beheld how, instead of the moon, a strange sun shone there; he heard the deep tones of bells, and saw them swinging. He saw a water-nixie rise from a bed of tall reeds; she turned to him, and her face was clearly visible, and she sang a song which penetrated his soul; then she approached him and nearly reached the surface of the water, on which she burst into laughter and again disappeared.

Did he see it or did he not see it? Was he dreaming or was he awake? But what was that below—wind or music? It sounded and drew nearer, and penetrated his soul like a song that rose and fell. "What is it?" he thought as he gazed into the depths, and still sped rapidly along.

The perspiration flowed from him in streams; he experienced simultaneously a strange feeling of oppression and delight in all his being. Often he felt as though he had no longer a heart, and pressed his hand on his breast with alarm.

Weary to death, he began to repeat all the prayers which he knew, and all the formulas of exorcism against evil spirits. Suddenly he experienced a certain relief. He felt that his pace was slackening; the witch weighed less heavily on his shoulders, and the thick herbage of the plain was again beneath his feet, with nothing especial to remark about it.

"Splendid!" thought the philosopher Thomas, and began to repeat his exorcisms in a still louder voice.

Then suddenly he wrenched himself away from under the witch, and sprang on her back in his turn. She began to run, with short, trembling steps indeed, but so rapidly that he could hardly breathe. So swiftly did she run that she hardly seemed to touch the ground. They were still on the plain, but owing to the rapidity of their flight everything seemed indistinct and confused before his eyes. He seized a stick that was lying on the ground, and began to belabour the hag with all his might. She uttered a wild cry, which at first sounded raging and threatening; then it became gradually weaker and more gentle, till at last it sounded quite low like the pleasant tones of a silver bell, so that it penetrated his innermost soul. Involuntarily the thought passed through his mind:

"Is she really an old woman?"

"Ah! I can go no farther," she said in a faint voice, and sank to the earth.

He knelt beside her, and looked in her eyes. The dawn was red in the sky, and in the distance glimmered the gilt domes of the churches of Kiev. Before him lay a beautiful maiden with thick, dishevelled hair and long eyelashes. Unconsciously she had stretched out her white, bare arms, and her tear-filled eyes gazed at the sky.

Thomas trembled like an aspen-leaf. Sympathy, and a strange feeling of excitement, and a hitherto unknown fear overpowered him. He began to run with all his might. His heart beat violently, and he could not explain to himself what a strange, new feeling had seized him. He did not wish to return to the village, but hastened towards Kiev, thinking all the way as he went of his weird, unaccountable adventure.

There were hardly any students left in the town; they were all scattered about the country, and had either taken tutors' posts or simply lived without occupation; for at the farms in Little Russia one can live comfortably and at ease without paying a farthing. The great half-decayed building in which the seminary was established was completely empty; and however much the philosopher searched in all its corners for a piece of lard and bread, he could not find even one of the hard biscuits which the seminarists were in the habit of hiding.

But the philosopher found a means of extricating himself from his difficulties by making friends with a certain young widow in the marketplace who sold ribbons, etc. The same evening he found himself being stuffed with cakes and fowl; in fact it is impossible to say how many things were placed before him on a little table in an arbour shaded by cherry-trees.

Later on the same evening the philosopher was to be seen in an alehouse.

He lay on a bench, smoked his pipe in his usual way, and threw the Jewish publican a gold piece. He had a jug of ale standing before him, looked on all who went in and out in a cold-blooded, self-satisfied way, and thought no more of his strange adventure.

About this time a report spread about that the daughter of a rich colonel, whose estate lay about fifty versts distant from Kiev, had returned home one day from a walk in a quite broken-down condition. She had scarcely enough strength to reach her father's house; now she lay dying, and had expressed a wish that for three days after her death the prayers for the dead should be recited by a Kiev seminarist named Thomas Brutus.

This fact was communicated to the philosopher by the rector of the seminary himself, who sent for him to his room and told him that he must start at once, as a rich colonel had sent his servants and a kibitka for him. The philosopher trembled, and was seized by an uncomfortable feeling which he could not define. He had a gloomy foreboding that some evil was about to befall him. Without knowing why, he declared that he did not wish to go.

"Listen, Thomas," said the rector, who under certain circumstances spoke very politely to his pupils; "I have no idea of asking you whether you wish to go or not. I only tell you that if you think of disobeying, I will have you so soundly flogged on the back with young birch-rods, that you need not think of having a bath for a long time."

The philosopher scratched the back of his head, and went out silently, intending to make himself scarce at the first opportunity. Lost in thought, he descended the steep flight of steps which led to the courtyard, thickly planted with poplars; there he remained standing for a moment, and heard quite distinctly the rector giving orders in a loud voice to his steward, and to another person, probably one of the messengers sent by the colonel.

"Thank your master for the peeled barley and the eggs," said the rector; "and tell him that as soon as the books which he mentions in his note are ready, I will send them. I have already given them to a clerk to be copied. And don't forget to remind your master that he has some excellent fish, especially prime sturgeon, in his ponds; he might send me some when he has the opportunity, as here in the market the fish are bad and dear. And you, Jantukh, give the colonel's man a glass of brandy. And mind you tie up the philosopher, or he will show you a clean pair of heels."

"Listen to the scoundrel!" thought the philosopher. "He has smelt a rat, the long-legged stork!"

He descended into the courtyard and beheld there a kibitka, which he at first took for a barn on wheels. It was, in fact, as roomy as a kiln, so that bricks might have been made inside it. It was one of those remarkable Krakow vehicles in which Jews travelled from town to town in scores, wherever they thought they would find a market. Six stout, strong, though somewhat elderly Cossacks were standing by it. Their gold-braided coats of fine cloth showed that their master was rich and of some importance; and certain little scars testified to their valour on the battlefield.

"What can I do?" thought the philosopher. "There is no escaping one's destiny." So he stepped up to the Cossacks and said "Good day, comrades."

"Welcome, Mr. Philosopher!" some of them answered.

"Well, I am to travel with you! It is a magnificent vehicle," he continued as he got into it. "If there were only musicians present, one might dance in it."

"Yes, it is a roomy carriage," said one of the Cossacks, taking his seat by the coachman. The latter had tied a cloth round his head, as he had already found an opportunity of pawning his cap in the alehouse. The other five, with the philosopher, got into the capacious kibitka, and sat upon sacks which were filled with all sorts of articles purchased in the city.

"I should like to know," said the philosopher, "if this equipage were laden with salt or iron, how many horses would be required to draw it?"

"Yes," said the Cossack who sat by the coachman, after thinking a short time, "it would require a good many horses."

After giving this satisfactory answer, the Cossack considered himself entitled to remain silent for the whole of the rest of the journey.

The philosopher would gladly have found out who the colonel was, and what sort of a character he had. He was also curious to know about his daughter, who had returned home in such a strange way and now lay dying, and whose destiny seemed to be mingled with his own; and wanted to know the sort of life that was lived in the colonel's house. But the Cossacks were probably philosophers like himself, for in answer to his inquiries they only blew clouds of tobacco and settled themselves more comfortably on their sacks.

Meanwhile, one of them addressed to the coachman on the box a brief command: "Keep your eyes open, Overko, you old sleepyhead, and when you come to the alehouse on the road to Tchukrailoff, don't forget to pull up and wake me and the other fellows if we are asleep." Then he began to snore pretty loud. But in any case his admonition was quite superfluous; for scarcely had the enormous equipage begun to approach the aforesaid alehouse, than they all cried with one mouth "Halt! Halt!" Besides this, Overko's horse was accustomed to stop outside every inn of its own accord.

In spite of the intense July heat, they all got out and entered a low, dirty room where a Jewish innkeeper received them in a friendly way as old acquaintances. He brought in the skirt of his long coat some sausages, and laid them on the table, where, though forbidden by the Talmud, they looked very seductive. All sat down at table, and it was not long before each of the guests had an earthenware jug standing in front of him. The philosopher Thomas had to take part in the feast, and as the Little Russians when they are intoxicated always begin to kiss each other or to weep, the whole room soon began to echo with demonstrations of affection.

"Come here, come here, Spirid, let me embrace thee!"

"Come here, Dorosch, let me press you to my heart!"

One Cossack, with a grey moustache, the eldest of them all, leant his head on his hand and began to weep bitterly because he was an orphan and alone in God's wide world. Another tall, loquacious man did his best to comfort him, saying, "Don't weep, for God's sake, don't weep! For over there—God knows best."

The Cossack who had been addressed as Dorosch was full of curiosity, and addressed many questions to the philosopher Thomas. "I should like to know," he said, "what you learn in your seminary; do you learn the same things as the deacon reads to us in church, or something else?"

"Don't ask," said the consoler; "let them learn what they like. God knows what is to happen; God knows everything."

"No, I will know," answered Dorosch, "I will know what is written in their books; perhaps it is something quite different from that in the deacon's book."

"O good heavens!" said the other, "why all this talk? It is God's will, and one cannot change God's arrangements."

"But I will know everything that is written; I will enter the seminary too, by heaven I will! Do you think perhaps I could not learn? I will learn everything, everything."

"Oh, heavens!" exclaimed the consoler, and let his head sink on the table, for he could no longer hold it upright.

The other Cossacks talked about the nobility, and why there was a moon in the sky.

When the philosopher Thomas saw the state they were in, he determined to profit by it, and to make his escape. In the first place he turned to the grey-headed Cossack, who was lamenting the loss of his parents. "But, little uncle," he said to him, "why do you weep so? I too am an orphan! Let me go, children; why do you want me?"

"Let him go!" said some of them, "he is an orphan, let him go where he likes."

They were about to take him outside themselves, when the one who had displayed a special thirst for knowledge, stopped them, saying, "No, I want to talk with him about the seminary; I am going to the seminary myself."

Moreover, it was not yet certain whether the philosopher could have executed his project of flight, for when he tried to rise from his chair, he felt as though his feet were made of wood, and he began to see such a number of doors leading out of the room that it would have been difficult for him to have found the right one.

It was not till evening that the company remembered that they must continue their journey. They crowded into the kibitka, whipped up the horses, and struck up a song, the words and sense of which were hard to understand. During a great part of the night, they wandered about, having lost the road which they ought to have been able to find blindfolded. At last they drove down a steep descent into a valley, and the philosopher noticed, by the sides of the road, hedges, behind which he caught glimpses of small trees and house-roofs. All these belonged to the colonel's estate.

It was already long past midnight. The sky was dark, though little stars glimmered here and there; no light was to be seen in any of the houses. They drove into a large courtyard, while the dogs barked. On all sides were barns and cottages with thatched roofs. Just opposite the gateway was a house, which was larger than the others, and seemed to be the colonel's dwelling. The kibitka stopped before a small barn, and the travellers hastened into it and laid themselves down to sleep. The philosopher however attempted to look at the exterior of the house, but, rub his eyes as he might, he could distinguish nothing; the house seemed to turn into a bear, and the chimney into the rector of the seminary. Then he gave it up and lay down to sleep.

When he woke up the next morning, the whole house was in commotion; the young lady had died during the night. The servants ran hither and thither in a distracted state; the old women wept and lamented; and a number of curious people gazed through the enclosure into the courtyard, as though there were something special to be seen. The philosopher began now to inspect the locality and the buildings, which he had not been able to do during the night.

The colonel's house was one of those low, small buildings, such as used formerly to be constructed in Russia. It was thatched with straw; a small, high-peaked gable, with a window shaped like an eye, was painted all over with blue and yellow flowers and red crescent-moons; it rested on little oaken pillars, which were round above the middle, hexagonal below, and whose capitals were adorned with quaint carvings. Under this gable was a small staircase with seats at the foot of it on either side.

The walls of the house were supported by similar pillars. Before the house stood a large pear-tree of pyramidal shape, whose leaves incessantly trembled. A double row of buildings formed a broad street leading up to the colonel's house. Behind the barns near the entrance-gate stood two three-cornered wine-houses, also thatched with straw; each of the stone walls had a door in it, and was covered with all kinds of paintings. On one was represented a Cossack sitting on a barrel and swinging a large pitcher over his head; it bore the inscription "I will drink all that!" Elsewhere were painted large and small bottles, a beautiful girl, a running horse, a pipe, and a drum bearing the words "Wine is the Cossack's joy."

In the loft of one of the barns one saw through a huge round window a drum and some trumpets. At the gate there stood two cannons. All this showed that the colonel loved a cheerful life, and the whole place often rang with sounds of merriment. Before the gate were two windmills, and behind the house gardens sloped away; through the treetops the dark chimneys of the peasants' houses were visible. The whole village lay on a broad, even plateau, in the middle of a mountain-slope which culminated in a steep summit on the north side. When seen from below, it looked still steeper. Here and there on the top the irregular stems of the thick steppe-brooms showed in dark relief against the blue sky. The bare clay soil made a melancholy impression, worn as it was into deep furrows by rainwater. On the same slope there stood two cottages, and over one of them a huge apple-tree spread its branches; the roots were supported by small props, whose interstices were filled with mould. The apples, which were blown off by the wind, rolled down to the courtyard below. A road wound round the mountain to the village.

When the philosopher looked at this steep slope, and remembered his journey of the night before, he came to the conclusion that either the colonel's horses were very sagacious, or that the Cossacks must have very strong heads, as they ventured, even when the worse for drink, on such a road with the huge kibitka.

When the philosopher turned and looked in the opposite direction, he saw quite another picture. The village reached down to the plain; meadows stretched away to an immense distance, their bright green growing gradually dark; far away, about twenty versts off, many other villages were visible. To the right of these meadows were chains of hills, and in the remote distance one saw the Dnieper shimmer and sparkle like a mirror of steel.

"What a splendid country!" said the philosopher to himself. "It must be fine to live here! One could catch fish in the Dnieper, and in the ponds, and shoot and snare partridges and bustards; there must be quantities here. Much fruit might be dried here and sold in the town, or, better still, brandy might be distilled from it, for fruit-brandy is the best of all. But what prevents me thinking of my escape after all?"

Behind the hedge he saw a little path which was almost entirely concealed by the high grass of the steppe. The philosopher approached it mechanically, meaning at first to walk a little along it unobserved, and then quite quietly to gain the open country behind the peasants' houses. Suddenly he felt the pressure of a fairly heavy hand on his shoulder.

Behind him stood the same old Cossack who yesterday had so bitterly lamented the death of his father and mother, and his own loneliness. "You are giving yourself useless trouble, Mr. Philosopher, if you think you can escape from us," he said. "One cannot run away here; and besides, the roads are too bad for walkers. Come to the colonel; he has been waiting for you for some time in his room."

"Yes, of course! What are you talking about? I will come with the greatest pleasure," said the philosopher, and followed the Cossack.

The colonel was an elderly man; his moustache was grey, and his face wore the signs of deep sadness. He sat in his room by a table, with his head propped on both hands. He seemed about five-and-fifty, but his attitude of utter despair, and the pallor on his face, showed that his heart had been suddenly broken, and that all his former cheerfulness had forever disappeared.

When Thomas entered with the Cossack, he answered their deep bows with a slight inclination of the head.

"Who are you, whence do you come, and what is your profession, my good man?" asked the colonel in an even voice, neither friendly nor austere.

"I am a student of philosophy; my name is Thomas Brutus."

"And who was your father?"

"I don't know, sir."

"And your mother?"

"I don't know either; I know that I must have had a mother, but who she was, and where she lived, by heavens, I do not know."

The colonel was silent, and seemed for a moment lost in thought. "Where did you come to know my daughter?"

"I do not know her, gracious sir; I declare I do not know her."

"Why then has she chosen you, and no one else, to offer up prayers for her?"

The philosopher shrugged his shoulders. "God only knows. It is a well-known fact that grand people often demand things which the most learned man cannot comprehend; and does not the proverb say, 'Dance, devil, as the Lord commands!'"

"Aren't you talking nonsense, Mr. Philosopher?"

"May the lightning strike me on the spot if I lie."

"If she had only lived a moment longer," said the colonel sadly, "then I had certainly found out everything. She said, 'Let no one offer up prayers for me, but send, father, at once to the seminary in Kiev for the student Thomas Brutus; he shall pray three nights running for my sinful soul—he knows.' But what he really knows she never said. The poor dove could speak no more, and died. Good man, you are probably well known for your sanctity and devout life, and she has perhaps heard of you."

"What? Of me?" said the philosopher, and took a step backward in amazement. "I and sanctity!" he exclaimed, and stared at the colonel. "God help us, gracious sir! What are you saying? It was only last Holy Thursday that I paid a visit to the tart-shop."

"Well, she must at any rate have had some reason for making the arrangement, and you must begin your duties today."

"I should like to remark to your honour—naturally everyone who knows the Holy Scripture at all can in his measure—but I believe it would be better on this occasion to send for a deacon or subdeacon. They are learned people, and they know exactly what is to be done. I have not got a good voice, nor any official standing."

"You may say what you like, but I shall carry out all my dove's wishes. If you read the prayers for her three nights through in the proper way, I will reward you; and if not—I advise the devil himself not to oppose me!"

The colonel spoke the last words in such an emphatic way that the philosopher quite understood them.

"Follow me!" said the colonel.

They went into the hall. The colonel opened a door which was opposite his own. The philosopher remained for a few minutes in the hall in order to look about him; then he stepped over the threshold with a certain nervousness.

The whole floor of the room was covered with red cloth. In a corner under the icons of the saints, on a table covered with a gold-bordered, velvet cloth, lay the body of the girl. Tall candles, round which were wound branches of the *kalina*, stood at her head and feet, and burned dimly in the broad daylight. The face of the dead was not to be seen, as the inconsolable father sat before his daughter, with his back turned to the philosopher. The words which the latter overheard filled him with a certain fear:

"I do not mourn, my daughter, that in the flower of your age you have prematurely left the earth, to my grief; but I mourn, my dove, that I do not know my deadly enemy who caused your death. Had I only known that anyone could even conceive the idea of insulting you, or of speaking a disrespectful word to you, I swear by heaven he would never have seen his children again, if he had been as old as myself; nor his father and mother, if he had been young. And I would have thrown his corpse to the birds of the air, and the wild beasts of the steppe. But woe is me, my flower, my dove, my light! I will spend the remainder of my life without joy, and wipe the bitter tears which flow out of my old eyes, while my enemy will rejoice and laugh in secret over the helpless old man!"

He paused, overpowered by grief, and streams of tears flowed down his cheeks.

The philosopher was deeply affected by the sight of such inconsolable sorrow. He coughed gently in order to clear his throat. The colonel turned and signed to him to take his place at the head of the dead girl, before a little prayer-desk on which some books lay.

"I can manage to hold out for three nights," thought the philosopher; "and then the colonel will fill both my pockets with ducats."

He approached the dead girl, and after coughing once more, began to read, without paying attention to anything else, and firmly resolved not to look at her face.

Soon there was deep silence, and he saw that the colonel had left the room. Slowly he turned his head in order to look at the corpse. A violent shudder thrilled through him; before him lay a form of such beauty as is seldom seen upon earth. It seemed to him that never in a single face had so much intensity of expression and harmony of feature been united. Her brow, soft as snow and pure as silver, seemed to be thinking; the fine, regular eyebrows shadowed proudly the closed eyes, whose lashes gently rested on her cheeks, which seemed to glow with secret longing; her lips still appeared to smile. But at the same time he saw something in these features which appalled him; a terrible depression seized his heart, as when in the midst of dance and song someone begins to chant a dirge. He felt as though those ruby lips were coloured with his own heart's blood. Moreover, her face seemed dreadfully familiar.

"The witch!" he cried out in a voice which sounded strange to himself; then he turned away and began to read the prayers with white cheeks. It was the witch whom he had killed.

II

WHEN THE SUN had sunk below the horizon, the corpse was carried into the church. The philosopher supported one corner of the black-draped coffin upon his shoulder, and felt an ice-cold shiver run through his body. The colonel walked in front of him, with his right hand resting on the edge of the coffin.

The wooden church, black with age and overgrown with green lichen, stood quite at the end of the village in gloomy solitude; it was adorned with three round cupolas. One saw at the first glance that it had not been used for divine worship for a long time.

Lighted candles were standing before almost every icon. The coffin was set down before the altar. The old colonel kissed his dead daughter once more, and then left the church, together with the bearers of the bier, after he had ordered his servants to look after the philosopher and to take him back to the church after supper.

The coffin-bearers, when they returned to the house, all laid their hands on the stove. This custom is always observed in Little Russia by those who have seen a corpse.

The hunger which the philosopher now began to feel caused him for a while to forget the dead girl altogether. Gradually all the domestics of the house assembled in the kitchen; it was really a kind of club, where they were accustomed to gather. Even the dogs came to the door, wagging their tails in order to have bones and offal thrown to them.

If a servant was sent on an errand, he always found his way into the kitchen to rest there for a while, and to smoke a pipe. All the Cossacks of the establishment lay here during the whole day on and under the benches—in fact, wherever a place could be found to lie down in. Moreover, everyone was always leaving something behind in the kitchen—his cap, or his whip, or something of the sort. But the numbers of the club were not complete till the evening, when the groom came in after tying up his horses in the stable, the cowherd had shut up his cows in their stalls, and others collected there who were not usually seen in the daytime. During supper-time even the tongues of the laziest were set in motion. They talked of all and everything—of the new pair of breeches which someone had ordered for himself, of what might be in the centre of the earth, and of the wolf which someone had seen. There were a number of wits in the company—a class which is always represented in Little Russia.

The philosopher took his place with the rest in the great circle which sat round the kitchen door in the open-air. Soon an old woman with a red cap issued from it, bearing with both hands a large vessel full of hot *galuchkis*, which she distributed among them. Each drew out of his pocket a wooden spoon, or a one-pronged wooden fork. As soon as their jaws began to move a little more slowly, and their wolfish hunger was somewhat appeased, they began to talk. The conversation, as might be expected, turned on the dead girl.

"Is it true," said a young shepherd, "is it true—though I cannot understand it—that our young mistress had traffic with evil spirits?"

"Who, the young lady?" answered Dorosch, whose acquaintance the philosopher had already made in the kibitka. "Yes, she was a regular witch! I can swear that she was a witch!"

"Hold your tongue, Dorosch!" exclaimed another—the one who, during the journey, had played the part of a consoler. "We have nothing to do with that. May God be merciful to her! One ought not to talk of such things."

But Dorosch was not at all inclined to be silent; he had just visited the wine-cellar with the steward on important business, and having stooped two or three times over one or two casks, he had returned in a very cheerful and loquacious mood.

"Why do you ask me to be silent?" he answered. "She has ridden on my own shoulders, I swear she has."

"Say, uncle," asked the young shepherd, "are there signs by which to recognise a sorceress?"

"No, there are not," answered Dorosch; "even if you knew the Psalter by heart, you could not recognise one."

"Yes, Dorosch, it is possible; don't talk such nonsense," retorted the former consoler. "It is not for nothing that God has given each some special peculiarity; the learned maintain that every witch has a little tail."

"Every old woman is a witch," said a grey-headed Cossack quite seriously.

"Yes, you are a fine lot," retorted the old woman who entered at that moment with a vessel full of fresh *galuchkis*. "You are great fat pigs!"

A self-satisfied smile played round the lips of the old Cossack whose name was Javtuch, when he found that his remark had touched the old woman on a tender point. The shepherd burst into such a deep and loud explosion of laughter as if two oxen were lowing together.

This conversation excited in the philosopher a great curiosity, and a wish to obtain more exact information regarding the colonel's daughter. In order to lead the talk back to the subject, he turned to his next neighbour and said, "I should like to know why all the people here think that the young lady was a witch. Has she done harm to anyone, or killed them by witchcraft?"

"Yes, there are reports of that kind," answered a man, whose face was as flat as a shovel. "Who does not remember the huntsman Mikita, or the—"

"What has the huntsman Mikita got to do with it?" asked the philosopher.

"Stop; I will tell you the story of Mikita," interrupted Dorosch.

"No, I will tell it," said the groom, "for he was my godfather."

"I will tell the story of Mikita," said Spirid.

"Yes, yes, Spirid shall tell it," exclaimed the whole company; and Spirid began.

"You, Mr. Philosopher Thomas, did not know Mikita. Ah! he was an extraordinary man. He knew every dog as though he were his own father. The present huntsman, Mikola, who sits three places away from me, is not fit to hold a candle to him, though good enough in his way; but compared to Mikita, he is a mere milksop."

"You tell the tale splendidly," exclaimed Dorosch, and nodded as a sign of approval.

Spirid continued.

"He saw a hare in the field quicker than you can take a pinch of snuff. He only needed to whistle 'Come here, Rasboy! Come here, Bosdraja!' and flew away on his horse like the wind, so that you could not say whether he went quicker than the dog or the dog than he. He could empty a quart pot of brandy in the twinkling of an eye. Ah! he was a splendid huntsman, only for some time he always had his eyes fixed on the young lady. Either he had fallen in love with her or she had bewitched him—in short, he went to the dogs. He became a regular old woman; yes, he became the devil knows what—it is not fitting to relate it."

"Very good," remarked Dorosch.

"If the young lady only looked at him, he let the reins slip out of his hands, called Bravko instead of Rasboy, stumbled, and made all kinds of mistakes. One day when he was currycombing a horse, the young lady came to him in the stable. 'Listen, Mikita,' she said. 'I should like for once to set my foot on you.' And he, the booby, was quite delighted, and answered, 'Don't only set your foot there, but sit on me altogether.' The young lady lifted her white little foot, and as soon as he saw it, his delight robbed him of his senses. He bowed his neck, the idiot, took her feet in both hands, and began to trot about like a horse all over the place. Whither they went he could not say; he returned more dead than alive, and from that time he wasted away and became as dry as a chip of wood. At last someone coming into the stable one day found instead of him only a handful of ashes and an empty jug; he had burned completely out. But it must be said he was a huntsman such as the world cannot match."

When Spirid had ended his tale, they all began to vie with one another in praising the deceased huntsman.

"And have you heard the story of Cheptchicha?" asked Dorosch, turning to Thomas.

"No."

"Ha! Ha! One sees they don't teach you much in your seminary. Well, listen. We have here in our village a Cossack called Cheptoun, a fine fellow. Sometimes indeed he amuses himself by stealing and lying without any reason; but he is a fine fellow for all that. His house is not far away from here. One evening, just about this time, Cheptoun and his wife went to bed after they had finished their day's work. Since it was fine weather, Cheptchicha went to sleep in the courtyard, and Cheptoun in the house—no! I mean Cheptchicha went to sleep in the house on a bench and Cheptoun outside—"

"No, Cheptchicha didn't go to sleep on a bench, but on the ground," interrupted the old woman who stood at the door.

Dorosch looked at her, then at the ground, then again at her, and said after a pause, "If I tore your dress off your back before all these people, it wouldn't look pretty."

The rebuke was effectual. The old woman was silent, and did not interrupt again.

Dorosch continued.

"In the cradle which hung in the middle of the room lay a one-year-old child. I do not know whether it was a boy or a girl. Cheptchicha had lain down, and heard on the other side of the door a dog scratching and howling loud enough to frighten anyone. She was afraid, for women are such simple folk that if one puts out one's tongue at them behind the door in the dark, their hearts sink into their boots. 'But,' she thought to herself, 'I must give this cursed dog one on the snout to stop his howling!' So she seized the poker and opened the door. But hardly had she done so than the dog rushed between her legs straight to the cradle. Then Cheptchicha saw that it was not a dog but the young lady; and if it had only been the young lady as she knew her it wouldn't have mattered, but she looked quite blue, and her eyes sparkled like fiery coals. She seized the child, bit its throat, and began to suck its blood. Cheptchicha shrieked, 'Ah! my darling child!' and rushed out of the room. Then she saw that the house-door was shut and rushed up to the attic and sat there, the stupid woman, trembling all over. Then the young lady came after her and bit her too, poor fool! The next morning Cheptoun carried his wife, all bitten and wounded, down from the attic, and the next day she died. Such strange things happen in the world. One may wear fine clothes, but that does not matter; a witch is and remains a witch."

After telling his story, Dorosch looked around him with a complacent air, and cleaned out his pipe with his little finger in order to fill it again. The story of the witch had made a deep impression on all, and each of them had something to say about her. One had seen her come to the door of his house in the form of a hayrick; from others she had stolen their caps or their pipes; she had cut off the hair-plaits of many girls in the village, and drunk whole pints of the blood of others.

At last the whole company observed that they had gossiped over their time, for it was already night. All looked for a sleeping place—some in the kitchen and others in the barn or the courtyard.

"Now, Mr. Thomas, it is time that we go to the dead," said the grey-headed Cossack, turning to the philosopher. All four—Spirid, Dorosch, the old Cossack, and the philosopher—betook themselves to the church, keeping off with their whips the wild dogs who roamed about the roads in great numbers and bit the sticks of passersby in sheer malice.

Although the philosopher had seized the opportunity of fortifying himself beforehand with a stiff glass of brandy, yet he felt a certain secret fear which increased as he approached the church, which was lit up within. The strange tales he had heard had made a deep impression on his imagination. They had passed the thick hedges and trees, and the country became more open. At last they reached the small enclosure round the church; behind it there were no more trees, but a huge, empty plain dimly visible in the darkness. The three Cossacks ascended the steep steps with Thomas, and entered the church. Here they left the philosopher, expressing their hope that he would successfully accomplish his duties, and locked him in as their master had ordered.

He was left alone. At first he yawned, then he stretched himself, blew on both hands, and finally looked round him. In the middle of the church stood the black bier; before the dark pictures of saints burned the candles, whose light only illuminated the icons, and cast a faint glimmer into the body of the church; all the corners were in complete darkness. The lofty icons seemed to be of considerable age; only a little of the original gilt remained on their broken traceries; the faces of the saints had become quite black and looked uncanny.

Once more the philosopher cast a glance around him. "Bother it!" said he to himself. "What is there to be afraid about? No living creature can get in, and as for the dead and those who come from the 'other side,' I can protect myself with such effectual prayers that they cannot touch me with the tips of their fingers. There is nothing to fear," he repeated, swinging his arms. "Let us begin the prayers!"

As he approached one of the side-aisles, he noticed two packets of candles which had been placed there.

"That is fine," he thought. "I must illuminate the whole church, till it is as bright as day. What a pity that one cannot smoke in it."

He began to light the candles on all the wall-brackets and all the candelabra, as well as those already burning before the holy pictures; soon the whole church was brilliantly lit up. Only the darkness in the roof above seemed still denser by contrast, and the faces of the saints peering out of the frames looked as unearthly as before. He approached the bier, looked nervously at the face of the dead girl, could not help shuddering slightly, and involuntarily closed his eyes. What terrible and extraordinary beauty!

He turned away and tried to go to one side, but the strange curiosity and peculiar fascination which men feel in moments of fear, compelled him to look again and again, though with a similar shudder. And in truth there was something terrible about the beauty of the dead girl. Perhaps she would not have inspired so much fear had she been less beautiful; but there was nothing ghastly or deathlike in the face, which wore rather an expression of life, and it seemed to the philosopher as though she were watching him from under her closed eyelids. He even thought he saw a tear roll from under the eyelash of her right eye, but when it was halfway down her cheek, he saw that it was a drop of blood.

He quickly went into one of the stalls, opened his book, and began to read the prayers in a very loud voice in order to keep up his courage. His deep voice sounded strange to himself in the grave-like silence; it aroused no echo in the silent and desolate wooden walls of the church.

"What is there to be afraid of?" he thought to himself. "She will not rise from her bier, since she fears God's word. She will remain quietly resting. Yes, and what sort of a Cossack should I be, if I were afraid? The fact is, I have drunk a little too much—that is why I feel so queer. Let me take a pinch of snuff. It is really excellent—first-rate!"

At the same time he cast a furtive glance over the pages of the prayer-book towards the bier, and involuntarily he said to himself, "There! See! She is getting up! Her head is already above the edge of the coffin!"

But a deathlike silence prevailed; the coffin was motionless, and all the candles shone steadily. It was an awe-inspiring sight, this church lit up at midnight, with the corpse in the midst, and no living soul near but one. The philosopher began to sing in various keys in order to stifle his fears, but every moment he glanced across at the coffin, and involuntarily the question came to his lips, "Suppose she rose up after all?"

But the coffin did not move. Nowhere was there the slightest sound nor stir. Not even did a cricket chirp in any corner. There was nothing audible but the slight sputtering of some distant candle, or the faint fall of a drop of wax.

"Suppose she rose up after all?"

He raised his head. Then he looked round him wildly and rubbed his eyes. Yes, she was no longer lying in the coffin, but sitting upright. He turned away his eyes, but at once looked again, terrified, at the coffin. She stood up; then she walked with closed eyes through the church, stretching out her arms as though she wanted to seize someone.

She now came straight towards him. Full of alarm, he traced with his finger a circle round himself; then in a loud voice he began to recite the prayers and formulas of exorcism which he had learnt from a monk who had often seen witches and evil spirits.

She had almost reached the edge of the circle which he had traced; but it was evident that she had not the power to enter it. Her face wore a bluish tint like that of one who has been several days dead.

Thomas had not the courage to look at her, so terrible was her appearance; her teeth chattered and she opened her dead eyes, but as in her rage she saw nothing, she turned in another direction and felt with outstretched arms among the pillars and corners of the church in the hope of seizing him.

At last she stood still, made a threatening gesture, and then lay down again in the coffin.

The philosopher could not recover his self-possession, and kept on gazing anxiously at it. Suddenly it rose from its place and began hurtling about the church with a whizzing sound. At one time it was almost directly over his head; but the philosopher observed that it could not pass over the area of his charmed circle, so he kept on repeating his formulas of exorcism. The coffin now fell with a crash in the middle of the church, and remained lying there motionless. The corpse rose again; it had now a greenish-blue colour, but at the same moment the distant crowing of a cock was audible, and it lay down again.

The philosopher's heart beat violently, and the perspiration poured in streams from his face; but heartened by the crowing of the cock, he rapidly repeated the prayers.

As the first light of dawn looked through the windows, there came a deacon and the grey-haired Javtuk, who acted as sacristan, in order to release him. When he had reached the house, he could not sleep for a long time; but at last weariness overpowered him, and he slept till noon. When he awoke, his experiences of the night appeared to him like a dream. He was given a quart of brandy to strengthen him.

At table he was again talkative and ate a fairly large sucking pig almost without assistance. But none the less he resolved to say nothing of what he had seen, and to all curious questions only returned the answer, "Yes, some wonderful things happened."

The philosopher was one of those men who, when they have had a good meal, are uncommonly amiable. He lay down on a bench, with his pipe in his mouth, looked blandly at all, and expectorated every minute.

But as the evening approached, he became more and more pensive. About suppertime nearly the whole company had assembled in order to play *krapli*. This is a kind of game of skittles, in which, instead of bowls, long staves are used, and the winner has the right to ride on the back of his opponent. It provided the spectators with much amusement; sometimes the groom, a huge man, would clamber on the back of the swineherd, who was slim and short and shrunken; another time the groom would present his own back, while Dorosch sprang on it shouting, "What a regular ox!" Those of the company who were more staid sat by the threshold of the kitchen. They looked uncommonly serious, smoked their pipes, and did not even smile when the younger ones went into fits of laughter over some joke of the groom or Spirid.

Thomas vainly attempted to take part in the game; a gloomy thought was firmly fixed like a nail in his head. In spite of his desperate efforts to appear cheerful after supper, fear had overmastered his whole being, and it increased with the growing darkness.

"Now it is time for us to go, Mr. Student!" said the grey-haired Cossack, and stood up with Dorosch. "Let us betake ourselves to our work."

Thomas was conducted to the church in the same way as on the previous evening; again he was left alone, and the door was bolted behind him.

As soon as he found himself alone, he began to feel in the grip of his fears. He again saw the dark pictures of the saints in their gilt frames, and the black coffin, which stood menacing and silent in the middle of the church.

"Never mind!" he said to himself. "I am over the first shock. The first time I was frightened, but I am not so at all now—no, not at all!"

He quickly went into a stall, drew a circle round him with his finger, uttered some prayers and formulas for exorcism, and then began to read the prayers for the dead in a loud voice and with the fixed resolution not to look up from the book nor take notice of anything.

He did so for an hour, and began to grow a little tired; he cleared his throat and drew his snuffbox out of his pocket, but before he had taken a pinch he looked nervously towards the coffin.

A sudden chill shot through him. The witch was already standing before him on the edge of the circle, and had fastened her green eyes upon him. He shuddered, looked down at the book, and began to read his prayers and exorcisms aloud. Yet all the while he was aware how her teeth chattered, and how she stretched out her arms to seize him. But when he cast a hasty glance towards her, he saw that she was not looking in his direction, and it was clear that she could not see him.

Then she began to murmur in an undertone, and terrible words escaped her lips—words that sounded like the bubbling of boiling pitch. The philosopher did not know their meaning, but he knew that they signified something terrible, and were intended to counteract his exorcisms.

After she had spoken, a stormy wind arose in the church, and there was a noise like the rushing of many birds. He heard the noise of their wings and claws as they flapped against and scratched at the iron bars of the church windows. There were also violent blows on the church door, as if someone were trying to break it in pieces.

The philosopher's heart beat violently; he did not dare to look up, but continued to read the prayers without a pause. At last there was heard in the distance the shrill sound of a cock's crow. The exhausted philosopher stopped and gave a great sigh of relief.

Those who came to release him found him more dead than alive; he had leant his back against the wall, and stood motionless, regarding them without any expression in his eyes. They were obliged almost to carry him to the house; he then shook himself, asked for and drank a quart of brandy. He passed his hand through his hair and said, "There are all sorts of horrors in the world, and such dreadful things happen that—" Here he made a gesture as though to ward off something. All who heard him bent their heads forward in curiosity. Even a small boy, who ran on everyone's errands, stood by with his mouth wide open.

Just then a young woman in a close-fitting dress passed by. She was the old cook's assistant, and very coquettish; she always stuck something in her bodice by way of ornament, a ribbon or a flower, or even a piece of paper if she could find nothing else.

"Good day, Thomas," she said, as she saw the philosopher. "Dear me! what has happened to you?" she exclaimed, striking her hands together.

"Well, what is it, you silly creature?"

"Good heavens! You have grown quite grey!"

"Yes, so he has!" said Spirid, regarding him more closely. "You have grown as grey as our old Javtuk."

When the philosopher heard that, he hastened into the kitchen, where he had noticed on the wall a dirty, three-cornered piece of looking-glass. In front of it hung some forget-me-nots, evergreens, and a small garland—a proof that it was the toilette-glass of the young coquette. With alarm he saw that it actually was as they had said—his hair was quite grizzled.

He sank into a reverie; at last he said to himself, "I will go to the colonel, tell him all, and declare that I will read no more prayers. He must send me back at once to Kiev." With this intention he turned towards the doorsteps of the colonel's house.

The colonel was sitting motionless in his room; his face displayed the same hopeless grief which Thomas had observed on it on his first arrival, only the hollows in his cheeks had deepened. It was obvious that he took very little or no food. A strange paleness made him look almost as though made of marble.

"Good day," he said as he observed Thomas standing, cap in hand, at the door. "Well, how are you getting on? All right?"

"Yes, sir, all right! Such hellish things are going on, that one would like to rush away as far as one's feet can carry one."

"How so?"

"Your daughter, sir.…When one considers the matter, she is, of course, of noble descent—no one can dispute that; but don't be angry, and may God grant her eternal rest!"

"Very well! What about her?"

"She is in league with the devil. She inspires one with such dread that all prayers are useless."

"Pray! Pray! It was not for nothing that she sent for you. My dove was troubled about her salvation, and wished to expel all evil influences by means of prayer."

"I swear, gracious sir, it is beyond my power."

"Pray! Pray!" continued the colonel in the same persuasive tone. "There is only one night more; you are doing a Christian work, and I will reward you richly."

"However great your rewards may be, I will not read the prayers any more, sir," said Thomas in a tone of decision.

"Listen, philosopher!" said the colonel with a menacing air. "I will not allow any objections. In your seminary you may act as you like, but here it won't do. If I have you knouted, it will be somewhat different to the rector's canings. Do you know what a strong *kantchuk* is?"

"Of course I do," said the philosopher in a low voice; "a number of them together are insupportable."

"Yes, I think so too. But you don't know yet how hot my fellows can make it," replied the colonel threateningly. He sprang up, and his face assumed a fierce, despotic expression, betraying the savagery of his nature, which had been only temporarily modified by grief. "After the first flogging they pour on brandy and then repeat it. Go away and finish your work. If you don't obey, you won't be able to stand again, and if you do, you will get a thousand ducats."

"That is a devil of a fellow," thought the philosopher to himself, and went out. "One can't trifle with him. But wait a little, my friend; I will escape you so cleverly, that even your hounds can't find me!"

He determined, under any circumstances, to run away, and only waited till the hour after dinner arrived, when all the servants were accustomed to take a nap on the hay in the barn, and to snore and puff so loudly that it sounded as if machinery had been set up there. At last the time came. Even Javtuch stretched himself out in the sun and closed his eyes. Tremblingly, and on tiptoe, the philosopher stole softly into the garden, whence he thought he could escape more easily into the open country. This garden was generally so choked up with weeds that it seemed admirably adapted for such an attempt. With the exception of a single path used by the people of the house, the whole of it was covered with cherry-trees, elder-bushes, and tall heath-thistles with fibrous red buds. All these trees and bushes had been thickly overgrown with ivy, which formed a kind of roof. Its tendrils reached to the hedge and fell down on the other side in snakelike curves among the small, wild field-flowers. Behind the hedge which bordered the garden was a dense mass of wild heather, in which it did not seem probable that anyone would care to venture himself, and the strong, stubborn stems of which seemed likely to baffle any attempt to cut them.

As the philosopher was about to climb over the hedge, his teeth chattered, and his heart beat so violently that he felt frightened at it. The skirts of his long cloak seemed to cling to the ground as though they had been fastened to it by pegs. When he had actually got over the hedge he seemed to hear a shrill voice crying behind him "Whither? Whither?"

He jumped into the heather and began to run, stumbling over old roots and treading on unfortunate moles. When he had emerged from the heather he saw that he still had a wide field to cross, behind which was a thick, thorny underwood. This, according to his calculation, must stretch as far as the road leading to Kiev, and if he reached it he would be safe. Accordingly he ran over the field and plunged into the thorny copse. Every sharp thorn he encountered tore a fragment from his coat. Then he reached a small open space; in the centre of it stood a willow, whose branches hung down to the earth, and close by flowed a clear spring bright as silver. The first thing the philosopher did was to lie down and drink eagerly, for he was intolerably thirsty.

"Splendid water!" he said, wiping his mouth. "This is a good place to rest in."

"No, better run farther; perhaps we are being followed," said a voice immediately behind him.

Thomas started and turned; before him stood Javtuch.

"This devil of a Javtuch!" he thought. "I should like to seize him by the feet and smash his hangdog face against the trunk of a tree."

"Why did you go round such a long way?" continued Javtuch. "You had much better have chosen the path by which I came; it leads directly by the stable. Besides, it is a pity about your coat. Such splendid cloth! How much did it cost an ell? Well, we have had a long enough walk; it is time to go home."

The philosopher followed Javtuch in a very depressed state.

"Now the accursed witch will attack me in earnest," he thought. "But what have I really to fear? Am I not a Cossack? I have read the prayers for two nights already; with God's help I will get through the third night also. It is plain that the witch must have a terrible load of guilt upon her, else the evil one would not help her so much."

Feeling somewhat encouraged by these reflections, he returned to the courtyard and asked Dorosch, who sometimes, by the steward's permission, had access to the wine-cellar, to fetch him a small bottle of brandy. The two friends sat down before a barn and drank a pretty large one. Suddenly the philosopher jumped up and said, "I want musicians! Bring some musicians!"

But without waiting for them he began to dance the *tropak* in the court-yard. He danced till teatime, and the servants, who, as is usual in such cases, had formed a small circle round him, grew at last tired of watching him, and went away saying, "By heavens, the man can dance!"

Finally the philosopher lay down in the place where he had been dancing, and fell asleep. It was necessary to pour a bucket of cold water on his head to wake him up for supper. At the meal he enlarged on the topic of what a Cossack ought to be, and how he should not be afraid of anything in the world.

"It is time," said Javtuch; "let us go."

"I wish I could put a lighted match to your tongue," thought the philosopher; then he stood up and said, "Let us go."

On their way to the church, the philosopher kept looking round him on all sides, and tried to start a conversation with his companions; but both Javtuch and Dorosch remained silent. It was a weird night. In the distance wolves howled continually, and even the barking of the dogs had something unearthly about it.

"That doesn't sound like wolves howling, but something else," remarked Dorosch.

Javtuch still kept silence, and the philosopher did not know what answer to make.

They reached the church and walked over the old wooden planks, whose rotten condition showed how little the lord of the manor cared about God and his soul. Javtuch and Dorosch left the philosopher alone, as on the previous evenings.

There was still the same atmosphere of menacing silence in the church, in the centre of which stood the coffin with the terrible witch inside it.

"I am not afraid, by heavens, I am not afraid!" he said; and after drawing a circle round himself as before, he began to read the prayers and exorcisms.

An oppressive silence prevailed; the flickering candles filled the church with their clear light. The philosopher turned one page after another, and noticed that he was not reading what was in the book. Full of alarm, he crossed himself and began to sing a hymn. This calmed him somewhat, and he resumed his reading, turning the pages rapidly as he did so.

Suddenly in the midst of the sepulchral silence the iron lid of the coffin sprang open with a jarring noise, and the dead witch stood up. She was this time still more terrible in aspect than at first. Her teeth chattered loudly and her lips, through which poured a stream of dreadful curses, moved convulsively. A whirlwind arose in the church; the icons of the saints fell on the ground, together with the broken windowpanes. The door was wrenched from its hinges, and a huge mass of monstrous creatures rushed into the church, which became filled with the noise of beating wings and scratching claws. All these creatures flew and crept about, seeking for the philosopher, from whose brain the last fumes of intoxication had vanished. He crossed himself ceaselessly and uttered prayer after prayer, hearing all the time the whole unclean swarm rustling about him, and brushing him with the tips of their wings. He had not the courage to look at them; he only saw one uncouth monster standing by the wall, with long, shaggy hair and two flaming eyes. Over him something hung in the air which looked like a gigantic bladder covered with countless crabs' claws and scorpions' stings, and with black clods of earth hanging from it. All these monsters stared about seeking him, but they could not find him, since he was protected by his sacred circle.

"Bring the Viy! Bring the Viy!" cried the witch.

A sudden silence followed; the howling of wolves was heard in the distance, and soon heavy footsteps resounded through the church. Thomas looked up furtively and saw that an ungainly human figure with crooked legs was being led into the church. He was quite covered with black soil, and his hands and feet resembled knotted roots. He trod heavily and stumbled at every step. His eyelids were of enormous length. With terror, Thomas saw that his face was of iron. They led him in by the arms and placed him near Thomas's circle.

"Raise my eyelids! I can't see anything!" said the Viy in a dull, hollow voice, and they all hastened to help in doing so.

"Don't look!" an inner voice warned the philosopher; but he could not restrain from looking.

"There he is!" exclaimed the Viy, pointing an iron finger at him; and all the monsters rushed on him at once.

Struck dumb with terror, he sank to the ground and died.

At that moment there sounded a cock's crow for the second time; the earth-spirits had not heard the first one. In alarm they hurried to the windows and the door to get out as quickly as possible. But it was too late; they all remained hanging as though fastened to the door and the windows.

When the priest came he stood amazed at such a desecration of God's house, and did not venture to read prayers there. The church remained standing as it was, with the monsters hanging on the windows and the door. Gradually it became overgrown with creepers, bushes, and wild heather, and no one can discover it now.

When the report of this event reached Kiev, and the theologian Khalava heard what a fate had overtaken the philosopher Thomas, he sank for a whole hour into deep reflection. He had greatly altered of late; after finishing his studies he had become bell-ringer of one of the chief churches in the city, and he always appeared with a bruised nose, because the belfry staircase was in a ruinous condition.

"Have you heard what has happened to Thomas?" said Tiberius Gorobetz, who had become a philosopher and now wore a moustache.

"Yes; God had appointed it so," answered the bell-ringer. "Let us go to the alehouse; we will drink a glass to his memory."

The young philosopher, who, with the enthusiasm of a novice, had made such full use of his privileges as a student that his breeches and coat and even his cap reeked of brandy and tobacco, agreed readily to the proposal.

"He was a fine fellow, Thomas," said the bell-ringer as the limping inn-keeper set the third jug of beer before him. "A splendid fellow! And lost his life for nothing!"

"I know why he perished," said Gorobetz; "because he was afraid. If he had not feared her, the witch could have done nothing to him. One ought to cross oneself incessantly and spit exactly on her tail, and then not the least harm can happen. I know all about it, for here, in Kiev, all the old women in the marketplace are witches."

The bell-ringer nodded assent. But being aware that he could not say any more, he got up cautiously and went out, swaying to the right and left in order to find a hiding-place in the thick steppe grass outside the town. At the same time, in accordance with his old habits, he did not forget to steal an old boot-sole which lay on the alehouse bench.

THE TALE OF HOW IVAN IVANOVICH QUARRELED WITH IVAN NIKIFOROVICH

I

IVAN IVANOVICH AND IVAN NIKIFOROVICH.

A FINE BEKESHA [short shooting-coat] has Ivan Ivanovich! splendid! And what lambskin! deuce take it, what lambskin! blue-black with silver lights. I'll forfeit, I know not what, if you find any one else owning any such. Look at it, for Heaven's sake, especially when he stands talking with any one! look at him from the side: what a pleasure it is! To describe it, is impossible: velvet! silver! fire! Heavens! Nikolai the Wonder-worker, saint of God! why have not I such a bekesha? He had it made before Agafya Fedosyevna went to Kief. You know Agafya Fedosyevna, the same who bit the assessor's ear off.

Ivan Ivanovich was a very handsome man. What a house he had in Mirgorod ! Around it on every side was a veranda on oaken pillars, and on the veranda everywhere were benches. Ivan Ivanovich, when the weather gets too warm, throws off his bekesha and his underclothing, remains in his shirt alone, and rests on the veranda, and observes what is going on in the court-yard and the street. What apples and pears he has under his very windows! You have but to open the window, and the branches force themselves through into the room. All this is in front of the house; but you should have seen what he had in the garden. What was there not there? Plums, cherries, black-hearts, every sort of vegetable, sunflowers, cucumbers, melons, peas, a threshing-floor, and even a forge.

A very fine man, Ivan Ivanovich! He is very fond of melons: they are his favorite food. Just as soon as he has dined, and come out on his veranda, in his shirt, he orders Gapka to fetch two melons, and immediately cuts them himself, collects the seeds in a paper, and begins to eat. Then he orders Gapka to fetch the ink-bottle, and, with his own hand, writes this inscription on the paper of seeds: *These melons were eaten on such and such a date*. If there was a guest present, then it reads, *Such and such a person assisted*.

The late judge of Mirgorod always gazed at Ivan Ivanovich's house with pleasure. Yes, the little house was very pretty. It pleased me because sheds, and still other little sheds, were built on to it on all sides; so that, looking at it from a distance, only roofs were visible, rising one above another, which greatly resembled a plate full of pancakes, or, better still, fungi growing on the trunk of a tree. Moreover, the roofs were all overgrown with weeds: a willow, an oak, and two apple-trees leaned their spreading branches against it. Through the trees peeped little windows with carved and whitewashed shutters, which projected even into the street.

A very fine man, Ivan Ivanovich! The commissioner of Poltava knows him also. Dorosh Tarasovich Pukhívochka, when he leaves Khorola, always goes to his house. And Father Peter, the Protopope who lives in Koliberda, when he invites a few guests, always says that he knows of no one who so well fulfils all his Christian duties, and understands so well how to live, as Ivan Ivanovich.

How time flies! More than ten years have already passed since he became a widower. He never had any children. Gapka has children, and they run about the court-yard. Ivan Ivanovich always gives each one of them either a round cake, or a slice of melon, or a pear.

Gapka carries the keys of his storerooms and cellars; but the key of the large chest which stands in his bedroom, and that of the centre storeroom, Ivan Ivanovich keeps himself; and he does not like to admit any one. Gapka is a healthy girl, and goes about in coarse cloth garments with ruddy cheeks and calves.

And what a pious man is Ivan Ivanovich! Every Sunday he dons his bekesha, and goes to church. On entering, Ivan Ivanovich bows on all sides, generally stations himself in the choir, and sings a very good bass. When the service is over, Ivan Ivanovich cannot refrain from passing the poor people in review. He probably would not have cared to undertake this tiresome work, if his natural goodness had not urged him to it. "Good-day, beggar!" he generally said, selecting the most crippled old woman in the most threadbare garment made of patches. "Whence come you, my poor woman?"

"I come from the farm, panochka [master dear]. "Tis two days since I have eaten or drunk: my own children drove me out."

"Poor soul! why did you come hither?"

"To beg alms, panochka, to see whether some one will not give at least enough for bread."

"Hm! so you want bread?" Ivan Ivanovich generally inquired.

"How should I not want it? I am as hungry as a dog."

"Hm!" replied Ivan Ivanovich usually, "and perhaps you would like butter too?"

"Yes; everything which your kindness will give; I will be content with all."

"Hm! Is butter better than bread?"

"How is a hungry person to choose? Any thing you please, all is good." Thereupon the old woman generally extended her hand.

"Well, go with God's blessing," said Ivan Ivanovich. "Why do you stand there? I'm not beating you." And turning to a second and a third with the same questions, he finally returns home, or goes to drink a little glass of vodka with his neighbor, Ivan Nikiforovich, or the judge, or the chief of police.

Ivan Ivanovich is very fond of receiving presents. This pleases him very much.

A very fine man also is Ivan Nikiforovich. They are such friends as the world never saw. Anton Prokofievich Golopuz, who goes about to this hour in his cinnamon-colored surtout with blue sleeves, and dines every Sunday with the judge, was in the habit of saying that the Devil himself had bound Ivan Ivanovich and Ivan Nikiforovich together with a rope: where one goes, the other follows.

Ivan Nikiforovich was never married. Although it was reported that he was married, it was completely false. I know Ivan Nikiforovich very well, and am able to state that he never even had any intention of marrying. Where do all these scandals originate? In the same way it was rumored that Ivan Nikiforovich was born with a tail! But this invention is so clumsy, and at the same time so horrible and indecent, that I do not even consider it necessary to refute it for the benefit of civilized readers, to whom it is doubtless known that only witches, and very few even of those, have tails. Witches, moreover, belong more to the feminine than to the masculine gender.

In spite of their great friendship, these rare friends were not always agreed between themselves. Their characters can best be known by comparing them. Ivan Ivanovich has the unusual gift of speaking in an extremely pleasant manner. Heavens! How he does speak! The feeling can best be described by comparing it to that which you experience when some one combs your head, or draws his finger softly across your heel. You listen and listen until you drop your head. Pleasant, exceedingly pleasant! like the sleep after a bath. Ivan Nikiforovich, on the contrary, is more reticent; but, if he once takes up the word, look out for yourself! He shaves better than any barber.

Ivan Ivanovich is tall and thin; Ivan Nikiforovich is rather shorter in stature, but he makes it up in thickness. Ivan Ivanovich's head is like a radish, tail down; Ivan Nikiforovich's like a radish with the tail up. Ivan Ivanovich lies on the veranda in his shirt after dinner only: in the evening he dons his bekesha, and goes out somewhere, either to the village store, where he supplies flour, or into the fields to catch quail. Ivan Nikiforovich lies all day on his porch; if the day is not too hot, he generally turns his back to the sun, and will not go anywhere. If it happens to occur to him in the morning, he walks through the yard, inspects the domestic affairs, and retires again to his room.

In early days he used to go to Ivan Ivanovich. Ivan Ivanovich is a very refined man, and in polite conversation never utters an impolite word, and is offended at once if he hears one. Ivan Nikiforovich is not always on his guard. On such occasions Ivan Ivanovich usually rises from his seat, and says, "Enough, enough, Ivan Nikiforovich! it's better to go out into the sun at once, than to utter such godless words."

Ivan Ivanovich goes into a terrible rage if a fly falls into his beet-soup; then he is fairly beside himself; and he flings away his plate, and the house-keeper catches it. Ivan Nikiforovich is exceedingly fond of bathing; and, when he gets up to the neck in water, he orders a table and a samovar to be placed on the water, and he is very fond of drinking tea in that cool position. Ivan Ivanovich shaves his beard twice a week; Ivan Nikiforovich, once. Ivan Ivanovich is extremely curious. God preserve you if you begin to tell him anything, and do not finish it! If he is displeased with anything, he lets it be seen at once. It is very hard to tell from Ivan Nikiforovich's countenance whether he is pleased or angry: even if he is rejoiced at anything, he will not show it.

Ivan Ivanovich is of a rather timid character: Ivan Nikiforovich, on the contrary, has such full folds in his trousers, that, if you were to inflate them, you might put the court-yard, with its store-houses and buildings, inside them. Ivan Ivanovich has large, expressive eyes, of a snuff color, and a mouth shaped something like the letter V Ivan Nikiforovich has small, yellowish eyes, quite concealed between heavy brows and fat cheeks; and his nose is the shape of a ripe plum. If Ivan Ivanovich treats you to snuff, he always licks the cover of his box first with his tongue, then taps on it with his finger, and says, as he raises it, if you are an acquaintance, "Dare I beg you, sir, to give me the pleasure?"—if a stranger, "Dare I beg you, sir, though I have not the honor of knowing your rank, name, and family, to do me the favor?" But Ivan Nikiforovich puts his box straight into your hand, and merely adds, "Do me the favor." Neither Ivan Ivanovich nor Ivan Nikiforovich loves fleas; and therefore, neither Ivan Ivanovich nor Ivan Nikiforovich will, on any account, admit a Jew with his wares, without purchasing of him elixir in various little boxes, as remedies against these insects, having first rated him well for belonging to the Hebrew faith.

But, in spite of numerous dissimilarities, Ivan Ivanovich and Ivan Nikiforovich are both very fine men.

II
FROM WHICH MAY BE SEEN WHAT IVAN IVANOVICH WANTED, WHENCE AROSE THE DISCUSSION BETWEEN IVAN IVANOVICH AND IVAN NIKIFOROVICH, AND WHERE IT ENDED.

ONE MORNING—IT was in July—Ivan Ivanovich was lying on his veranda. The day was warm; the air was dry, and came in gusts. Ivan Ivanovich had been to town, to the mowers, and at the farm, and had succeeded in asking all the muzhiks [peasants] and women whom he met, whence, whither, and why. He was fearfully tired, and had lain down to rest. As he lay there, he looked at the store-houses, the court-yard, the sheds, the chickens running about, and thought to himself, "My Heavens! What a master I am! What is there that I have not? Birds, buildings, granaries, everything I take a fancy to; genuine distilled vodka; pears and plums in the orchard; poppies, cabbages, peas, in the garden;…what is there which I have not? I should like to know what there is that I have not?"

As he put this profound question to himself, Ivan Ivanovich reflected; and meantime, his eyes, in their search after fresh objects, crossed the fence into Ivan Nikiforovich's yard, and involuntarily took note of a curious sight. A fat woman was bringing out clothes, which had been packed away, and spreading them out on the line to air. Presently an old uniform with worn trimmings was swinging its sleeves in the air, and embracing a brocade gown; from behind it peeped a court-coat, its buttons stamped with coats-of-arms, and with moth-eaten collar; white cassimere pantaloons with spots, which had once upon a time clothed Ivan Nikiforovich's legs, and might now, possibly, fit his fingers. Behind them were speedily hung some more in the shape of the letter II. Then came a blue Cossack jacket, which Ivan Nikiforovich had had made twenty years before, when he prepared to enter the militia, and allowed his mustache to grow. And finally, one after another, appeared a sword, projecting into the air like a spit; then the skirts of a grass-green caftan-like garment, with copper buttons the size of a five-kopek piece, unfolded themselves. From among the folds peeped a vest bound with gold, with a wide opening in front. The vest was soon concealed by an old petticoat belonging to his dead grandmother, with pockets which would have held a watermelon. All these things piled together formed a very interesting spectacle for Ivan Ivanovich, while the sun's rays, falling upon bits of a blue or green sleeve, a red binding, or a scrap of gold brocade, or playing on the point of the sword, formed an unusual sight, similar to the representations of the Nativity given at farmhouses by wandering bands; particularly that part where the throng of people, pressing close together, gaze at King Herod in his golden crown, or at Anthony leading his goat: at these exhibitions the fiddle whines, a gypsy taps on his lips in lieu of a drum, and the sun goes down, and the cool freshness of the young night presses more strongly on the shoulders and bosoms of the plump farmers' wives.

Presently the old woman crawled, grunting, from the storeroom, dragging after her an old-fashioned saddle with broken stirrups, worn leather pistol-cases, and saddle-cloth, once red, with gilt embroidery and copper disks.

"Here's a stupid woman," thought Ivan Ivanovich. "She'll be dragging Ivan Nikiforovich out and airing him next."

And with reason: Ivan Ivanovich was not so far wrong in his surmise. Five minutes later, Ivan Nikiforovich's nankeen trousers appeared, and took nearly half the yard to themselves. After that she fetched out a hat and a gun.

"What's the meaning of this?" thought Ivan Ivanovich. "I never saw Ivan Nikiforovich have a gun. What does he want with it? Whether he shoots, or not, he keeps a gun! Of what use is it to him? But it's a splendid thing. I have long wanted to get just such a one; I want that gun very much: I like to amuse myself with a gun. Hello, there, woman, woman!" shouted Ivan Ivanovich, beckoning to her.

The old woman approached the fence.

"What's that you have there, my good woman?"

"A gun, as you see."

"What sort of a gun?"

"Who knows what sort of a gun? If it were mine, perhaps I should know what it is made of; but it is my master's."

Ivan Ivanovich rose, and began to examine the gun on all sides, and forgot to reprove the old woman for hanging it and the sword to air.

"It must be iron," went on the old woman.

"Hm! iron! why iron?" said Ivan Ivanovich to himself. "Has your master had it long?"

"Yes; long, perhaps."

"It's a nice thing!" continued Ivan Ivanovich. "I will ask him for it. What can he do with it? I'll exchange with him for it. Is your master at home, my good woman?"

"Yes."

"What is he doing? lying down?"

"Yes, lying down."

"Very well, I will come to him."

Ivan Ivanovich dressed himself, took his well-seasoned stick for the benefit of the dogs (for, in Mirgorod, there are more dogs than people to be met in the street), and went out.

Although Ivan Nikiforovich's house was next door to Ivan Ivanovich's, so that you could have got from one to the other by climbing the fence, yet Ivan Ivanovich went by the street. From the street it was necessary to turn into an alley which was so narrow, that if two one-horse carts chanced to meet, they could not get out, and were forced to remain there until the drivers, seizing the hind-wheels, dragged them in opposite directions into the street, and pedestrians drew aside like flowers growing by the fence on either hand. Ivan Ivanovich's wagon-shed adjoined this alley on one side; and on the other, Ivan Nikiforovich's granary, gate, and pigeon-house.

Ivan Ivanovich went up to the gate, and rattled the latch. Within arose the barking of dogs; but the motley-haired pack ran back, wagging their tails, when they saw the well-known face. Ivan Ivanovich traversed the court-yard, in which were collected Indian doves fed by Ivan Nikiforovich's own hand, watermelon, and melon-rinds, vegetables, broken wheels, barrel-hoops, or a wallowing small boy with dirty blouse—a picture such as painters love. The shadows of the fluttering clothes covered nearly the whole of the yard, and lent it a degree of coolness. The woman greeted him with an inclination, and stood, gaping, in one spot. The front of the house was adorned with a small porch, its roof supported on two oak pillars—a welcome protection from the sun, which at that season in Little Russia [the Ukraine] loves not to jest, and bathes the pedestrian from head to foot in boiling perspiration. From this it may be judged how powerful was Ivan Ivanovich's desire to obtain an indispensable article, when he made up his mind, at such an hour, to depart from his usual custom, which was to walk about only in the evening.

The room which Ivan Ivanovich entered was quite dark, for the shutters were closed; and the ray of sunlight falling through a hole made in the shutter, took on the colors of the rainbow, and, striking the opposite wall, sketched upon it a party-colored picture of the outlines of roofs, trees, and the clothes suspended in the yard, only upside down. This gave the room a peculiar half-light.

"God assist you!" said Ivan Ivanovich.

"Ah! how do you do, Ivan Ivanovich?" replied a voice from the corner of the room. Then only did Ivan Ivanovich perceive Ivan Nikiforovich, lying upon a rug which was spread on the floor. "Excuse me for appearing before you in a state of nature."

"Not at all. You have been asleep to-day, Ivan Nikiforovich?"

"I have been asleep. Have you been asleep, Ivan Ivanovich?"

"I have."

"And now you have risen?"

"Now I have risen. Christ be with you, Ivan Nikiforovich! How can you sleep until this time? I have just come from the farm. There's very fine barley on the road, charming! and the hay is so tall and soft and golden!"

"Gorpina!" shouted Ivan Nikiforovich, "fetch Ivan Ivanovich some vodka, and some pastry and sour cream!"

"Fine weather, we're having to-day."

"Don't praise it, Ivan Ivanovich! Devil take it! You can't get away from the heat."

"Now, why need you mention the Devil! Ah, Ivan Nikiforovich! you will recall my words when it's too late. You will suffer in the next world for such godless words."

"How have I offended you, Ivan Ivanovich? I have not attacked your father nor your mother. I don't know how I have insulted you."

"Enough, enough, Ivan Nikiforovich!"

"By Heavens, Ivan Ivanovich, I did not insult you!"

"It's strange that the quails haven't come yet to the whistle."

"Think what you please, but I have not insulted you in any way"

"I don't know why they don't come," said Ivan Ivanovich, as if he did not hear Ivan Nikiforovich; "it is more than time for them already;...but they seem to need more time, for some reason."

"You say that the barley is good?"

"Splendid barley, splendid!"

A silence ensued.

"So you are having your clothes aired, Ivan Nikiforovich?" said Ivan Ivanovich, at length.

"Yes: those cursed women have ruined some beautiful clothes; almost new, they were, too. Now I'm having them aired: the cloth is fine and handsome. They only need turning to make them fit to wear again."

"One thing among them pleased me extremely, Ivan Nikiforovich."

"Which was that?"

"Tell me, please, what do you do with the gun that has been put to air with the clothes?" Here Ivan Ivanovich offered his snuff. "May I ask you to do me the favor?"

"By no means! take it yourself: I will use my own." Thereupon Ivan Nikiforovich felt about him, and got hold of his snuff-box. "That stupid woman! So she hung the gun out to air. That Jew makes good snuff in Sorochintzi. I don't know what he puts into it, but it is so fragrant. It is a little like tansy. Here, take a little, and chew it: isn't it like tansy?"

"Say, Ivan Nikiforovich, I want to talk about that gun: what are you going to do with it? You don't need it."

"Why don't I need it? I might want to shoot."

"God be with you, Ivan Nikiforovich! When will you shoot? At the millennium, perhaps? So far as I know, or any one can recollect, you never killed even a duck: yes, and your nature was not so constructed that you can shoot. You have a dignified bearing and figure: how are you to drag yourself about the marshes, when your garment, which it is not polite to mention in conversation by name, is being aired at this very moment? What then? No: you require rest, repose." (Ivan Ivanovich, as has been hinted at above, employed uncommonly picturesque language when it was necessary to persuade any one. How he talked! Heavens, how he could talk!) "Yes, and you require polite actions. See here, give it to me!"

"The idea! The gun is valuable: you can't find such guns anywhere nowadays. I bought it of a Turk when I joined the militia; and now, to give it away all of a sudden! Impossible! It is an indispensable article."

"Indispensable for what?"

"For what? What if robbers should attack the house?…Indispensable indeed! Glory to God! now I am at ease, and fear no one. And why? Because I know that a gun stands in my store-house."

"A fine gun that! Why, Ivan Nikiforovich, the hammer is spoiled."

"What! how spoiled? It can be repaired: all that needs to be done is to rub it with hemp-oil, so that it may not rust."

"I see in your words, Ivan Nikiforovich, anything but a friendly disposition towards me. You will do nothing for me in token of friendship."

"How can you say, Ivan Ivanovich, that I show you no friendship? You ought to be ashamed of yourself. Your oxen pasture on my steppes, and I have never interfered with them. When you go to Poltava, you always beg my wagon, and what then? Have I ever refused? Your children climb over the fence into my yard, and play with my dogs—I never say anything; let them play, so long as they touch nothing; let them play!"

"If you won't give it to me, then let us exchange."

"What will you give me for it?" Thereupon Ivan Nikiforovich raised himself on his elbow, and looked at Ivan Ivanovich.

"I will give you my dark-brown sow, the one I have fed in the sty. A magnificent sow. You'll see, she'll bring you a litter of pigs next year."

"I do not see, Ivan Ivanovich, how you can talk so. What could I do with your sow? Make a funeral dinner for the Devil?"

"Again! You can't get along without the Devil! It's a sin! by Heaven, it's a sin, Ivan Nikiforovich!"

"What do you mean, in fact, Ivan Ivanovich, by giving, the deuce knows what—a sow—for my gun?"

"Why is she 'the deuce knows what,' Ivan Nikiforovich?"

"Why? You can judge for yourself perfectly well: here's the gun, a known thing; but the deuce knows what that sow is! If it had not been you who said it, Ivan Ivanovich, I might have put an insulting construction on it."

"What defect have you observed in the sow?"

"For what do you take me, in fact—for a sow?"…

"Sit down, sit down! I won't…No matter about your gun; let it rot and rust where it stands, in the corner of the storeroom. I don't want to say anything more about it!"

After this a pause ensued.

"They say," began Ivan Ivanovich, "that three kings have declared war on our Tzar."

"Yes: Peter Feodorovich told me. What sort of a war is this, and why?"

"I cannot say exactly, Ivan Nikiforovich, what the cause is. I suppose the kings want us to adopt the Turkish faith."

"Fools! they would have it," said Ivan Nikiforovich, raising his head.

"So, you see, our Tzar declared war on them in consequence. 'No,' says he, 'do you adopt the faith of Christ!'"

"What? Why, our people will beat them, Ivan Ivanovich!"

"They will. So you won't swap the gun, Ivan Nikiforovich?"

"It's a strange thing to me, Ivan Ivanovich, that you, who seem to be a man distinguished for sense, should talk such nonsense. What a fool I should be!"

"Sit down, sit down. God be with it! let it burst! I won't mention it again."

At this moment, lunch was brought in.

Ivan Ivanovich drank a glass, and ate a pie with sour cream. "Listen, Ivan Nikiforovich: I will give you, besides the sow, two sacks of oats; you did not sow any oats. You'll have to buy oats this year, in any case."

"By Heaven, Ivan Ivanovich, I must tell you, you are very green! [This is nothing: Ivan Nikiforovich does not even stop at such phrases.] Who ever heard of swapping a gun for two sacks of oats? Never fear, you don't offer your coat."

"But you forget, Ivan Nikiforovich, that I am to give you the sow too."

"What! two sacks of oats and a sow for a gun?"

"Why, is it too little?"

"For a gun?"

"Of course, for a gun."

"Two sacks for a gun?"

"Two sacks, not empty, but filled with oats; and you've forgotten the sow."

"Kiss your sow; and, if you don't like that, then go to the Evil One!"

"Oh, get angry now, do! See here: they'll stick your tongue full of red-hot needles in the other world, for such godless words. After a conversation with you, one has to wash his face and hands, and fumigate himself."

"Permit me, Ivan Ivanovich: my gun is a noble thing, the most curious toy; and, besides, it is a very agreeable decoration in a room.".....

"You go on like a fool about that gun of yours, Ivan Nikiforovich," said Ivan Ivanovich with vexation; for he was beginning to be really angry.

"And you, Ivan Ivanovich, are a regular *goose!*"

If Ivan Nikiforovich had not uttered that word, then they would have quarreled, but would have parted friends as usual; but now things took quite another turn. Ivan Ivanovich flew into a rage.

"What was that you said, Ivan Nikiforovich?" he asked, raising his voice.

"I said you were like a goose, Ivan Ivanovich!"

"How dare you, sir, forgetful of decency, and the respect due a man's rank and family, insult him with such a disgraceful name!"

"What is there disgraceful about it? And why are you flourishing your hands so, Ivan Ivanovich?"

"How dared you, I repeat, in disregard of all decency, call me a goose?"

"I spit on your head, Ivan Ivanovich! What are you screaming so for?"

Ivan Ivanovich could no longer control himself: his lips quivered; his mouth lost its usual V shape, and became like the letter O; he winked so that he was terrible to look at. This very rarely happened with Ivan Ivanovich: it was necessary that he should be extremely angry first.

"Then, I declare to you," exclaimed Ivan Ivanovich, "that I will not know you!"

"A great pity! By Heaven, I shall never cry on that account!" retorted Ivan Nikiforovich. He lied, he lied, by Heaven, he lied! it was very annoying to him.

"I will never put my foot inside your house again!"

"Oho, ho!" said Ivan Nikiforovich, vexed, yet not knowing himself what to do, and rising to his feet, contrary to his custom. "Hey, there, woman, boy!" Thereupon, there appeared at the door the same fat woman, and small boy, enveloped in a long and wide surtout. "Take Ivan Ivanovich by the arms, and lead him to the door!"

"What! a nobleman?" shouted Ivan Ivanovich with a feeling of vexation and dignity. "Just do it if you dare! Come on! I'll annihilate you and your stupid master. The crow won't be able to find your bones." (Ivan Ivanovich spoke with uncommon force when his spirit was up.)

The group presented a striking picture: Ivan Nikiforovich standing in the middle of the room; the woman with her mouth wide open, and the most senseless, terrified look on her face; Ivan Ivanovich with uplifted hand, as the Roman tribunes are depicted. This was an extraordinary moment, a magnificent spectacle: and yet there was but one spectator; this was the boy in the extensive surtout, who stood quite quietly, and picked his nose with his finger.

Finally Ivan Ivanovich took his hat. "You have behaved well, Ivan Nikiforovich, extremely well! I shall remember it."

"Go, Ivan Ivanovich, go! and see that you don't come in my way: if you do, I'll beat your ugly face to a jelly, Ivan Ivanovich!"

"Take that, Ivan Nikiforovich!" retorted Ivan Ivanovich, making an insulting gesture, and banged the door, which squeaked and flew open behind him.

Ivan Nikiforovich appeared at the door, and wanted to add something more; but Ivan Ivanovich did not glance back, and hastened from the yard.

III

WHAT TOOK PLACE AFTER IVAN IVANOVICH'S QUARREL WITH IVAN NIKIFOROVICH.

AND THUS TWO respectable men, the pride and honor of Mirgorod, had quarreled, and about what? About a bit of nonsense—a goose. They would not see each other, broke off all connection, while hitherto they had been known as the most inseparable friends. Every day Ivan Ivanovich and Ivan Nikiforovich had sent to inquire about each other's health, and often conversed together from their balconies, and said such charming things as it did the heart good to listen to. On Sundays, Ivan Ivanovich, in his lambskin bekesha, and Ivan Nikiforovich, in his yellowish cinnamon-colored nankeen casaquin, used to set out for church almost arm in arm; and if Ivan Ivanovich, who had remarkably sharp eyes, was the first to catch sight of a puddle or any dirt in the street, which sometimes happened in Mirgorod, he always said to Ivan Nikiforovich, "Look out! don't put your foot there, it's dirty." Ivan Nikiforovich, on his side, exhibited the same touching tokens of friendship; and wherever he chanced to be standing, he always held out his hand to Ivan Ivanovich with his snuff-box, saying, "Do me the favor!" And what fine managers both were.... And these two friends...When I heard of it, it struck me like a flash of lightning. For a long time I would not believe it. Ivan Ivanovich had quarreled with Ivan Nikiforovich! Such worthy people! What is to be depended upon, then, in this world?

When Ivan Ivanovich reached home, he remained long in a state of strong excitement. He usually went, first of all, to the stable, to see whether his mare was eating her hay (Ivan Ivanovich had a bay mare, with a white star on her forehead: a very pretty little mare she was too), then to feed the turkeys and little pigs with his own hand, and then to his room, where he either made wooden dishes (he could make various vessels of wood very tastefully, quite as well as any turner), or read a book printed by Liubia, Garia and Popoff (Ivan Ivanovich never could remember the name, because the serving-maid had long before torn off the top part of the title page while amusing the children), or rested on the veranda. But now he did not betake himself to any of his ordinary occupations. Instead, on encountering Gapka, he began to scold because she was loitering about without any occupation, though she was carrying groats to the kitchen; flung a stick at a cock which came upon the veranda for his customary treat; and when the dirty little boy, in his little torn blouse, ran up to him, and shouted, "Papa, papa! give me a honey-cake," he threatened him and stamped at him so fiercely that the frightened child fled, God knows whither.

But at last he bethought himself, and began to busy himself with his every-day duties. He dined late, and it was almost night when he lay down to rest on the veranda. A good beet-soup with pigeons, which Gapka cooked for him, quite drove from his mind the occurrences of the morning. Again Ivan Ivanovich began to gaze at his belongings with satisfaction: at length his eye rested on the neighboring yard; and he said to himself, "I have not been to Ivan Nikiforovich's to-day: I'll go there now." So saying, Ivan Ivanovich took his stick and his hat, and directed his steps to the street; but scarcely had he passed through the gate, when he recollected the quarrel, spit, and turned back. Almost the same thing happened at Ivan Nikiforovich's house. Ivan Ivanovich saw the woman put her foot on the fence, with the intention of climbing over into his yard, when suddenly Ivan Nikiforovich's voice became audible. "Back! back! it won't do!" But Ivan Ivanovich found it very tiresome. It is quite possible that these worthy men would have made peace next day, if a certain occurrence in Ivan Ivanovich's house had not destroyed all hopes, and poured oil upon the fire of enmity which was ready to die out.

On the evening of that very day, Agafya Fedosyevna arrived at Ivan Nikiforovich's. Agafya Fedosyevna was not Ivan Nikiforovich's relative, nor his sister-in-law, nor even his fellow-godparent. There seemed to be no reason why she should come to him, and he was not particularly glad of her company; still, she came, and lived on him for weeks at a time, and even longer. Then she took possession of the keys, and took the whole house into her own hands. This was extremely displeasing to Ivan Nikiforovich; but he, to his amazement, minded her like a child; and although he occasionally attempted to dispute, yet Agafya Fedosyevna always got the better of him.

I must confess that I do not understand why things are so arranged, that women seize us by the nose as deftly as they do the handle of a teapot: either their hands are so constructed, or else our noses are good for nothing else. And notwithstanding the fact that Ivan Nikiforovich's nose somewhat resembled a plum, she grasped that nose, and led him about after her like a dog. He even, in her presence, involuntarily altered his ordinary manner of life.

Agafya Fedosyevna wore a cap on her head, three warts on her nose, and a coffee-colored cloak with yellow flowers. Her figure was like a cask, and it would have been as hard to tell where to look for her waist, as for her to see her nose without a mirror. Her feet were small, and formed in the shape of two cushions. She talked scandal, and ate boiled beet-soup in the morning, and swore extremely well; and amidst all these various occupations, her countenance never for one instant changed its expression, which phenomenon, as a rule, women alone are capable of displaying.

Just as soon as she arrived, everything went wrong side before. "Ivan Nikiforovich, don't you make peace with him, nor ask his forgiveness; he wants to ruin you; that's the kind of man he is! you don't know him yet!" that cursed woman whispered and whispered, and managed so that Ivan Nikiforovich would not even hear Ivan Ivanovich mentioned.

All assumed another aspect. If his neighbor's dog ran into the yard, it was beaten within an inch of its life; the children, who climbed over the fence, were sent back with howls, their little shirts stripped up, and marks of a switch behind; even the woman, when Ivan Ivanovich undertook to ask her about something, did something so insulting, that Ivan Ivanovich, being an extremely delicate man, only spit, and muttered, "What a nasty woman! even worse than her master!"

Finally, as a climax to all the insults, his hated neighbor built a goose-coop right against his fence where they usually climbed over, as if with the express intention of redoubling the insult. This coop, so hateful to Ivan Ivanovich, was constructed with diabolical swiftness—in one day.

This aroused wrath and a desire for revenge in Ivan Ivanovich. Nevertheless, he showed no signs of bitterness, in spite of the fact that the coop trespassed on his land; but his heart beat so violently, that it was extremely difficult for him to preserve this calm appearance.

He passed through the day in this manner. Night came.... Oh, if I were a painter, how magnificently I would depict the night's charms! I would describe how all Mirgorod sleeps; how steadily the myriads of stars gaze down upon it; how the apparent quiet is filled far and near with the barking of dogs; how the love-sick sacristan steals past them, and scales the fence with knightly fearlessness; how the white walls of the houses, bathed in the moonlight, grow whiter still, the overhanging trees darker; how the shadows of the trees fall blacker, the flowers and the silent grass become more fragrant, and the crickets, unharmonious cavaliers of the night, strike up their rattling song in friendly fashion on all sides. I would describe how, in one of these little, low-roofed, clay houses, the black-browed village maid, tossing on her lonely couch, dreams with heaving bosom of hussar's spurs and mustache, and how the moonlight smiles upon her cheeks. I would describe how the black shadows of the bats flit along the white road, before they alight upon the white chimneys of the cottages....

But it would hardly be within my power to depict Ivan Ivanovich, as he crept out that night, saw in hand; and the various emotions written on his countenance! Quietly, so quietly, he crawled along, and climbed upon the goose-coop. Ivan Nikiforovich's dogs knew nothing, as yet, of the quarrel between them; and so they permitted him, as an old friend, to enter the coop, which rested upon four oaken posts. Creeping up to the nearest post, he applied his saw, and began to cut. The noise produced by the saw caused him to glance about him every moment, but the recollection of the insult refreshed his courage. The first post was sawed through. Ivan Ivanovich began upon the next. His eyes burned, and he saw nothing for terror. All at once Ivan Ivanovich uttered an exclamation, and became petrified with fear: a dead man appeared to him; but he speedily recovered himself on perceiving that it was a goose, thrusting its neck out at him. Ivan Ivanovich spit with vexation, and proceeded with his work; and the second post was sawed through. The building trembled. Ivan Ivanovich's heart beat so violently, when he began on the third, that he had to stop several times. The post was more than half sawed through, when the frail building quivered violently....

Ivan Ivanovich had barely time to spring back when it tumbled down with a crash. Seizing his saw, he ran home in the greatest terror, and flung himself upon his bed, without having sufficient courage to peep from the window at the consequences of his terrible deed. It seemed to him as though Ivan Nikiforovich's entire household assembled: the old woman, Ivan Nikiforovich, the boy in the endless surtout, all with sticks,…led by Agafya Fedosyevna, were coming to tear down and destroy his house.

Ivan Ivanovich passed the whole of the following day in a perfect fever. It seemed to him that his detested neighbor would set fire to his house at least, in revenge for this; and so he gave orders to Gapka to look everywhere constantly, and see whether dry straw were laid against it anywhere. Finally, in order to forestall Ivan Nikiforovich, he determined to run ahead, like a hare, and enter a complaint against him before the district judge of Mirgorod. In what it consisted, can be learned from the following chapter.

IV
WHAT TOOK PLACE BEFORE THE DISTRICT JUDGE OF MIRGOROD.

A WONDERFUL TOWN is Mirgorod! How many buildings are there under straw, rush, and even wooden roofs! On the right is a street, on the left a street, and fine fences everywhere: over them twine hop-vines, upon them hang pots; from behind them the sunflowers show their sun-like heads, poppies blush, fat pumpkins peep,…luxury itself! The fence is always garnished with articles which render it still more picturesque: women's widespread undergarments of checked woollen stuff, shirts or trousers. There is no such thing as theft or rascality in Mirgorod, so everybody hangs upon his fence whatever strikes his fancy. If you will go to the square, you will surely stop and admire the view: a puddle, such a wonderful puddle, is there! the only one you ever saw. It occupies nearly the whole of the square. A truly magnificent puddle! The houses and cottages, which at a distance might be mistaken for hay-ricks, stand around it, lost in admiration of its beauty.

But I agree with those who think that there is no better house than that of the district judge. Whether it is of oak or birch, is nothing to the point; but it has, my dear sirs, eight windows! eight windows in a row, directly on the square, and upon that watery expanse, which I have just mentioned, and which the chief of police calls a lake. It alone is painted the color of granite. All the other houses in Mirgorod are merely whitewashed. Its roof is all of wood, and would have been even painted red, had not the government clerks eaten the oil which had been prepared for that purpose, having flavored it with garlic, as it happened, as if expressly, during a fast; and so the roof remained unpainted. Towards the square projects a porch, which the chickens frequently visit, because that porch is nearly always strewn with grain or some edible, not intentionally, but through the carelessness of visitors. The house is divided into two parts: one part is the court-room; the other, the jail. In the half which contains the court-room are two neat, whitewashed rooms—one, the front one, for clients, the other containing a table adorned with ink-spots. Upon the table is a looking-glass; there are four oak chairs with tall backs; along the wall stand iron-bound chests, in which are preserved bundles of district law-suit papers. Upon one of the chests stood at that time a pair of boots, polished with wax.

The court had been open since morning. The judge, a pretty large man, though thinner than Ivan Nikiforovich, with a good-natured face, a greasy dressing-gown, a pipe, and a cup of tea, was conversing with the clerk of the court.

The judges lips were directly under his nose, so that he could snuff his upper lip as much as he liked. This lip served him instead of a snuff-box, for the snuff intended for his nose almost always lodged upon it. So the judge was talking with the assistant. A barefooted girl held a tray with cups on one side of them. At the end of the table, the secretary was reading the decision in some case, but in such a mournful and monotonous voice, that the condemned man himself would have fallen asleep while listening to it. The judge, no doubt, would have been the first of all to do so, had he not entered into an engrossing conversation while it was going on.

"I expressly tried to find out," said the judge, sipping his tea from the already cold cup, "how they manage to sing so well. I had a splendid thrush two years ago. Well, all of a sudden he was completely spoiled, and began to sing God knows what: he got worse, and worse, and worse, as time went on; he began to rattle and get hoarse—just good for nothing! And it's all nonsense! this is why it happened: a little lump, not so big as a pea, came under his throat. It was only necessary to prick that little swelling with a needle. Zachar Prokofievich taught me that; and, if you like, I'll tell you just how it was. I go to him"…

"Shall I read another, Demyan Demyanovich?" broke in the secretary, who had not been reading for several minutes.

"Have you finished already? Just think how quick! And I did not hear a word of it! Where is it? Give it here, and I'll sign it. What else have you there?"

"The case of Cossack Bokitok for stealing a cow."

"Very good; read it! Yes, so I go to him.... I can even tell you in detail how he entertained me. There was vodka and dried sturgeon, excellent! Yes, not our sturgeon" (here the judge smacked his tongue, and smiled, upon which his nose took a snuff at its usual snuff-box), "such as our Mirgorod shops furnish us. I ate no herrings, for, as you know, they give me heart-burn; but I tasted the caviare—very fine caviare! There's no doubt about it, excellent. Then I drank some peach-brandy, real gentian. There was saffron-brandy too; but, as you know, I never take that. You see, it was very good. In the first place, to whet your appetite, as they say, and then to satisfy it...Ah! speak of an angel"...exclaimed the judge, all at once, catching sight of Ivan Ivanovich as he entered.

"God be with us! I wish you a good-morning," said Ivan Ivanovich, bowing all round with his usual politeness. My God! how well he under-stood the art of fascinating everybody with all his ways! I never beheld such refinement. He knew his own worth quite well, and therefore looked for universal respect as his due. The judge himself handed Ivan Ivanovich a chair; and his nose inhaled all the snuff from his upper lip, which, with him, was always a sign of great pleasure.

"What will you take, Ivan Ivanovich?" he inquired: "will you have a cup of tea?"

"No, much obliged," replied Ivan Ivanovich, bowed and seated himself.

"Do me the favor—one little cup," repeated the judge.

"No, thank you; much obliged for your hospitality," replied Ivan Ivanovich, and rose, bowed, and sat down.

"Just one little cup," repeated the judge.

"No, do not trouble yourself, Demyan Demyanovich." Whereupon Ivan Ivanovich again rose, bowed, and sat down.

"A little cup!"

"Very well, then, just a little cup," said Ivan Ivanovich, and reached out his hand to the tray

My Heavens! What a depth of refinement there was in that man! It is impossible to describe what a pleasant impression such manners produce!

"Will you not have another cup?"

"I thank you sincerely," answered Ivan Ivanovich, turning his cup upside down upon the tray, and bowing.

"Do me the favor, Ivan Ivanovich."

"I cannot; much obliged." Thereupon Ivan Ivanovich bowed, and sat down.

"Ivan Ivanovich, for the sake of our friendship, just one little cup!"

"No: I am extremely indebted for your hospitality." So saying, Ivan Ivanovich bowed, and seated himself.

"Only a cup, one little cup!"

Ivan Ivanovich put out his hand to the tray, and took a cup.

Oh, the deuce! How, how can a man contrive to support his dignity!

"Demyan Demyanovich," said Ivan Ivanovich, swallowing the last mouthful, "I have pressing business with you: I want to enter a complaint."

Then Ivan Ivanovich set down his cup, and drew from his pocket a sheet of stamped paper, written over. "A complaint against my enemy, my sworn enemy."

"And who is that?"

"Ivan Nikiforovich Dovgochkhun."

At these words, the judge nearly fell off his chair. "What do you say?" he exclaimed, clasping his hands: "Ivan Ivanovich, is this you?"

"You see yourself, that it is I."

"The Lord and all the saints be with you! What! You! Ivan Ivanovich! you have fallen out with Ivan Nikiforovich! Is it your mouth which says that? Repeat it! Is not some one hid behind you, who is speaking instead of you?"

"What is there incredible about it? I can't endure the sight of him: he has done me a deadly injury—he has insulted my honor."

"Holy Trinity! How am I to believe my mother now? Why every day, when I quarrel with my sister, the old woman says, 'Children, you live together like dogs. If you would only take pattern by Ivan Ivanovich and Ivan Nikiforovich, they are friends indeed! such friends! such worthy people!' There you are with your friend! Tell me what this is about. How is it?"

"It is a delicate business, Demyan Demyanovich; it is impossible to relate it in words: be pleased rather to read my petition. Here, take it by this side: it is more convenient."

"Read it, Taras Tikhonovich," said the judge, turning to the secretary. Taras Tikhonovich took the petition; and blowing his nose, as all district judges' secretaries blow their noses, with the assistance of two fingers, he began to read:

"From the nobleman and landed proprietor of the Mirgorod District, Ivan Pererepenko, son of Ivan, a petition: concerning which the following points are to be observed:

"1. Ivan Dovgochkhun, son of Nikifor, nobleman, known to all the world for his godless acts, which inspire disgust, and in lawlessness exceed all bounds, on the seventh day of July of this year 1810, conferred upon me a deadly insult, as touching my personal honor, and likewise as tending to the humiliation and confusion of my rank and family. The said nobleman, of repulsive aspect, has also a pugnacious disposition, and is full to overflowing of various sorts of blasphemy and quarrelsome words."...

Here the reader paused for an instant, to blow his nose again; but the judge folded his hands in approbation, and murmured to himself, "What a ready pen! Lord! how that man does write!"

Ivan Ivanovich requested that the reading might proceed, and Taras Tikhonovich went on:

"The said Ivan Dovgochkhun, son of Nikifor, when I went to him with a friendly proposition, called me publicly by an epithet insulting and injurious to my honor, namely, a goose, whereas it is known to the whole district of Mirgorod, that I never was named after that disgusting animal, and have no intention of ever being named after it. And the proof of my noble extraction is, that, in the baptismal register to be found in the Church of the Three Bishops, the day of my birth, and likewise the fact of my baptism, are inscribed. But a goose, as is well known to every one who has any knowledge of science, cannot be inscribed in the baptismal register; for a goose is not a man, but a fowl; which, likewise, is sufficiently well known, even to persons who have not been to a seminary. But the said evil-minded nobleman, being privy to all these facts, for no other purpose than to offer a deadly insult to my rank and calling, affronted me with the aforesaid foul word.

"2. And the same impolite and indecent nobleman, moreover, attempted injury to my property, inherited by me from my father, a member of the clerical profession, Ivan Pererépenko, son of Onisieff, of blessed memory, in that he, contrary to all law, transported directly opposite my porch, a goose-coop, which was done with no other intention than to emphasize the insult offered me; for the said coop had, up to that time, stood in a very good situation, and was still sufficiently strong. But the loathsome intention of the aforesaid nobleman consisted simply in this: viz., in making me a witness of unpleasant occurrences; for it is well known, that no man goes into a coop, much less into a goose-coop, for polite purposes. In the commission of his lawless deed, the two front posts trespassed on my land, received by me during the lifetime of my father, Ivan Pererépenko, son of Onisieff, of blessed memory, beginning at the granary, thence in a straight line to the spot where the women wash the pots.

"3. The above-described nobleman, whose very name and surname inspire thorough disgust, cherishes in his mind a malicious design to burn me in my own house. Which the infallible signs, hereinafter mentioned, fully demonstrate: in the first place, the said wicked nobleman has begun to emerge frequently from his apartments, which he never did formerly on account of his laziness and the disgusting corpulence of his body; in the second place, in his servants' apartments, adjoining the fence, surrounding my own land, received by me from my father, of blessed memory, Ivan Pererépenko, son of Onisieff, a light burns every day, and for a remarkably long period of time, which is also a clear proof of the fact. For hitherto, owing to his repulsive niggardliness, not only the tallow-candle, but also the grease-lamp, has been extinguished.

"And therefore I pray that the said nobleman, Ivan Dovgochkhun, son of Ivan, being plainly guilty of incendiarism, of insult to my rank, name, and family, and of illegal appropriation of my property, and, worse than all else, of malicious and deliberate addition to my surname, of the nickname of goose, be condemned by the court, to fine, satisfaction, costs, and damages, and that the aforesaid be put in irons as a criminal, and, being chained, be removed to the town jail, and that judgment be rendered upon this, my petition, immediately and without delay.

"Written and composed by Ivan Pererépenko, son of Ivan, nobleman, and landed proprietor of Mirgorod."

After the reading of the petition was concluded, the judge approached Ivan Ivanovich, took him by the button, and began to talk to him after this fashion. "What are you doing, Ivan Ivanovich? Fear God! throw away that petition, let it go! may Satan carry it off! Better take Ivan Nikiforovich by the hand, and kiss him, and buy some Santurinski or Nikopolski liquor, simply make a punch, and call me. We will drink it up together, and forget all."

"No, Demyan Demyanovich! its not that sort of an affair," said Ivan Ivanovich, with the dignity which always became him so well; "it is not an affair which can be arranged by a friendly agreement. Farewell! Good-day to you also, gentlemen," he continued with the same dignity, turning to them all. "I hope that my petition will give rise to the proper action." And out he went, leaving all present in a state of stupefaction.

The judge sat down without uttering a word; the secretary took a pinch of snuff; the clerks upset some broken fragments of bottles which served for ink-stands; and the judge himself, in absence of mind, spread out a puddle of ink upon the table with his finger.

"What do you say to this, Dorofei Trofimovich?" said the judge, turning to the assistant after a pause.

"I've nothing to say," replied the clerk.

"What things do go on!" continued the judge. He had not finished saying this, when the door creaked, and the front half of Ivan Nikiforovich presented itself in the court-room: the rest of him remained in the ante-room. The appearance of Ivan Nikiforovich, and in court, too, seemed so extraordinary, that the judge screamed; the secretary stopped reading; and one clerk, in his frieze imitation of a dress-coat, took his pen in his lips; and the other swallowed a fly; even the constable on service, and the watchman, a discharged soldier, who up to that moment had stood by the door scratching about his dirty blouse, with its chevrons of merit on the shoulder, even this invalid dropped his jaw, and trod on some ones foot.

"What chance brings you here? What and how? How is your health, Ivan Nikiforovich?"

But Ivan Nikiforovich was neither dead nor alive; for he was stuck fast in the door, and could not take a step either forwards or backwards. In vain did the judge shout into the ante-room that some one there should push Ivan Nikiforovich forward into the court-room. In the ante-room was only one old woman with a petition, who, in spite of all the efforts of her bony hands, could accomplish nothing. Then one of the clerks, with thick lips, wide shoulders, and a thick nose, with eyes which looked askance and intoxicated, and with ragged elbows, approached the front half of Ivan Nikiforovich, crossed his hands for him as though he had been a child, and winked at the old soldier, who braced his knee against Ivan Nikiforovich's belly. In spite of the latter's piteous moans, he was squeezed out into the ante-room. Then they pulled the bolts, and opened the other half of the door. Meanwhile the clerk and his assistant, the soldier, breathing hard with their friendly exertions, exhaled such a strong odor that the court-room seemed temporarily converted into a drinking-room.

"Did you hurt yourself, Ivan Nikiforovich? I will tell my mother to send you a decoction of brandy, with which you need but to rub your back and stomach, and all your bad feelings will disappear."

But Ivan Nikiforovich dropped into a chair, and could utter no word beyond prolonged oh's. Finally, in a voice feeble and barely audible from fatigue, he exclaimed, "Wouldn't you like some?" and, drawing his snuff box from his pocket, he added, "Help yourself, if you please."

"Very glad to see you," replied the judge; "but I cannot conceive what made you put yourself to so much trouble, and favor us with so unexpected an honor."

"A petition!"…Ivan Nikiforovich managed to ejaculate.

"A petition? What petition?"

"A complaint"…(here the asthma entailed a prolonged pause)—"Oh!—a complaint against the rascal—Ivan Ivanovich Pererépenko!"

"And you too! Such particular friends! A complaint against such a benevolent man!"

"He's Satan himself!" ejaculated Ivan Nikiforovich abruptly.

The judge crossed himself.

"Take my petition, and read it."

"There is nothing to be done. Read it, Taras Tikhonovich," said the judge, turning to the secretary with an expression of displeasure, which caused his nose to sniff at his upper lip, which generally occurred only as a sign of great enjoyment. This independence on the part of his nose caused the judge still greater vexation. He pulled out his handkerchief, and rubbed off all the snuff from his upper lip, in order to punish it for its daring.

The secretary, having gone through his usual performance, which he always indulged in before he began to read—that is to say, without the aid of a pocket-handkerchief-began in his ordinary voice, in the following manner:

"Ivan Dovgochkhun, son of Nikofor, nobleman of the Mirgorod District, offers a petition, and begs attention to the following points:

"1. Through his hateful malice, and plainly manifested ill will, the person calling himself a nobleman, Ivan Pererépenko, son of Ivan, commits against me every manner of injury damage, and other spiteful deeds, which inspire me with terror; and yesterday at afternoon, like a brigand and a thief, with axes, saws, chisels, and various locksmith's tools, he came by night into my yard, and into my own goose-coop located within it, and with his own hand, and in outrageous manner, destroyed it; for which very illegal and burglarious deed, on my side I gave no manner of cause.

"2. The same nobleman Pererépenko has designs upon my life; and on the 7th of last month, cherishing this design in secret, he came to me, and began, in a friendly and sly manner, to demand of me a gun which was in my chamber, and offered me for it, with the miserliness peculiar to him, many worthless objects, such as a brown sow and two sacks of oats. But, divining at that time his criminal intentions, I endeavored in every way to dissuade him from it; but the said rascal and scoundrel, Ivan Pererépenko, son of Ivan, abused me like a muzhik, and since that time has cherished against me an irreconcilable enmity. His sister was well known to all the world as a loose character, and went off with a regiment of chasseurs which was stationed at Mirgorod, five years ago; but she inscribed her husband as a peasant. His father and mother also were not law-abiding people, and both were inconceivable drunkards. The aforementioned nobleman and robber Pererépenko, in his beastly and blameworthy actions, goes beyond all his family, and under the guise of piety does the most immoral things. He does not observe the fasts; for on the eve of St. Philips this atheist bought a sheep, and the next day he ordered his mistress, Gapka, to kill it, alleging that he needed tallow for lamps and candles at once.

"Therefore I pray that the said nobleman, a manifest robber, church-thief, rascal, convicted of plundering and stealing, may be put in irons, and confined in the jail or the government prison, and there, under supervision, deprived of his rank and nobility, he may be well flogged by barbarians, and banished to forced labor in Siberia for cause, and that he may be commanded to pay damages, losses, and that judgment may be rendered on this my petition.

"To this petition, Ivan Dovgochkhun, son of Nikofor, noble of the Mirgorod District, has set his hand."

As soon as the secretary had finished reading, Ivan Nikiforovich seized his hat, and bowed, with the intention of departing.

"Where are you going, Ivan Nikiforovich?" the judge called after him. "Sit yet a little while. Drink some tea. Orishko, why are you standing there, you stupid girl, winking at the clerks? Go, bring tea."

But Ivan Nikiforovich, in terror at having got so far from home, and at having undergone such a fearful quarantine, made haste to crawl through the door, saying, "Don't trouble yourself. It is with pleasure that I"—and closed it after him, leaving all present stupefied.

There was nothing to be done. Both petitions were entered; and the affair promised to assume a sufficiently serious aspect, when an unforeseen occurrence gave an added interest to it. As the judge was leaving the court, in company with the clerk and secretary, and the employees were thrusting into sacks the fowls, eggs, chunks of bread, pies, cracknels, and other odds and ends brought by plaintiffs—just at that moment a brown sow rushed into the room, and snatched, to the amazement of the spectators, neither a pie nor a crust of bread, but Ivan Nikiforovich's petition, which lay on the end of the table, with its leaves hanging over. Having seized the document, mistress sow ran off so briskly that not one of the clerks or officials could catch her, in spite of the rulers and ink-bottles they hurled after her.

This extraordinary occurrence produced a terrible muddle, for there had not even a copy been taken of the petition. The judge—that is to say, his secretary—and the assistant debated for a long time upon such an unheard-of affair. Finally it was decided to write a report of the matter to the prefect, as the investigation of the matter pertained more to the department of the city police. Report No. 389 was despatched to him that same day; and also upon that day there came to light a sufficiently curious explanation, which the reader can learn from the following chapter.

V

IN WHICH ARE DETAILED THE DELIBERATIONS OF TWO IMPORTANT
PERSONAGES OF MIRGOROD.

As SOON AS Ivan Ivanovich had arranged his domestic affairs, and stepped out upon the veranda, according to his custom, to lie down, then, to his indescribable amazement, he saw something red at the gate. This was the red facings of the chief of police's coat, which were polished equally with his collar, and had turned on the edges into varnished leather. Ivan Ivanovich thought to himself, "It's not bad that Peter Feodorovich has come to talk it over." But he was very much surprised to see that the chief was walking remarkably fast, and flourishing his hands, which very rarely happened with him. There were eight buttons planted about on the chief of police's uniform; the ninth, torn off in some manner during the procession at the consecration of the church two years before, the *desyatskie* [constables] had not been able to find up to this time; although the chief, on the occasion of the daily reports made to him by the sergeants of police, always asked, "Has that button been found?" These eight buttons were strewn about him as women sow beans—one to the right, and one to the left. His left foot had been struck by a ball in the last campaign, and therefore he limped, and threw it out so far to one side as to almost counteract the efforts of the right foot. The more briskly the chief of police worked his walking apparatus, the less progress it made in advance; and so, while the chief was getting to the veranda, Ivan Ivanovich had plenty of time to lose himself in surmises as to why the chief was flourishing his hands so vigorously. This interested him the more, as the matter seemed one of unusual importance; for the chief had on a new dagger.

"Good-morning, Peter Feodorovich!" cried Ivan Ivanovich, who was, as has already been stated, exceedingly curious, and could not restrain his impatience at the sight as the chief of police began to ascend to the veranda, yet never raised his eyes, and scolded at his foot, which could not be persuaded to mount the step at only one flourish.

"I wish my good friend and benefactor, Ivan Ivanovich, a good-day," replied the chief.

"Pray sit down. I see that you are weary, as your lame foot hinders"...

"My foot!" screamed the chief, bestowing upon Ivan Ivanovich a glance such as a giant might cast upon a pygmy, a pedant upon a dancing-master: thereupon he stretched out his foot, and stamped upon the floor with it. But this boldness cost him dear; for his whole body wavered, and his nose struck the railing; but the brave preserver of order, with the purpose of making light of it, righted himself immediately, and began to feel in his pocket as if to get his snuff-box. "I must report to you, my dear friend and benefactor, Ivan Ivanovich, that never in all my days have I made such a march. Yes, seriously. For instance, during the campaign of 1807.... Ah! I will relate to you in what manner I crawled through the enclosure to see a pretty little German." Here the chief closed one eye, and executed a diabolically sly smile.

"Where have you been to-day?" asked Ivan Ivanovich, wishing to cut the chief short, and bring him more speedily to the object of his visit. He would have very much liked to inquire what the chief meant to tell him, but his extensive knowledge of the world showed him all the impropriety of such a question; and so Ivan Ivanovich had to keep himself well in hand, and await a solution, his heart, meanwhile, beating with unusual force.

"Ah, excuse me! I was going to tell you—where was I?" answered the chief of police. "In the first place, I report that the weather is fine to-day"...

At these last words, Ivan Ivanovich nearly died.

"But permit me," went on the chief. "I came to you to-day about a very important affair." Here the chief's face and bearing assumed the same careworn guise with which he had ascended to the veranda. Ivan Ivanovich lived again, and shook as if in a fever, omitting not, as was his habit, to put a question. "What is the important matter? Is it important?"

"Pray judge for yourself: first I venture to report to you, dear friend and benefactor, Ivan Ivanovich, that you…I beg you to observe that, for my own part, I should have nothing to say; but the rules of government require it… you have transgressed the rules of propriety."

"What do you say, Peter Feodorovich? I don't understand at all."

"Pardon me, Ivan Ivanovich! how is it that you do not understand? Your own beast has destroyed a very important government document; and you can still say, after that, that you do not understand!"

"What beast?"

"Your own brown sow, with your permission, be it said."

"How am I responsible? Why did the janitor of the court open the door?"

"But, Ivan Ivanovich, your own brown sow You must be responsible."

"I am extremely obliged to you for comparing me to a sow."

"But I did not say that, Ivan Ivanovich! By Heavens! I did not say it! Pray judge from your own clear conscience. It is known to you without doubt, that, in accordance with the views of the government, unclean animals are forbidden to roam about the city, particularly in the principal streets. Confess, now, that it is prohibited."

"God knows what you are talking about! A mighty important business, that a sow got into the street!"

"Permit me to inform you, Ivan Ivanovich, permit me, permit me, that this is utterly impossible. What is to be done? The authorities command, we must obey. I don't deny, that sometimes chickens and geese run about the streets, and even about the square—pray observe, chickens and geese; but only last year, I gave orders that pigs and goats were not to be admitted to the public squares, which regulations I directed to be read aloud at the time, in the assembly before all the people."

"No, Peter Feodorovich, I see nothing here except that you are doing your best to insult me."

"But you cannot say, my dearest friend and benefactor, that I have tried to insult you. Bethink yourself: I never said a word to you last year when you built a roof a whole arshin higher than was fixed by law On the contrary, I pretended not to have observed it. Believe me, my dearest friend, even now, I would, so to speak…but my duty, in a word, my obligations, demand that I should have an eye to cleanliness. Just judge for yourself, when suddenly in the principal street"…

"Fine principal streets yours are! Every woman goes there and throws down any rubbish she chooses."

"Permit me to inform you, Ivan Ivanovich, that it is you who are insulting me. In fact, that does sometimes happen, but, as a rule, only beside fences, sheds, or store-houses; but that a filthy sow should intrude herself in the main street, in the square, now that's a matter"...

"What sort of a matter? Peter Feodorovich! surely a sow is one of God's creatures!"

"Agreed. Everybody knows that you are a learned man, that you are acquainted with sciences and various other subjects. In short, I never studied the sciences: I began to learn to write in my thirteenth year. Of course you know that I was a soldier in the ranks."

"Hm!" said Ivan Ivanovich.

"Yes," continued the chief of police, "in 1801 I was in the Forty-second Regiment of chasseurs, lieutenant in the Fourth Battalion. The commander of our battalion was, if I may be permitted to mention it, Capt. Eremeeff." Thereupon the chief of police thrust his fingers into the snuff-box which Ivan Ivanovich was holding open, and stirred up the snuff.

Ivan Ivanovich answered, "Hm!"

"But my duty," went on the chief of police, "is to obey the commands of the authorities. Do you know, Ivan Ivanovich, that a person who purloins a government document in the court-room incurs capital punishment, equally with other criminals?"

"I know it; and, if you like, I can give you lessons. It is so ordered with regard to people—as if you, for instance, were to steal a document; but a sow is an animal, one of God's creatures."

"Certainly; but the law reads, 'Those guilty of theft'...I beg you to listen most attentively—'*Those* guilty!' Here is indicated neither race nor sex nor rank: of course, an animal can be guilty. You may say what you please; but the animal, until the sentence is pronounced by the court, should be committed to the charge of the police, as a transgressor of the law."

"No, Peter Feodorovich," retorted Ivan Ivanovich coolly, "that shall not be."

"As you like: only I must carry out the orders of the authorities."

"What are you threatening me with? Probably you want to send that one-armed soldier after her. I shall order the woman who tends the door to drive him off with the poker: he'll get his last arm broken."

"I dare not dispute with you. In case you will not commit her to the charge of the police, then do what you please with her: kill her for Christmas, if you like, and make hams of her, or eat her as she is. Only I should like to ask you, in case you make sausages, to send me a couple, such as your Gapka makes so well of blood and lard. My Agrafena Trofimovna is extremely fond of them."

"I will send you a couple of sausages if you permit."

"I shall be extremely obliged to you, dear friend and benefactor. Now permit me to say one word more. I am commissioned by the judge, as well as by all our acquaintances, so to speak, to effect a reconciliation between you and your friend, Ivan Nikiforovich."

"What! with that brute! I am to be reconciled to that clown! Never! It shall not be, it shall not be!" Ivan Ivanovich was in a remarkably determined frame of mind.

"As you like," replied the chief of police, treating both nostrils to snuff. "I will not venture to advise you; but permit me to mention—here you live at enmity, and if you make peace"…

But Ivan Ivanovich began to talk about catching quail, as he usually did when he wanted to put an end to a conversation. So the chief of police was obliged to retire without having achieved any success whatever.

VI.
FROM WHICH THE READER CAN EASILY DISCOVER WHAT Is CONTAINED IN IT.

IN SPITE OF all the judges efforts to keep the matter secret, all Mirgorod knew by the next day that Ivan Ivanovich's sow had stolen Ivan Nikiforovich's petition. The chief of police himself, in a moment of forgetfulness, was the first to betray himself. When Ivan Nikiforovich was informed of it, he said nothing: he merely inquired, "Was it the brown one?"

But Agafya Fedosyevna, who was present, began again to urge Ivan Nikiforovich. "What's the matter with you, Ivan Nikiforovich? People will laugh at you as at a fool if you let it pass. How can you remain a nobleman after that? You will be worse than the old woman who sells the honey-cakes with hemp-seed oil, you are so fond of And the mischief maker persuaded him. She hunted up somewhere a middle-aged man with black complexion, and spots all over his face, and a dark-blue surtout patched on the elbows—a regular official scribbler. He blacked his boots with tar, wore three pens behind his ear, and a glass bubble tied to his button-hole with a string, instead of an ink-bottle: he ate as many as nine pies at once, and put the tenth in his pocket, and wrote so many slanders of all sorts on a single sheet of stamped paper, that no reader could get through all at one time without interspersing coughs and sneezes. This poor imitation of a man labored, toiled, and wrote, and finally concocted the following document:

"To the District judge of Mirgorod, from the noble, Ivan Dovgochkhun, son of Nikifor.

"In pursuance of my petition which was presented by me, Ivan Dovgochkhun, son of Nikifor, in connection with the nobleman Ivan Pererépenko, son of Ivan; to which also, the judge of the Mirgorod district court exhibited his indifference. And the shameless, high-handed deed of the brown sow being kept secret, and coming to my ears from outside parties.

"And the said allowing and neglect, plainly malicious, lies incontestably at the judge's door; for the sow is a stupid animal, and therefore less fitted for the theft of papers. From which it plainly appears, that the said frequently mentioned sow was not otherwise than instigated to the same by the opponent, Ivan Pererépenko, son of Ivan, calling himself a nobleman, and already convicted of theft, conspiracy against life, and desecration of a church. But the said Mirgorod judge, with the partisanship peculiar to him, gave his private consent to this individual; for without such consent the said sow could by no possible means have been admitted to carry off the document; for the judge of the district court of Mirgorod is well provided with servants: it was only necessary to summon a soldier, who is always on duty in the reception-room, and who, although he has but one eye and one somewhat damaged arm, has powers quite adequate to driving out a sow, and to beating it with a club, from which is credibly evident the criminal neglect of the said Mirgorod judge, and the incontestable sharing of the Jew-like spoils therefrom resulting between these mutual conspirators. And the aforesaid robber and nobleman, Ivan Pererépenko, son of Ivan, having disgraced himself, finished his turning on his lathe. Wherefore I, the noble Ivan Dovgochkhun, son of Nikifor, declare to the said district judge, in proper form, that if the said brown sow, or the man Pererépenko, who was mentioned in the petition, in league with her, be not summoned to the court, and judgment in accordance with justice and my advantage pronounced upon her, then I, Ivan Dovgochkhun, son of Nikifor, shall present a complaint, with observance of all due formalities, against the said district judge, for his illegal partisanship, to the superior courts.

"Ivan Dovgochkhun, son of Nikifor, noble of the Mirgorod District."

This petition produced its effect. The judge was a man of timid disposition, as all good people generally are. He betook himself to the secretary. But the secretary emitted from his lips a thick *hm*, and exhibited in his countenance that indifferent and diabolically equivocal expression which Satan alone assumes when he sees his victim hasting to his feet. One resource remained—to reconcile the two friends. But how set about it, when all attempts up to that time had been so unsuccessful? Nevertheless, it was decided to make another effort; but Ivan Ivanovich declared downright that he would not hear to it, and even flew into a violent passion. Ivan Nikiforovich, in lieu of an answer, turned his back, and would not utter a word.

Then the case went on with the unusual promptness upon which courts usually pride themselves. Documents were dated, labelled, numbered, sewed together, registered, all in one day, and the matter laid on the shelf, where it continued to lie, lie, lie, for one, two, or three years. Many brides were married; a new street was laid out in Mirgorod; one of the judges double teeth fell out, and two of his eye-teeth; more children than ever ran about Ivan Ivanovich's yard; Ivan Nikiforovich, as reproof to Ivan Ivanovich, had constructed a new goose-coop, although a little farther off than the first, and built himself completely off from Ivan Ivanovich, so that these worthy people almost never beheld each other's faces; and still the case lay on, in the very best order, in the cabinet, which had become marbled with ink-spots.

In the mean time a very important event for all Mirgorod had taken place. The chief of police had given a reception. Whence shall I obtain the brush and colors to depict this varied gathering, and this magnificent feast? Take your watch, open it, and observe what is going on there. A fearful confusion, is it not? Now, imagine almost the same, if not a greater, number of wheels standing in the chief of police's court-yard. How many brichkas [traps] and wagons were there! One was wide behind and narrow in front; another narrow behind and wide in front. One was a brichka and wagon combined; another neither a brichka nor a wagon. One resembled a huge hayrick, or a fat merchants wife; another a dilapidated Jew, or a skeleton not quite freed from the skin. One was a perfect pipe with long stem in profile; another, resembling nothing whatever, suggested some strange, utterly formless, and exceedingly fantastic, being. In the midst of this chaos of wheels and carriage-boxes, rose the semblances of coaches, with windows like those of a room, crossed with broad frames.

The coachmen, in gray Cossack coats, svitkas [tunics], and white hare coats, with sheepskin hats and caps of various patterns, and pipes in their hands, drove the unharnessed horses through the yard. What a reception the chief of police gave! Permit me to run through the list of those who were there: Taras Tarasovich, Evpl Akinfovich, Evtikhii Evtikhievich, Ivan Ivanovich—not that Ivan Ivanovich, but another—Gabba Gavrilo-novich, our Ivan Ivanovich, Elevferii Elevferievich, Makar Nazarevich, Foma Grigorovich...I can do no more: my powers fail me, my hand ceases to write.

And how many ladies were there! dark and fair and short, fat like Ivan Nikiforovich, and some so thin that it seemed as though each one might hide herself in the scabbard of the chief's sword. What head-dresses! what costumes!—red, yellow, coffee-color, green, blue, new, turned, made over—dresses, ribbons, reticules. Farewell, poor eyes! you will never be good for any thing any more after this spectacle.

And how long the table was drawn out! and how all talked! and what a humming they made! What is a mill with its driving-wheel, stones, beams, hammers, wheels, in comparison with this? I cannot tell you exactly what they talked about, but presumably of many agreeable and useful things, such as the weather, dogs, wheat, caps, and dice. At length Ivan Ivanovich—not that Ivan Ivanovich, but the other, who had but one eye—said, "It strikes me as strange that my right eye [one-eyed Ivan Ivanovich always spoke sarcastically about himself] does not see Ivan Nikiforovich, Mr. Dovgochkhun."

"He would not come," said the chief of police.

"Why not?"

"It's two years now, glory to God! since they quarreled; that is, Ivan Ivanovich and Ivan Nikiforovich: and where one goes, the other will not go."

"You don't say so!" Thereupon one-eyed Ivan Ivanovich raised his eye, and clasped his hands. "Well, if people with good eyes cannot live in peace, how am I to live amicably, with my bad eye?" At these words, all laughed at the tops of their voices. All loved one-eyed Ivan Ivanovich, because he cracked jokes quite in the style of the present one. A tall, thin man in a frieze coat, with a plaster on his nose, who up to this time had sat in the corner, and never once altered the expression of his face, even when a fly lighted on his nose—this gentleman rose from his seat, and approached nearer to the crowd which surrounded one-eyed Ivan Ivanovich. "Listen," said one-eyed Ivan Ivanovich, when he perceived that quite a throng had collected about him; "see here: instead of gazing at my bad eye, suppose we make peace between our friends. Ivan Ivanovich is talking with the women and girls;...let us go quietly for Ivan Nikiforovich, and bring them together."

Ivan Ivanovich's proposal was unanimously agreed to; and it was decided to send at once to Ivan Nikiforovich's house, and beg him, at any rate, to come to the chief of police's for dinner. But the difficult question as to who was to be intrusted with this weighty commission rendered all thoughtful. They debated long as to who was the most fitted for, and expert in, diplomatic matters. At length it was unanimously agreed to depute Anton Prokofievich Golopuz for this business.

But it is necessary, first of all, to make the reader somewhat acquainted with this noteworthy person. Anton Prokofievich was a truly virtuous man, in the fullest meaning of the term. If any one in Mirgorod gives him a neckerchief or underclothes, he returns thanks; if any one gives him a fillip on the nose—he returns thanks then also. If he was asked, "Why, Anton Prokofievich, have you a light brown coat with blue sleeves?" he generally replied, "Ah, you haven't one like it! Wait: it will wear off, and it will be alike all over." And, in point of fact, the blue cloth, from the effects of the sun, began to turn cinnamon-color, and had now become of the same tint as the rest of the coat. But the strange part of it was that Anton Prokofievich had a habit of wearing woollen clothing in summer and nankeen in winter. Anton Prokofievich has no house of his own. He used to have one at the extremity of the town; but he sold it, and with the purchase-money bought a troika [three-horse carriage] of brown horses, and a little brichka in which he drove about to stay with the squires. But as the horses made a good deal of trouble, and money was required for oats, Anton Prokofievich swapped them off for a violin and a house-maid, with twenty-five paper rubles to boot. Afterwards Anton Prokofievich sold the violin, and swapped the girl for a morocco and gold tobacco-pouch; and now he has such a tobacco-pouch as no one else has. As a result of this luxury, he can no longer go about among the country-houses, but must remain in the city, and pass the night at different houses, especially of those gentlemen who take pleasure in tapping him on the nose. Anton Prokofievich is very fond of good eating, and plays well at *durak* and *melnik*.[4] Obeying orders always was his forte; so, taking his hat and cane, he set out at once on his way.

But, as he walked along, he began to ponder in what manner he should contrive to induce Ivan Nikiforovich to come to the assembly. The rather unbending character of the latter, who was otherwise a worthy man, rendered his undertaking almost hopeless. Yes, and how, in fact, was he to persuade him to come, when even rising from his bed cost him so great an effort? But supposing that he does rise, how can he get him there, where, as he doubtless knows, his irreconcilable enemy already is? The more Anton Prokofievich reflected, the more difficulties he perceived. The day was sultry, the sun beat down, the perspiration poured from him in streams. Anton Prokofievich was a tolerably sharp man in many respects (though they did tap him on the nose). In swapping, however, he was not fortunate. He knew very well when to play the fool, and sometimes contrived to turn things to his own profit, amid circumstances and surroundings from which a wise man could rarely escape without loss.

His ingenious mind had contrived a means of persuading Ivan Nikiforovich; and he was proceeding bravely to face everything, when an unexpected occurrence somewhat disturbed his equanimity. There is no harm, at this point, in admitting to the reader, that, among other things, Anton Prokofievich was the owner of a pair of trousers of such singular properties, that, when he put them on, the dogs always bit his calves. Unfortunately, on this day he had donned that particular pair of trousers; and so he had hardly resigned himself to meditation when a fearful barking on all sides saluted his ears. Anton Prokofievich raised such a yell (no one could scream louder than he) that not only did the well-known woman and the inhabitant of the endless surtout rush out to meet him, but even the small boys from Ivan Ivanovich's yard strewed themselves over him; and although the dogs succeeded in tasting only one of his calves, yet this sensibly diminished his courage, and he entered the veranda with a certain amount of timidity.

VII AND LAST.

"Ah! How do you do? Why do you irritate the dogs?" said Ivan Nikiforovich, on perceiving Anton Prokofievich; for no one spoke otherwise than jestingly with Anton Prokofievich.

"Hang them! who's been irritating them?" retorted Anton Prokofievich.

"You lie!"

"By Heavens, no!—You are invited to dinner by Peter Feodorovich."

"Hm!"

"He invited you more pressingly than I can tell you. 'Why,' says he, 'does Ivan Nikiforovich shun me like an enemy? He never comes round to have a chat, or make a call.'"

Ivan Nikiforovich stroked his beard.

"'If,' says he, 'Ivan Nikiforovich does not come now, I shall not know what to think: surely, he must have some design against me. Pray, Anton Prokofievich, persuade Ivan Nikiforovich!' Come, Ivan Nikiforovich, let us go! a very choice company is already assembled there."

Ivan Nikiforovich began to regard a cock, which was perched on the roof, and crowing with all its might.

"If you only knew, Ivan Nikiforovich," pursued the zealous ambassador, "what fresh sturgeon and caviare Peter Feodorovich has had sent to him!" Whereupon Ivan Nikiforovich turned his head, and began to listen attentively. This encouraged the messenger. "Come quick: Foma Grigorovich is there too. Why don't you come?" he added, seeing that Ivan Nikiforovich still lay in the same position. "Why, shall we go, or not?"

"I won't!"

This "*I won't*" startled Anton Prokofievich: he had fancied that his alluring representations had quite moved this very worthy man; but instead, he heard that decisive "*I won't.*"

"Why won't you?" he asked, almost with vexation, which he very rarely exhibited, even when they put burning paper on his head, a trick which the judge and the chief of police were particularly fond of indulging in.

Ivan Nikiforovich took a pinch of snuff.

"As you like, Ivan Nikiforovich. I do not know what detains you."

"Why won't I go?" said Ivan Nikiforovich at length: "that brigand will be there!" This was his ordinary way of alluding to Ivan Ivanovich. "Just God! and is it long"…

"He will not be there, he will not be there! May the lightning kill me on the spot!" returned Anton Prokofievich, who was ready to perjure himself ten times in an hour. "Come along, Ivan Nikiforovich!"

"Yes, you lie, Anton Prokofievich! he is there!"

"By Heavens, by Heavens, he's not! May I never stir from this place if he's there! Now, just think for yourself, what object have I in lying? May my hands and feet wither!…Why, don't you believe me now? May I perish right here in your presence! Don't you believe me yet?"

Ivan Nikiforovich was entirely re-assured by these asseverations, and ordered his valet, in the boundless surtout, to fetch his trousers and nankeen casaquin.

I suppose that to describe how Ivan Nikiforovich put on his trousers, how they wound his neckerchief about his neck, and finally dragged on his casaquin, which burst under the left sleeve, would be quite superfluous. Suffice it to say that during all that time he preserved a becoming calmness of demeanor, and answered not a word to Anton Prokofievich's proposition to swap something for his Turkish tobacco-pouch.

Meanwhile the assembly awaited with impatience the decisive moment when Ivan Nikiforovich should make his appearance, and at length comply with the general desire, that these worthy people should be reconciled to each other. Many were almost convinced that Ivan Nikiforovich would not come. Even the chief of police offered to bet with one-eyed Ivan Ivanovich that he would not come; and he only desisted because one-eyed Ivan Ivanovich demanded that he should wager his shot foot against his own bad eye, at which the chief of police was greatly offended, and the company enjoyed a quiet laugh. No one had yet sat down to the table, although it was long past two o'clock, an hour before which in Mirgorod, even on ceremonious occasions, every one had already long dined.

No sooner did Anton Prokofievich show himself in the doorway than he was instantly surrounded by all. Anton Prokofievich, in answer to all inquiries, shouted one all-decisive word, "He will not come!" No sooner had he uttered this, than a hailstorm of reproaches, scoldings, and, possibly, even fillips, prepared to descend upon his head for the ill success of his mission, when all at once the door opened, and—Ivan Nikiforovich entered.

If Satan himself or a corpse had appeared, it would not have caused such consternation throughout the company as Ivan Nikiforovich's unexpected arrival created. But Anton Prokofievich only went off into a fit of laughter, and held his sides with delight at having played such a joke upon the company.

At all events, it was almost past the belief of all that Ivan Nikiforovich could, in so brief a space of time, have attired himself like a respectable gentleman. Ivan Ivanovich was not there at the moment: he had stepped out somewhere. Recovering from their amazement, the public took an interest in Ivan Nikiforovich's health, and expressed their pleasure at his increase in breadth. Ivan Nikiforovich kissed every one, and said, "Very much obliged!"

Meantime the fragrance of the beet-soup was wafted through the apartment, and tickled the nostrils of the hungry guests very agreeably. All rushed headlong to the table. The line of ladies, loquacious and silent, thin and thick, swept on, and the long table glittered with all the hues of the rainbow. I will not describe the courses: I will make no mention of the curd dumplings with sour cream, nor of the dish of haslets that was served with the soup, nor of the turkey with plums and raisins, nor of the dish which greatly resembled in appearance a boot soaked in kvas, nor of the sauce, which is the swan's song of the old-fashioned cook, nor of that other sauce which was brought in all enveloped in the flames of wine, which amused as well as frightened the ladies extremely. I will say nothing of these dishes, because I like better to eat them than to spend many words in discussing them.

Ivan Ivanovich was exceedingly pleased with the fish prepared with horseradish. He devoted himself particularly to this useful and nourishing preparation. Picking out all the fine bones from the fish, he laid them on his plate; and happening to glance across the table...Heavenly Creator! but this was strange! Opposite him sat Ivan Nikiforovich.

At the very same instant Ivan Nikiforovich glanced up also...No...I can do no more...Give me a fresh pen! My pen is flabby, dead,...with a fine point for this picture! Their faces seemed to turn to stone, still keeping their defiant expression. Each beheld a long familiar face, to which it seemed the most natural of things to step up as to an unexpected friend, involuntarily, and offer a snuff-box, with the words, "Do me the favor," or "Dare I beg you to do me the favor?" Instead of this, that face was terrible as a forerunner of evil. The perspiration poured in streams from Ivan Ivanovich and Ivan Nikiforovich.

All the guests at table grew dumb with attention, and never took their eyes from the former friends. The ladies, who had been busy up to that time with a sufficiently interesting discussion as to the preparation of capons, suddenly cut their conversation short. All was silence. It was a picture worthy the brush of a great artist.

At length Ivan Ivanovich pulled out his handkerchief, and began to blow his nose; but Ivan Nikiforovich glanced about, and his eye rested on the open door. The chief of police at once perceived this movement, and ordered the door to be strongly fastened. Then both of the friends began to eat, and never once glanced at each other again.

As soon as dinner was done, both of the former friends rose from their seats, and began to look for their hats, with a view to departure. Then the chief beckoned; and Ivan Ivanovich—not that Ivan Ivanovich, but the other, the one with the one eye—stood behind Ivan Nikiforovich, and the chief stepped behind Ivan Ivanovich, and both began to drag them backwards, in order to bring them together, and not release them until they had shaken hands with each other. Ivan Ivanovich, the one-eyed Ivan, pushed Ivan Nikiforovich, though rather crookedly, yet with tolerable success, towards the spot where stood Ivan Ivanovich; but the chief of police directed his course too much to one side, because he could not steer himself with his refractory leg, which obeyed no orders whatever on this occasion, and, as if with malice aforethought, swung itself uncommonly far, and in quite the contrary direction (which possibly resulted from the fact that there had been an unusual amount of fruit-wine after dinner), so that Ivan Ivanovich fell over a lady in a red gown, who had thrust herself into the very centre, out of curiosity. Such an omen foreboded nothing good. Nevertheless, the judge, in order to set the matter to rights, took the chief of police's place, and, sweeping all the snuff from his upper lip with his nose, pushed Ivan Ivanovich in the opposite direction. In Mirgorod this is the usual manner of effecting a reconciliation: it somewhat resembles a game of ball. As soon as the judge pushed Ivan Ivanovich, Ivan Ivanovich with the one eye exerted all his strength, and pushed Ivan Nikiforovich, from whom the perspiration streamed like rain-water from the roofs. In spite of the fact that the friends resisted to the best of their ability, nevertheless they were brought together, for the two active movers received re-enforcements from the ranks of the guests.

Then they were closely surrounded on all sides, not to be released until they had decided to give each other their hands. "God be with you, Ivan Nikiforovich and Ivan Ivanovich! declare upon your honor now, what you quarreled about; trifles, wasn't it? aren't you ashamed of yourselves before people and before God?"

"I do not know," said Ivan Nikiforovich, panting with fatigue (it is to be observed that he was not at all disinclined to a reconciliation), "I do not know what I did to Ivan Ivanovich; but why did he destroy my coop, and plot against my life?"

"I am innocent of any evil designs!" said Ivan Ivanovich, never looking at Ivan Nikiforovich. "I swear before God and before you, honorable noblemen, I did nothing to my enemy! Why does he calumniate me, and injure my rank and family?"

"What injury have I done you, Ivan Ivanovich?" said Ivan Nikiforovich. One moment more of explanation, and the long enmity was on the point of being extinguished. Ivan Nikiforovich was already feeling in his pocket for his snuff-box, and was about to say, "Do me the favor."

"Is it no injury," answered Ivan Ivanovich, without raising his eyes, "when you, my dear sir, insulted my honor and my family with a word which it is improper to repeat here?"

"Permit me to observe, in a friendly manner, Ivan Ivanovich (here Ivan Nikiforovich touched Ivan Ivanovich's button with his finger, which clearly indicated the disposition of his mind), that you took offence, the deuce only knows at what, because I called you a *goose.* "…

It came over Ivan Nikiforovich that he had made a mistake in uttering that word; but it was too late: the word was out. Everything went to the deuce. If, on the utterance of this word without witnesses, Ivan Ivanovich lost control of himself, and flew into such a passion as God preserve us from beholding any man in, what was to be expected now? I put it to you, dear readers, what was to be expected now, when the fatal word was uttered in an assemblage of persons among whom were ladies, in whose presence Ivan Ivanovich liked to be particularly polite? If Ivan Nikiforovich had set to work in any other manner, if he had only said *bird* and not *goose,* it might still have been arranged; but…all was at an end.

He cast one glance upon Ivan Nikiforovich, and such a glance! If that glance had possessed active power, then it would have turned Ivan Nikiforovich into dust. The guests understood the glance, and hastened to separate them. And this man, the very model of gentleness, who never let a single poor woman go without interrogating her, rushed out in a fearful rage. Such violent storms do passions produce!

For a whole month nothing was heard of Ivan Ivanovich. He shut himself up at home. His ancestral chest was opened; from the chest was taken—what? silver rubles, his grandfather's old silver rubles! And these rubles passed into the ink-stained hands of legal advisers. The case was sent up to the higher court; and when Ivan Ivanovich received the joyful news that it would be decided on the morrow, then only did he look out upon the world, and resolve to emerge from his house. Alas! from that time forth, the council gave notice day by day, that the case would be finished on the morrow, for the space of ten years.

Five years ago, I passed through the town of Mirgorod. I came at a bad time. It was autumn, with its damp, melancholy weather, mud and mists. An unnatural verdure, the result of tiresome and incessant rains, covered with a watery network the fields and meadows, to which it is as well suited as youthful pranks to an old man, or roses to an old woman. The weather made a deep impression on me at that time: when it was dull, I was dull; but in spite of that, when I came to pass through Mirgorod, my heart beat violently. God, what reminiscences! I had not beheld Mirgorod for twenty years. Here then had lived, in touching friendship, two inseparable friends. And how many prominent people had died! Judge Demyan Demyanovich was already gone: Ivan Ivanovich (with the one eye) had long ceased to live. I entered the main street. All about stood poles with bundles of straw on top: some new grading was being done. Several izbás had been removed. The remnants of board and wattled fences projected sadly, here and there.

It was a festival day. I ordered my basket kibitka [hooded cart] to stop in front of the church, and entered softly that no one might turn round. To tell the truth, there was no need of this: the church was empty; there were very few people; it was evident that even the most pious feared the mud. The candles seemed strangely unpleasant in that gloomy, or, better still, sickly, light. The dim vestibule was melancholy; the long windows, with their circular panes, were bedewed with tears of rain; I retired into the vestibule, and addressed myself to a respectable old man, with grayish hair: "May I inquire if Ivan Nikiforovich is still living?" At that moment the lamp before the ikon burned up more brightly, and the light fell directly upon the face of my companion. What was my surprise, on looking more closely, to behold features with which I was acquainted! It was Ivan Nikiforovich himself! But how he had changed!

"Are you well, Ivan Nikiforovich? How old you have grown!"

"Yes, I have grown old. I have just come from Poltava to-day," answered Ivan Nikiforovich.

"You don't say so! you have been to Poltava in this bad weather?"

"What was to be done? that lawsuit"…

At this I sighed involuntarily.

Ivan Nikiforovich observed my sigh, and said, "Do not be troubled: I have reliable information that the case will be decided next week, and in my favor."

I shrugged my shoulders, and went to get some news of Ivan Ivanovich.

"Ivan Ivanovich is here," some one said to me, "in the choir."

Then I saw a gaunt form. Was that Ivan Ivanovich? His face was covered with wrinkles, his hair was perfectly white; but the bekesha was the same as ever. After the first greetings were over, Ivan Ivanovich, turning to me with the joyous smile which always became his funnel-shaped face, said, "Have you been informed of the pleasant news?"

"What news?" I inquired.

"My case is to be decided to-morrow without fail: the court has announced it decisively."

I sighed more deeply than before, and made haste to take my leave (for I was bound on very important business), and seated myself in my kibitka.

The lean nags known in Mirgorod as "courier's horses" started, producing with their hoofs, which were buried in a gray mass of mud, a sound very displeasing to the ear. The rain poured in torrents upon the Jew seated on the box, covered with a rug. The dampness penetrated through and through me. The gloomy barrier with a sentry-box, in which an old soldier was repairing his gray weapons, passed slowly by. Again the same fields, in some places black where they had been dug up, in others of a greenish hue; wet daws and crows; monotonous rain; a tearful sky, without one gleam of light!…It is dull in this world, gentlemen!

THE DIARY OF A MADMAN

3 OCTOBER—Today an extraordinary event occurred. I got up rather late in the morning, and when Mavra brought me my cleaned boots I asked her the time. Hearing that it was long past ten I made haste to dress. I own I wouldn't have gone to the department at all, knowing the sour face the chief of our section will make me. For a long time past he has been saying to me: "How is it, my man, your head always seems in a muddle? Sometimes you rush about as though you were crazy and do your work so that the devil himself could not make head or tail of it, you write the title with a small letter, and you don't put in the date or the number." The damned heron! To be sure he is jealous because I sit in the director's room and mend pens for his Excellency. In short I wouldn't have gone to the department if I had not hoped to see the counting-house clerk and to find out whether maybe I could not get something of my month's salary in advance out of that wretched Jew. That's another creature! Do you suppose he would ever let one have a month's pay in advance? Good gracious! The heavens would fall before he'd do it! You may ask till you burst, you may be at your last farthing, but the grey-headed devil won't let you have it—and when he is at home his own cook slaps him in the face; everybody knows it. I can't see the advantage of serving in a department; there are absolutely no possibilities in it. In the provincial government, or in the civil and crown offices, it's quite a different matter: there you may see some wretched man squeezed into the corner, copying away, with a nasty old coat on and such a face that it nearly makes you sick, but look what a villa he takes! It's no use offering him a gilt china cup: "That's a doctor's present," he will say. You must give him a pair of trotting horses or a droshky or a beaver fur worth three hundred roubles. He is such a quiet fellow to look at, and says in such a refined way: "Oblige

me with a penknife just to mend a pen," but he fleeces the petitioners so that he scarcely leaves them a shirt to their backs. It is true that ours is a gentlemanly office, there is a cleanliness in everything such as is never seen in provincial offices, the tables are mahogany and all the heads address you formally…I must confess that if it were not for the gentlemanliness of the service I should have left the department long ago.

I put on my old greatcoat and took my umbrella, as it was raining in torrents. There was no one in the streets; some women pulling their skirts up to cover themselves, and some Russian merchants under umbrellas and some messengers met my eye. I saw none of the better class except one of ourselves. I saw him at the crossroads. As soon as I saw him I said to myself: "No, my dear man, you are not on your way to the department; you are running after that girl who is racing ahead and looking at her feet." What sad dogs clerks are! Upon my soul, they are as bad as any officer: if any female goes by in a hat they are bound to be after her. While I was making this reflection I saw a carriage driving up to the shop which I was passing. I recognised it at once. It was our director's carriage. "But he can have nothing to go to the shop for," I thought; "I suppose it must be his daughter." I flattened myself against the wall. The footman opened the carriage door and she darted out like a bird. How she glanced from right to left, how her eyes and eyebrows gleamed…Good God, I am done for, done for utterly! And why does she drive out in such rain! Don't tell me that women have not a passion for all this frippery. She didn't know me, and, indeed, I tried to muffle myself up all I could, because I had on a very muddy greatcoat of an old-fashioned cut. Now people wear cloaks with long collars while I had short collars one above the other, and, indeed, the cloth was not at all rainproof. Her little dog, who had been too late to dash in at the door, was left in the street. I know the dog—her name is Madgie. I had hardly been there a minute when I heard a thin little voice: "Good morning, Madgie."

"Well, upon my soul! Who's that speaking?"

I looked round me and saw two ladies walking along under an umbrella: one old and the other young; but they had passed already and again I heard beside me: "It's too bad of you, Madgie!"

What the devil! I saw that Madgie was sniffing at a dog that was following the ladies. "Aha," I said to myself, "but come, surely I am drunk! Only I fancy that very rarely happens to me."

"No, Fido, you are wrong there," said Madgie—I saw her say it with my own eyes. "I have been, wow, wow, I have been very ill, wow, wow, wow!"

"Oh, so it's you, you little dog! Goodness me!" I must own I was very much surprised to hear her speaking like a human being; but afterwards, when I thought it was all over, I was no longer surprised. A number of similar instances have as a fact occurred. They say that in England a fish popped up and uttered two words in such a strange language that the learned men have been for three years trying to interpret them and have not succeeded yet. I have read in the papers of two cows also who went into a shop and asked for a pound of tea. But I must own I was much more surprised when Madgie said: "I did write to you, Fido; I expect Polkan did not take my letter." Dash it all! I never in all my life heard of a dog being able to write. No one but a gentleman born can write correctly. It's true, of course, that some shopmen and even serfs can sometimes write a little; but their writing is for the most part mechanical: they have no commas, no stops, no style.

It amazed me. I must confess that of late I have begun seeing and hearing things such as no one has ever seen or heard before. "I'll follow that dog," I said to myself, "and find out what she is like and what she thinks." I opened my umbrella and set off after the two ladies. They passed into Gorohovy Street, turned into Myeshtchansky and from there into Stolyarny Street; at last they reached Kokushin Bridge and stopped in front of a big edifice. "I know that building," I said to myself. "That's Zvyerkov's Buildings. What a huge mechanism! All sorts of people live in it: such a lot of cooks, of visitors from all parts! And our friends the clerks, one on the top of another, with a third trying to squeeze in, like dogs. I have a friend living there, who plays capitally on the horn." The ladies went up to the fifth storey. "Good," I thought, "I won't go in now, but I will note the place and I will certainly take advantage of the first opportunity."

4 OCTOBER—Today is Wednesday, and so I was in our chief's study. I came a little early on purpose and, sitting down, began mending the pens. Our director must be a very clever man. His whole study is lined with bookshelves. I have read the titles of some of them: they are all learned, so learned that they are quite beyond anyone like me—they are all either in French or in German. And just look into his face! Ough! What importance shining in his eyes! I have never heard him say a word too much. Only sometimes when one hands him the papers he'll ask: "What's it like out of doors?" "Damp, your Excellency." Yes, he is a cut above anyone like me! He's a statesman. I notice, however, he is particularly fond of me. If his daughter, too, were...Ah, you rascal!... Never mind, never mind, silence! I read *The*

Bee. They are stupid people, the French! What do they want? I'd take the lot of them, upon my word I would, and thrash them all soundly! In it I read a very pleasant description of a ball written by a country gentleman of Kursk. The country gentlemen of Kursk write well. Then I noticed it was half-past twelve and that our chief had not come out of his bedroom. But about half-past one an event occurred which no pen could describe. The door opened, I thought it was the director and jumped up from my chair with my papers, but it was she, she herself! Holy saints, how she was dressed! Her dress was white as a swan—ough, how sumptuous! And the look in her eye—like sunshine, upon my soul, like sunshine. She bowed and said: "Hasn't Papa been here?" Aïe, aïe, aïe, what a voice! A canary, a regular canary. "Your Excellency," I was on the point of saying, "do not bid them punish me, but if you want to punish, then punish with your own illustrious hand." But devil take it, my tongue would not obey me, and all I said was: "No, madam."

She looked at me, looked at the books, and dropped her handkerchief. I dashed forward, slipped on the damned parquet and almost smashed my nose but recovered myself and picked up the handkerchief. Saints, what a handkerchief! The most delicate batiste—amber, perfect amber! You would know from the very scent that it belonged to a general's daughter. She thanked me and gave a faint smile, so that her sugary lips scarcely moved, and after that went away. I stayed on another hour, when a footman came in and said: "You can go home, Aksenty Ivanovitch, the master has gone out." I cannot endure the flunkey set: they are always lolling about in the vestibule and don't as much as trouble themselves to nod. That's nothing: once one of the beasts had the effrontery to offer me his snuffbox without even getting up from his seat. Don't you know, you dull fellow, that I am a government clerk, that I am a gentleman by birth! However, I took my hat and put on my greatcoat myself, for these gentry never help me on with it, and went off. At home I spent most of the time lying on my bed. Then I copied out some very good verses:

> *My love for one hour I did not see,*
> *And a whole year it seemed to me.*
> *My life is now a hated task,*
> *How can I live this life, I ask.*

It must have been written by Pushkin.

In the evening, wrapping myself up in my greatcoat, I went to the front door of her Excellency's house and waited about for a long time on the chance of her coming out to get into her carriage, that I might snatch another glimpse of her, but she never came out.

6 NOVEMBER—The head of our section put me in such a fury today. When I came into the department he called me into his room and began like this: "Come, kindly tell me what you are doing?"

"How do you mean?" I said. "I am doing nothing."

"Come, think what you are about! Why, you are over forty. It's time you had a little sense. What do you imagine yourself to be? Do you suppose I don't know all the tricks you are up to? Why, you are dangling after the director's daughter! Come, look at yourself; just think what you are! Why, you are a nonentity and nothing else! Why, you haven't a penny to bless yourself with. And just look at yourself in the looking-glass—how could you think of such a thing!"

Dash it all, because his face is rather like a medicine bottle and he has a clump of hair on his head curled in a tuft, and pomades it into a kind of rosette, and holds his head in the air, he imagines he is the only one who may do anything. I understand, I understand why he is in such a rage with me. He is envious: he has seen perhaps signs of preference shown to me. But I spit on him! As though a court councillor were of so much consequence! He hangs a gold chain on his watch and orders boots at thirty roubles—but deuce take him! Am I some plebeian—a tailor or a son of a non-commissioned officer? I am a gentleman. Why, I may rise in the service too. I am only forty-two, a time of life in which a career in the service is really only just beginning. Wait a bit, my friend! We too shall be a colonel and perhaps, please God, something better. We shall establish a reputation, and better maybe than your own. A queer notion you have got into your head that no one is a gentleman but yourself. Give me a fashionably cut coat and let me put on a cravat like yours—and then you wouldn't hold a candle to me. I haven't the means, that's the trouble.

8 NOVEMBER—I have been to the theatre. It was a performance of the Russian fool Filatka. I laughed very much. There was a vaudeville too, with some amusing verses about lawyers, and especially about a collegiate registrar, very freely written so that I wondered that the censor had passed it; and about the merchants they openly said that they cheat people and that their sons are debauched and ape the gentry. There was a very amusing

couplet about the journalists too; saying that they abused everyone and that an author begged the public to defend him against them. The authors do write amusing plays nowadays. I love going to the theatre. As soon as I have a coin in my pocket I can't resist going. And among our dear friends the officials there are such pigs; they positively won't go to the theatre, the louts; unless perhaps you give them a free ticket. One actress sang very nicely. I thought of her…ah, you rascal!… Never mind, never mind…silence!

9 November—At eight o'clock I went to the department. The head of our section put on a look as though he did not see me come in. On my side, too, I behaved as though nothing had passed between us. I looked through and checked some papers. I went out at four o'clock. I walked by the director's quarters, but no one was to be seen. After dinner for the most part lay on my bed.

11 November—Today I sat in our director's study. I mended twenty-three pens for him and for her…aïe, aïe! For her Excellency four pens. He likes to have a lot of pens. Ooh, he must have a head! He always sits silent, and I expect he is turning over everything in his head. I should like to know what he thinks most about. What is going on in that head? I should like to get a close view of the life of these gentlemen, of all these *équivoques* and court ways. How they go on and what they do in their circle—that's what I should like to find out! I have several times thought of beginning a conversation with his Excellency, but, dash it all! I couldn't bring my tongue to it; one says it's cold or warm today and can't utter another word. I should like to look into the drawing-room, of which one sees the open door and another room beyond it. Ah, what sumptuous furniture! What mirrors and china! I long to have a look in there, into the part of the house where her Excellency is, that's where I should like to go! Into her boudoir where there are all sorts of little jars, little bottles and such flowers that one is frightened even to breathe on them, to see her dresses lying scattered about, more like ethereal gossamer than dresses. I long to glance into her bedroom, there I fancy there must be marvels…a paradise, such as is not to be found in the heavens. To look at the little stool on which she puts her little foot when she gets out of bed and the way she puts a stocking on that little snow-white foot…Aïe, aïe, aïe! Never mind, never mind…silence.

But today a light as it were dawned upon me. I remembered the conversation between the two dogs that I heard on Nevsky Prospect. "Good,"

I thought to myself, "now I will learn all. I must get hold of the correspondence that these wretched dogs have been carrying on. Then I shall certainly learn something." I must own I once called Madgie to me and said to her: "Listen, Madgie; here we are alone. If you like, I will shut the door too, so that no one shall see you; tell me all you know about your young lady; what she is like and how she behaves. I swear I won't tell anyone." But the sly little dog put her tail between her legs, doubled herself up and went quickly to the door as though she hadn't heard. I have long suspected that dogs are far more intelligent than men; I am even convinced that they can speak, only there is a certain doggedness about them. They are extremely diplomatic: they notice everything, every step a man takes. Yes, whatever happens I will go tomorrow to Zvyerkov's Buildings, I will question Fido, and if I am successful I will seize all the letters Madgie has written her.

12 NOVEMBER—At two o'clock in the afternoon I set out determined to see Fido and question her. I can't endure cabbage, the smell of which reeks from all the little shops in Myeshtchansky Street; moreover, such a hellish reek rises from under every gate that I raced along at full speed holding my nose. And the nasty workmen let off such a lot of soot and smoke from their workshops that a gentleman cannot walk there. When I climbed up to the sixth storey and rang the bell, a girl who was not at all bad-looking, with little freckles, came to the door. I recognised her: it was the girl who was with the old lady. She turned a little red, and I said to myself at once: "You are on the look-out for a young man, my dear."

"How can I be of help?" she asked.

"I want to have a few words with your doggie."

The girl was silly. I saw at once that she was silly. At that moment the doggie ran out barking; I tried to catch hold of her, but the nasty wretch almost snapped at my nose. However, I saw her bed in the corner. Ah, that was just what I wanted.

I went up to it, rummaged in the straw in the wooden box, and to my indescribable delight pulled out a packet of little slips of paper. The wretched dog, seeing this, first bit my calf, and then when she perceived that I had taken her letters began to whine and fawn on me, but I said, "No, my dear, goodbye," and took to my heels. I believe the girl thought I was a madman, as she was very much frightened. When I got home I wanted to set to work at once to decipher the letters, for I don't see very well by candlelight; but Mavra had taken it into her head to wash the floor. These stupid Finnish women always clean at the wrong moment. And so I went out to walk about and think over the incident. Now I shall find out all their doings and ways of thinking, all the hidden springs, and shall get to the bottom of it all. These letters will reveal everything. Dogs are a clever people, they understand all the diplomatic relations, and so no doubt I shall find there everything about our gentleman: the portrait and all the doings of the man. There will be something in them too about her who…never mind, silence! Towards evening I came home. For the most part I lay on my bed.

13 NOVEMBER—Well, we shall see! The writing is fairly distinct, at the same time there is something doggy about the hand. Let us read:

> DEAR FIDO—I never can get used to your plebeian name. As though they could not have given you a better one? Fido, Rose—what vulgarity! No more about that, however. I am very glad we thought of writing to each other.

The letter is very well written. The punctuation and even the spelling are quite correct. Even the chief of our section could not write like this, though he does talk of having studied at some university. Let us see what comes next.

"It seems to me that to share one's ideas, one's feelings and one's impressions with others is one of the greatest blessings on earth."

Hm!… an idea taken from a work translated from the German. I don't remember the name of it.

"I say this from experience, though I have not been about the world, beyond the gates of our house. Is not my life spent in comfort? My young lady, whom her papa calls Sophie, loves me passionately."

Aïe, aïe! Never mind, never mind! Silence!

"Papa, too, often caresses me. I drink tea and coffee with cream. Ah, *ma chère*, I ought to tell you that I see nothing agreeable at all in big, gnawed bones such as our Polkan crunches in the kitchen. The only bones that are nice are those of game, and then only when the marrow hasn't been sucked out of them by someone. What is very good is several sauces mixed together, only they must be free from capers and green stuff; but I know of nothing worse than giving dogs little balls of bread. A gentleman sitting at the table who has been touching all sorts of nasty things with his hands begins with those hands rolling up bread, calls one up and thrusts the ball upon one. To refuse seems somehow discourteous—well, one eats it—with repulsion, but one eats it…"

What the devil's this! What nonsense! As though there were nothing better to write about. Let us look at another page and see if there is nothing more sensible.

"I shall be delighted to let you know about everything that happens here. I have already told you something about the chief gentleman, whom Sophie calls Papa. He is a very strange man."

Ah, here we are at last! Yes, I knew it; they have a very diplomatic view of everything. Let us see what Papa is like.

"…a very strange man. For the most part he says nothing; he very rarely speaks. But about a week ago he was continually talking to himself: 'Shall I receive it or shall I not?' He would take a paper in one hand and close the other hand empty and say: 'Shall I receive it or shall I not?' Once he turned to me with the question: 'What do you think, Madgie, shall I receive it or not?' I couldn't understand a word of it, I sniffed at his boots and walked away. A week later, *ma chère*, he came in in high glee. All the morning gentlemen in uniform were coming to see him and congratulating him on something. At table he was merrier than I have ever seen him; he kept telling stories. And after dinner, he lifted me up to his neck and said: 'Look, Madgie, what's this?' I saw a little ribbon. I sniffed it, but could discover no aroma whatever; at last I licked it on the sly: it was a little bit salt."

Hm! This doggie seems to me to be really too…She ought to be thrashed! And so he is ambitious! One must take that into consideration.

"Farewell, *ma chère*! I fly, and so on…and so on…I will finish my letter tomorrow. Well, good day, I am with you again. Today my young lady Sophie…"

Oh come, let us see about Sophie. Ah, you rascal…Never mind, never mind…let us go on.

"My young lady Sophie was in a great fluster. She was getting ready to go to a ball, and I was delighted that in her absence I could write to you. My Sophie is always very glad to go to a ball, though she always gets almost angry when she is being dressed. I cannot understand why people dress. Why don't they go about as we do, for instance? It's nice and it's comfortable. I can't understand, *ma chère*, what pleasure there is in going to balls. Sophie always comes home from balls at six o'clock in the morning, and I can almost always guess from her pale and exhausted face that they had given the poor thing nothing to eat. I must own I couldn't live like that.

If I didn't get grouse and gravy or the roast wing of a chicken, I don't know what would become of me. Gravy is nice too with grain in it, but carrots, turnips and artichokes are never good."

Extraordinary inequality of style! You can see at once that it is not a man writing; it begins as it ought and ends with dogginess. Let us look at one more letter. It's rather long. Hm! And there's no date on it.

"Ah, my dear, how one feels the approach of spring! My heart beats as though I were always expecting someone. There is always a noise in my ears so that I often stand for some minutes with my foot in the air listening at doors. I must confide to you that I have a number of suitors. I often sit at the window and look at them. Oh, if only you knew what ugly creatures there are among them. One is a very ungainly yard-dog, fearfully stupid, stupidity is painted on his face; he walks about the street with an air of importance and imagines that he is a distinguished person and thinks that everybody is looking at him. Not a bit of it. I don't take any notice of him—I behave exactly as though I didn't see him. And what a terrible Great Dane stops before my window! If he were to stand upon his hind legs, which I expect the clumsy fellow could not do, he would be a whole head taller than my Sophie's papa, though he is fairly tall and stout. That blockhead must be a frightfully insolent fellow. I growled at him, but much he cared: he hardly frowned, he put out his tongue, dangled his huge ears and looked up at the window—such a country bumpkin! But can you suppose, *ma chère*, that my heart makes no response to any overture? Ah no…If only you could see one of my suitors climbing over the fence next door, by name Tresor…Ah, *ma chère*, what a face he has!…"

Ough, the devil!… What rubbish! How can anyone fill a letter with such foolishness! Give me a man! I want to see a man. I want spiritual sustenance—in which my soul might find food and enjoyment; and instead of that I have this nonsense…Let us turn over the page and see whether it is better!

"Sophie was sitting at the table sewing something, I was looking out of the window because I am fond of watching passers-by, when all at once the footman came in and said 'Teplov!' 'Ask him in,' cried Sophie, and rushed to embrace me. 'Ah, Madgie, Madgie! If only you knew who that is: a dark young man, a kammer-junker, and such eyes, black and bright as fire!' And Sophie ran off to her room. A minute later a kammer-junker with black whiskers came in, walked up to the looking-glass, smoothed his hair and looked about the room. I growled and sat in my place. Sophie soon came in and bowed gaily in response to his scraping; and I just went on looking out of the window as though I were noticing nothing. However, I bent my head a little on one side and tried to hear what they were saying. Oh, *ma chère*, the nonsense they talked! They talked about a lady who had mistaken one figure for another at the dance; and said that someone called Bobov with a ruffle on his shirt looked just like a stork and had almost fallen down on the floor, and that a girl called Lidin imagined that her eyes were blue when they were really green—and that sort of thing. 'Well,' I thought to myself, 'if one were to compare that kammer-junker to Tresor, heavens, what a difference!' In the first place, the kammer-junker has a perfectly flat face with whiskers all round as though he had tied it up in a black handker-chief; while Tresor has a delicate little countenance with a white patch on the forehead. It's impossible to compare the kammer-junker's figure with Tresor's. And his eyes, his ways, his manners are all quite different. Oh, what a difference! I don't know, *ma chère*, what she sees in her Teplov. Why she is so enthusiastic about him…"

Well, I think myself that there is something wrong about it. It's impossi-ble that she can be fascinated by the kammer-junker. Let us see what next.

"It seems to me that if she is attracted by that kammer-junker she will soon be attracted by that clerk that sits in Papa's study. Oh, *ma chère*, if you know what an ugly fellow that is! A regular tortoise in a bag…"

What clerk is this?

"He has a very queer surname. He always sits mending the pens. The hair on his head is very much like hay. Papa sometimes sends him out instead of a servant…"

I do believe the nasty little dog is alluding to me. But my hair isn't like hay!

"Sophie can never help laughing when she sees him."

That's a lie, you damned little dog! What an evil tongue! As though I didn't know that that is the work of envy! As though I didn't know whose tricks were at the bottom of that! This is all the doing of the chief of my section. The man has vowed eternal hatred, and here he tried to injure me again and again, at every turn. Let us look at one more letter though. Perhaps the thing will explain itself.

MY DEAR FIDO,—Forgive me for not writing for so long. I have been in a perfect delirium. How truly has some writer said that love is a second life. Moreover, there are great changes in the house here. The kammer-junker is here every day. Sophie is frantically in love with him. Papa is very good-humoured. I have even heard from our Grigory, who sweeps the floor and almost always talks to himself, that there will soon be a wedding because Papa is set on seeing Sophie married to a general or a kammer-junker or to a colonel in the army...

Deuce take it! I can't read any more...It's always a kammer-junker or a general. Everything that's the best in the world falls to the kammer-junkers or the generals. If you find some poor treasure and think it is almost within your grasp, a kammer-junker or a general will snatch it from you. The devil take it! I should like to become a general myself, not in order to receive her hand and all the rest of it; no, I should like to be a general only to see how they would wriggle and display all their court manners and *équivoques* and then to say to them: I spit on you both. Deuce take it, it's annoying! I tore the silly dog's letters to bits.

3 DECEMBER—It cannot be. It's idle talk! There won't be a wedding! What if he is a kammer-junker? Why, that is nothing but a dignity, it's not a visible thing that one could pick up in one's hands. You don't get a third eye in your head because you are a kammer-junker. Why, his nose is not made of gold but is just like mine and everyone else's; he sniffs with it and doesn't eat with it, he sneezes with it and doesn't cough with it. I have often tried to make out from what all these differences arise. Why am I a titular councillor and on what grounds am I a titular councillor? Perhaps I am not a titular councillor at all? Perhaps I am a count or a general, and only somehow appear to be a titular councillor. Perhaps I don't know myself who I am. How many instances there have been in history: some simple, humble tradesman or peasant, not even a nobleman, is suddenly discovered to be a grand gentleman or the sovereign, or what do you call it...If a peasant can sometimes turn into something like that, what may not a nobleman turn into? I shall suddenly, for instance, enter wearing a general's uniform: with an epaulette on my right shoulder and an epaulette on my left shoulder, and a blue ribbon across my chest; well, my charmer will sing a different tune then, and what will her papa, our director, himself say? Ah, he is very ambitious! He is a mason, he is certainly a mason; though he does pretend to be this and that, but I noticed at once that he was a mason: if he shakes hands with anyone, he only offers him two fingers. Might I not be appointed a

governor-general this very minute or an intendant, or something of that sort? I should like to know why I am a titular councillor. Why precisely a titular councillor?

5 DECEMBER—I spent the whole morning reading the newspaper. Strange things are going on in Spain. In fact, I can't really make it out. They write that the throne is vacant, and that they are in a difficult position about choosing an heir, and that there are insurrections in consequence. It seems to me that it is extremely queer. How can the throne be vacant? They say that some *doña* ought to ascend to the throne. A *doña* cannot ascend the throne, she cannot possibly. There ought to be a king on the throne. "But," they say, "there is not a king." It cannot be that there is no king. A kingdom cannot exist without a king. There is a king, only probably he is in hiding somewhere. He may be there, but either family reasons or danger from some neighbouring State, such as France or some other country, may compel him to remain in hiding, or there may be some other reasons.

8 DECEMBER—I quite wanted to go to the department, but various reasons and considerations detained me. I cannot get the affairs of Spain out of my head. How can it be that a *doña* should be made queen? They won't allow it. England in the first place won't allow it. And besides, the politics of all Europe, the Emperor of Austria and our Tsar...I must own these events have so overwhelmed and shaken me that I haven't been able to do anything all day. Mavra remarked that I was extremely absent-minded at table. And I believe I did accidentally throw two plates on the floor, which smashed immediately. After dinner I went for a walk to the winter festival: I could deduce nothing edifying from it. For the most part I lay on my bed and reflected on the affairs of Spain.

43 APRIL 2000 AD—This is the day of the greatest public rejoicing! There is a king of Spain! He has been discovered. I am that king. I only heard of it this morning. I must own it burst upon me like a flash of lightning. I can't imagine how I could believe and imagine myself to be a titular councillor. How could that crazy, mad idea ever have entered my head? It's a good thing that no one thought of putting me in a madhouse. Now everything has been revealed to me. Now it is all as plain as possible. But until now I did not understand, everything was in a sort of mist. And I believe it all arose from believing that the brain is in the head. It's not so at all; it comes with

the wind from the direction of the Caspian Sea. First of all, I told Mavra who I am. When she heard that the King of Spain was standing before her, she threw up her hands and almost died of horror; the silly woman had never seen a king of Spain before. I tried to reassure her, however, and in gracious words tried to convince her of my benevolent feeling towards her, saying that I was not angry with her for having sometimes cleaned my boots so badly. Of course they are benighted people; it is no good talking of elevated subjects to them. She is frightened because she is convinced that all kings of Spain are like Philip II. But I assured her that there was no resemblance between me and Philip II and that I have not even one Capuchin. I didn't go to the department. The devil take it! No, my friends, you won't lure me there again; I am not going to copy your nasty papers!

MARTOBER 86, BETWEEN DAY AND NIGHT—Our office messenger arrived today to tell me to go to the department, and to say that I had not been there for more than three weeks.

But people are unjust: they do their reckoning by weeks. It's the Jews brought that in because their Rabbi washes once a week. However, I did go to the department for a joke. The head of our section thought that I should bow to him and apologise, but I looked at him indifferently, not too angrily and not too graciously, and sat down in my place as though I did not notice anything. I looked at all the scum of the office and thought: "If only you knew who is sitting among you!" Good gracious! Wouldn't there be an upset! And the head of our section would bow to me as he bows now to the director. They put a paper before me to make some sort of an extract from it. But I didn't touch it. A few minutes later everyone was in a bustle. They said the director was coming. A number of clerks ran forward to show off to him, but I didn't stir. When he walked through our room they all buttoned up their coats, but I didn't do anything at all. What's a director? Am I going to tremble before him? Never! He's a fine director! He is a cork, he is not a director. An ordinary cork, a simple cork and nothing else—such as you cork a bottle with. What amused me most of all was when they put a paper before me to sign. They thought I should write at the bottom of the paper, "So-and-so, head clerk of the table"—how else should it be! But in the most important place, where the director of the department signs his name, I wrote "Ferdinand VIII." You should have seen the awe-struck silence that followed; but I only waved my hand and said, "I don't insist on any signs of allegiance!" and walked out. From there I walked straight to the director's. He was not at home. The footman did not want to let me in, but I spoke to him in such a way that he let his hands drop. I went straight to her dressing-room. She was sitting before the looking-glass, she jumped up and stepped back on seeing me. I did not tell her that I was the King of Spain, however; I only told her that there was a happiness awaiting her such as she could not imagine, and that in spite of the wiles of our enemies we should be together. I didn't care to say more and walked out. Oh, woman is a treacherous creature! I have discovered now what women are. Hitherto no one has found out with whom woman is in love: I have been the first to discover it. Woman is in love with the devil. Yes, joking apart. Scientific men write nonsense saying that she is this or that—she cares for nothing but the devil. You will see her from a box in the first tier fixing her lorgnette. You imagine she is looking at the fat man with decorations. No, she is looking at the devil who is standing behind his back. There he is, hidden in his coat. There he is, making signs to her! And she will marry him, she will marry him.

And all these people, their dignified fathers who fawn on everybody and push their way to court and say that they are patriots and one thing and another: profit, profit is all that these patriots want! They would sell their father and their mother and God for money, ambitious creatures, Judases! All this is ambition, and the ambition is because of a little pimple under the tongue and in it a little worm no bigger than a pin's head, and it's all the doing of a barber who lives in Gorohovy Street, I don't remember his name; but I know for a fact that, in collusion with a midwife, he is trying to spread Mahometanism all over the world, and that is how it is, I am told, that the majority of people in France profess the Mahometan faith.

No DATE. THE DAY HAD NO NUMBER.—I walked incognito along Nevsky Prospect. His Majesty the Tsar drove by. All the people took off their caps and I did the same, but I made no sign that I was the King of Spain. I thought it improper to discover myself so suddenly before everyone, because I ought first to be presented at court. The only thing that has prevented my doing so is the lack of a royal dress. If only I could get hold of a royal mantle. I should have liked to order it from a tailor, but they are perfect asses; besides, they neglect their work so, they have given themselves up to speculating and for the most part are employed in laying the pavement in the street. I determined to make the mantle out of my new uniform, which I had only worn twice. And that the scoundrels should not ruin it I decided to make it myself, shutting the door that no one might see me at it. I ripped it all up with the scissors because the cut has to be completely different.

I DON'T REMEMBER THE DATE. THERE WAS NO MONTH EITHER. GOODNESS KNOWS WHAT TO MAKE OF IT.—The mantle is completely finished. Mavra gave a shriek when she saw me in it. However, I can't make up my mind to present myself at court, for so far there is no deputation from Spain. It wouldn't be proper to go without deputies: there would be nothing to give weight to my dignity. I expect them from hour to hour.

THE 1ST—I am extremely surprised at the tardiness of the deputies. What can be detaining them? Can it be the machinations of France? Yes, that is the most malignant of States. I went to enquire at the post office whether the Spanish deputies had not arrived; but the postmaster was excessively stupid and knew nothing. "No," he said, "there are no deputies here, but if you care to write a letter I will send it off in accordance with the regulations." Dash it all, what's the use of a letter? A letter is nonsense. Letters are written by chemists, and even then they have to moisten their tongues with vinegar or else their faces would be all over scabs.

MADRID, FEBRUARY THIRTIETH—And so here I am in Spain, and it happened so quickly that I can hardly realise it yet. This morning the Spanish deputies arrived and I got into a carriage with them. The extraordinary rapidity of our journey struck me as strange. We went at such a rate that within half an hour we had reached the frontiers of Spain. But of course now there are railroads all over Europe, and steamers go very rapidly. Spain is a strange land! When we went into the first room I saw a number of people with shaven heads. I guessed at once that these were either grandees or soldiers because they do shake their heads. I thought the behaviour of the High Chancellor, who led me by the hand, extremely strange. He thrust me into a little room and said: "Sit there, and if you persist in calling yourself King Ferdinand, I'll knock the inclination out of you." But knowing that this was only to try me, I answered in the negative, whereupon the Chancellor hit me twice on the back with the stick and it hurt so that I almost cried out, but I restrained myself, remembering that this is the custom of chivalry on receiving any exalted dignity, for customs of chivalry persist in Spain to this day.

When I was alone I decided to occupy myself with the affairs of state.

I discovered that Spain and China are one and the same country, and it is only through ignorance that they are considered to be a different kingdoms. I recommend everyone to try and write "Spain" on a bit of paper and it will always turn out "China." But I was particularly distressed by an event which will take place tomorrow. Tomorrow at seven o'clock a strange phenomenon will occur: the earth will sit on the moon. The celebrated English chemist Wellington has written about it. I must confess that I experience a tremor in my heart when I reflect on the extreme softness and fragility of the moon. You see, the moon is generally made in Hamburg, and very badly made too. I am surprised that England hasn't taken notice of it. It was made by a lame cooper, and it is evident that the fool had no idea what a moon should be. He put in tarred cord and one part of olive oil; and that is why there is such a fearful stench all over the world that one has to stop up one's nose. And that's how it is that the moon is such a soft globe that man cannot live on it and that nothing lives there but noses. And it is for that very reason that we can't see our noses, because they are all in the moon. And when I reflected that the earth is a heavy body and when it sits down may ground our noses to powder, I was overcome by such uneasiness that, putting on my shoes and stockings, I hastened to the hall of the Imperial Council to give orders to the police not to allow the earth to sit on the moon. The grandees with shaven heads whom I found in great numbers in the hall of the Imperial Council were very intelligent people, and when I said, "Gentlemen, let us save the moon, for the earth is trying to fall upon it!" they all rushed to carry out my sovereign wishes, and several climbed up the walls to try and get at the moon, but at that moment the High Chancellor walked in. Seeing him they all ran in different directions. I as King remained alone. But, to my amazement, the Chancellor struck me with his stick and drove me back to my room! So great is the power of national customs in Spain.

JANUARY OF THE SAME YEAR (IT CAME AFTER FEBRUARY)—So far I have not been able to make out what sort of a country Spain is. The national traditions and the customs of the court are quite extraordinary. I can't make it out, I can't make it out, I absolutely can't make it out. Today they shaved my head, although I shouted at the top of my voice that I didn't want to become a monk. But I can't even remember what happened afterwards when they poured cold water on my head. I have never endured such hell. I was almost going frantic so that they had a difficulty in holding me. I cannot understand the meaning of this strange custom. It's a stupid, senseless practice! The lack of good sense in the kings who have not abolished it to this day is beyond my comprehension. Judging from all the circumstances, I wonder whether I have not fallen into the hands of the Spanish Inquisition, and whether the man I took to be the Grand Chancellor isn't the Grand Inquisitor. Only I cannot understand how a king can be subject to the Inquisition. It can only be through the influence of France, especially of Polignac. Oh, that beast of a Polignac! He has sworn to me enmity to the death. And he pursues me and pursues me; but I know, my friend, that you are the tool of England. The English are great politicians. They poke their noses into everything. All the world knows that when England takes a piece of snuff, France sneezes.

THE TWENTY-FIFTH—Today the Grand Inquisitor came into my room again, but hearing his steps in the distance I hid under a chair. Seeing I wasn't there, he began calling me. At first he shouted "Popristchin!" I didn't say a word. Then: "Aksenty Ivanov! Titular councillor! Nobleman!" I still remained silent. "Ferdinand VIII, King of Spain!" I was on the point of sticking out my head, but then I thought: "No, my friend, you won't take me in. I know you: you will be pouring cold water on my head again." However, he caught sight of me and drove me from under the chair with a stick. That damned stick does hurt. However, I was rewarded for all this by the discovery I made today. I found out that every cock has a Spain, that it is under his wings not far from his tail.

The Grand Inquisitor went away, however, very wroth, threatening me with some punishment. But I disdain his impotent malice, knowing that he is simply an instrument, a tool of England.

34 MARCH. FEBRUARY, 349—No, I haven't the strength to endure more. My God! The things they are doing to me! They pour cold water on my head! They won't listen to me, they won't see me, they won't hear me. What have I done to them? Why do they torture me? What do they want of a poor creature like me? What can I give them? I have nothing. It's too much for me, I can't endure these agonies, my head is burning and everything is going round. Save me, take me away! Give me a troika and horses swift as a whirlwind! Take your seat, my driver, ring out, my bells, fly upwards, my steeds, and bear me away from this world! Far away, far away, so that nothing can be seen, nothing. Yonder the sky whirls before me, a star sparkles in the distance; the forest floats by with dark trees and the moon, blue-grey mist lies stretched under my feet; a chord resounds in the mist; on one side

the sea, on the other Italy, yonder the huts of Russia can be seen. Is that my home in the distance? Is it my mother sitting before the window? Mother, save your poor son! Drop a tear on his sick head! See how they torment him! Press your poor orphan to your bosom! There is nowhere in the world for him! He is persecuted! Mother, have pity on your sick child!

And do you know that the King of France has a boil just under his nose?

THE NOSE

I

AN EXTRAORDINARILY STRANGE incident took place in Petersburg on the 25th of March. The barber, Ivan Yakovlevitch, who lives in the Voznesensky Prospect (his surname is lost, and nothing more appears even on his signboard, where a gentleman is depicted with his cheeks covered with soapsuds, together with the inscription ALSO LETS BLOOD)—the barber Ivan Yakovlevitch woke up rather early and was aware of a smell of hot bread. Raising himself in bed he saw his spouse, a rather portly lady who was very fond of drinking coffee, engaged in taking out of the oven some freshly baked loaves.

"I won't have coffee today, Praskovya Osipovna," said Ivan Yakovlevitch; "instead I should like some hot bread with onion." (The fact is that Ivan Yakovlevitch would have liked both, but he knew that it was utterly impossible to ask for two things at once, for Praskovya Osipovna greatly disliked such caprices.)

"Let the fool have bread, so much the better for me," thought his spouse to herself, "there will be an extra cup of coffee left," and she flung one loaf on the table.

For the sake of propriety Ivan Yakovlevitch put a tail-coat over his shirt, and sitting down to the table, sprinkled with salt and prepared two onions, took a knife in his hand and, making a solemn face, set to work to cut the bread. After dividing the loaf in two halves he looked into the middle of it—and to his amazement saw there something that looked white. Ivan Yakovlevitch scooped at it carefully with his knife and felt it with his finger: "It's solid," he said to himself. "Whatever can it be?"

He thrust in his finger and drew it out—it was a nose!... Ivan

Yakovlevitch's hand dropped with astonishment, he rubbed his eyes and felt it: it actually was a nose, and, what's more, it looked to him somehow familiar. A look of horror came into Ivan Yakovlevitch's face. But that horror was nothing to the indignation with which his wife was overcome.

"Where have you cut that nose off, you brute?" she cried wrathfully. "You scoundrel, you drunkard, I'll go to the police myself to tell of you! You bandit! Here I have heard from three men that when you are shaving them you pull at their noses till you almost tug them off."

But Ivan Yakovlevitch was more dead than alive: he perceived that the nose was no other than that of Kovalyov, the collegiate assessor, whom he shaved every Wednesday and every Sunday.

"Stay, Praskovya Osipovna! I'll wrap it up in a rag and put it in a corner. Let it stay there for a bit; I'll take it out later on."

"I won't hear of it! As though I would allow a cut-off nose to lie about in my room. You dried-up biscuit! To be sure, he can do nothing but sharpen his razors on the strop, but soon he won't be fit to do his duties at all, the gad-about, the rake! As though I were going to answer to the police for you…Oh, you sloven, you stupid blockhead. Away with it, away with it! Take it where you like! Don't let me get even a whiff of it again!"

Ivan Yakovlevitch stood as though utterly crushed. He thought and thought, and did not know what to think.

"The devil only knows how it happened," he said at last, scratching behind his ear. "Did I come home drunk last night or not? I can't say for certain now. But from all the signs and tokens it must be a thing quite unheard of, for bread is a thing that is baked, while a nose is something quite different. I can't make head or tail of it."

Ivan Yakovlevitch sank into silence. The thought that the police might make a search there for the nose and throw the blame of it on him reduced him to complete prostration. Already the red collar, beautifully embroidered with silver, the sabre, hovered before his eyes, and he trembled all over. At last he got his breeches and his boots, pulled on these wretched objects, and, accompanied by the stern upbraidings of Praskovya Osipovna, wrapped the nose in a rag and went out into the street.

He wanted to thrust it out of sight somewhere, under a gate, or somehow accidentally to drop it and then turn off into a side street, but as ill-luck would have it he kept coming upon someone he knew, who would at once begin by asking "Where are you going?" or "Whom are you going to shave so early?" so that Ivan Yakovlevitch could never find a good moment.

Another time he really did drop it, but a sentry pointed to it with this halberd from a long way off, saying as he did so, "Pick it up, you have dropped something!" and Ivan Yakovlevitch was obliged to pick up the nose and put it in his pocket. He was overcome by despair as the number of people in the street was continually increasing as the shops and stalls began to open.

He made up his mind to go to St Isaac's Bridge in the hope of being able to fling it into the Neva…But I am rather in fault for not having hitherto said anything about Ivan Yakovlevitch, a worthy man in many respects.

Ivan Yakovlevitch, like every self-respecting Russian workman, was a terrible drunkard, and though every day he shaved other people's chins, his own went forever unshaven. Ivan Yakovlevitch's tail-coat (he never wore any other shape) was piebald, that is, it was black dappled all over with brown and yellow and grey; the collar was shiny, and instead of three buttons there were only hanging threads. Ivan Yakovlevitch was a great cynic, and when Kovalyov, the collegiate assessor, said to him while he was being shaved, "Your hands always stink, Ivan Yak," the latter would reply with the question: "What should make them stink?" "I can't tell, my good man, but they do stink," the collegiate assessor would say, and, taking a pinch of snuff, Ivan Yakovlevitch lathered him for it on his cheeks and under his nose and behind his ears and under his beard—in fact wherever he chose.

The worthy citizen found himself by now on St Isaac's Bridge. First of all he looked about him, then bent over the parapet as though to look under the bridge to see whether there were a great number of fish racing by, and stealthily flung in the rag with the nose. He felt as though with it a heavy weight had rolled off his back. Ivan Yakovlevitch even grinned. Instead of going to shave the chins of government clerks, he repaired to an establishment bearing the inscription TEA AND REFRESHMENTS and asked for a glass of punch, when he suddenly observed at the end of the bridge a police inspector of respectable appearance with full whiskers, a three-cornered hat and sword. He turned cold, and meanwhile the inspector beckoned to him and said: "Come this way, my good man."

Ivan Yakovlevitch, knowing the etiquette, took off his hat some way off and, as he approached, said, "I wish your honour good health."

"No, no, old fellow, I am not 'your honour.' Tell me what you were about, standing on the bridge."

"Upon my soul, sir, I was on my way to shave my customers, and I was only looking to see whether the current was running fast."

"That's a lie, that's a lie! You won't get off with that. Kindly answer!"

"I am ready to shave you, gracious sir, two or even three times a week with no conditions whatever," answered Ivan Yakovlevitch.

"No, my friend, that is nonsense; I have three barbers to shave me and they think it is a great honour, too. But be so kind as to tell me what you were doing there?"

Ivan Yakovlevitch turned pale...but the incident is completely veiled in obscurity, and absolutely nothing is known of what happened next.

II

KOVALYOV THE COLLEGIATE assessor woke up early next morning and made the sound *brrrr* with his lips as he always did when he woke up, though he could not himself have explained the reason for his doing so. Kovalyov stretched and asked for a little looking-glass that was standing on the table. He wanted to look at a pimple which had come out upon his nose on the previous evening, but to his great astonishment there was a completely flat space where his nose should have been. Kovalyov in a fright asked for some water and a towel to rub his eyes: there really was no nose. He began feeling around with his hand to see whether he was still asleep: it appeared that he was not asleep. The collegiate assessor, Kovalyov, jumped out of bed, he shook himself—there was still no nose...He ordered his clothes to be given him at once and flew off straight to the head police-master.

But meanwhile we must say a word about Kovalyov in order that the reader may have some idea of what kind of collegiate assessor he was. Collegiate assessors who receive that title through learned diplomas cannot be compared with those who are created collegiate assessors in the Caucasus. They are two quite different species. The learned collegiate assessors...But Russia is such a wonderful country that, if you say a word about one collegiate assessor, all the collegiate assessors from Roga to Kamchatka would certainly take it to themselves, and it is the same, of course, with all grades and titles. Kovalyov was a collegiate assessor from the Caucasus. He had only been of that rank for the last two years, and so could not forget it for a moment, and to give himself greater weight and dignity he did not call himself simply collegiate assessor but always spoke of himself as a major. "Listen, my dear," he would usually say when he met in the street a woman selling shirt-fronts, "you go to my house; I live in Sadovoy Street; just ask, 'Does Major Kovalyov live here?' Anyone will show you." If he met some prepossessing little baggage he would give her besides a secret instruction, adding: "You ask for Major Kovalyov's flat, my love." For this reason we will for the future speak of him as the major.

Major Kovalyov was in the habit of walking every day up and down Nevsky Prospect. The collar on his shirt-front was always extremely clean and well starched. His whiskers were such as one may see nowadays on provincial and district surveyors, on architects and army doctors, also on those employed on special commissions, and in general on all such men as have full ruddy checks and are very good hands at a game of boston: these whiskers start from the middle of the cheek and go straight up to the nose. Major Kovalyov used to wear a number of cornelian seals, some with crests on them and others on which were carved Wednesday, Thursday, Monday and so on. Major Kovalyov had come to Petersburg on business, that is, to look for a post befitting his rank: if he were successful, the post of a vice-governor, and failing that the situation of an executive clerk in some prominent department. Major Kovalyov was not averse to matrimony, but only on the condition he could find a bride with a fortune of two hundred thousand. And so the reader may judge for himself what was the major's position when he saw, instead of a nice-looking, well-proportioned nose, an extremely stupid level space.

As ill-luck would have it, not a cab was to be seen in the street, and he was obliged to walk, wrapping himself in his cloak and hiding his face in his handkerchief, as though his nose were bleeding. "But perhaps it was my imagination: it's impossible I could have been so silly as to lose my nose," he thought, and went into a confectioner's on purpose to look at himself in the looking-glass. Fortunately there was no one in the shop: some boys were sweeping the floor and putting all the chairs straight; others with sleepy faces were bringing in hot turnovers on trays: yesterday's papers covered with coffee stains were lying about on the tables and chairs. "Well, thank God, there is nobody here," he thought, "now I can look." He went timidly up to the mirror and looked. "What the devil's the meaning of it? How nasty!" he commented, spitting. "If only there had been something instead of a nose, but there is nothing!…"

Biting his lips, he went out of the confectioner's with annoyance, and resolved, contrary to his usual practice, not to look or smile at anyone. All at once he stood as though rooted to the spot before the door of a house. Something inexplicable took place before his eyes: a carriage was stopping at the entrance; the carriage door flew open; a gentleman in uniform, bending down, sprang out and ran up the steps. What was the horror and at the same time amazement of Kovalyov when he recognised that this was his own nose! At this extraordinary spectacle it seemed to him that everything was heaving before his eyes; he felt that he could scarcely stand; but he made up his mind, come what may, to await the gentleman's return to the carriage, and he stood trembling all over as though in fever. Two minutes later the nose actually did come out. He was in a gold-laced uniform with a big stand-up collar; he had on chamois-leather breeches, at his side was a sword. From his plumed hat it might be gathered that he was of the rank of a civil councillor. Everything showed that he was going somewhere to pay a visit. He looked to both sides, called to the coachman to open the carriage door, got in and drove off.

Poor Kovalyov almost went out of his mind; he did not know what to think of such a strange occurrence. How was it possible for a nose—which had only yesterday been on his face and could neither drive nor walk—to be in uniform! He ran after the carriage, which luckily did not go far, but stopped before Kazan Cathedral.

He hurried into the cathedral, made his way through a row of old beggar women with their faces wrapped up and two chinks in place of their eyes at whom he used to laugh so merrily, and went into the church. There were not many worshippers inside the church, and they were all huddled around the door. Kovalyov was so agitated that he was utterly unable to pray, and he looked in every corner of the church trying to catch a glimpse of this gentleman. At last he saw him standing off to one side. The nose was completely covering up his face with a large stiff collar and was praying with an expression of the greatest devoutness.

"How am I to approach him?" thought Kovalyov. "One can see by everything—from his uniform, from his hat—that he is a civil councillor. The devil only knows how to do it!"

He began by coughing at his side; but the nose never changed his devout attitude and continued to bow very low.

"Sir," said Kovalyov, inwardly forcing himself to speak confidently. "Sir..."

"What do you want?" answered the nose, turning around.

"It seems...strange to me, sir...You ought to know your proper place, and all at once I find you, where?... In church. You will admit..."

"Excuse me, I cannot understand what you are talking about...Explain."

"How am I to explain to him?" thought Kovalyov, and plucking up his courage he began: "Of course I…I am a major, by the way. For me to go about without a nose you must admit is improper. An old woman selling peeled oranges on Voskresensky Bridge may sit there without a nose; but having prospects of obtaining…and being besides acquainted with a great many ladies in the families of Tchehtarev, the civil councillor and others…You can judge for yourself…I don't know, sir –" at this point Major Kovalyov shrugged his shoulders—"excuse me…if you look at the matter in accordance with the principles of duty and honour…you can understand of yourself…"

"I don't understand a word," said the nose. "Explain it more satisfactorily."

"Sir," said Kovalyov, with a sense of his own dignity, "I don't know how to understand your words. The matter appears to me perfectly obvious… either you wish…Why, you are my own nose!"

The nose looked at the major and his eyebrows slightly quivered.

"You are mistaken, sir, I am an independent individual. Moreover, there can be no sort of close relations between us. I see, sir, from the buttons of your uniform, you must be serving in a different department." Saying this, the nose turned away and continued to pray.

Kovalyov was utterly confused, not knowing what to do or even what to think. Meanwhile they heard the agreeable rustle of a lady's dress: an elderly lady was approaching, all decked out in lace, and with her a slim lady in a white dress which looked very charming on her slender figure, in a straw-coloured hat as light as a pastry puff. Behind them stood, opening his snuffbox, a tall footman with big whiskers and quite a dozen collars.

Kovalyov came nearer, pulled out the cambric collar of his shirt-front, arranged the seals on his gold watch-chain, and, smiling from side to side, turned his attention to the ethereal lady who, like a spring flower, faintly swayed forward and put her white hand with its half-transparent fingers to her brow. The smile of Kovalyov's face broadened when he saw under her hat the round, dazzlingly white chin and part of her cheek flushed with the hues of the first spring rose; but all at once he skipped away as though he had been scalded. He recollected that he had absolutely nothing on his face in place of a nose, and tears oozed from his eyes. He turned away to tell the gentleman in uniform straight out that he was only pretending to be a civil councillor, that he was a rogue and a scoundrel, and that he was nothing else than his own nose…But the nose was no longer there; he had managed to gallop off, probably again to call on someone.

This reduced Kovalyov to despair. He went back and stood for a minute or two under the colonnade, carefully looking in all directions to see whether the nose was anywhere about. He remembered very well that there was a plume in his hat and gold lace on his uniform; but he had not noticed his greatcoat nor the colour of his carriage, nor his horses, nor even whether he had a footman behind him and if so in what livery. Moreover, such numbers of carriages were driving backwards and forwards and at such a speed that it was difficult even to distinguish them; and if he had distinguished one of them he would have had no means of stopping it. It was a lovely, sunny day. There were masses of people on Nevsky; ladies were scattered like a perfect cataract of flowers all over the pavement from Politseysky to Anitchkin Bridge. Here he saw coming towards him an upper-court councillor of his acquaintance whom he used to call "Lieutenant-Colonel," particularly if he were speaking to other people. There he saw Yaryzhkin, a head clerk in the senate, a great friend of his, who always lost points when he went eight at boston. And here was another major who had received the rank of assessor in the Caucasus, beckoning to him…

"Ah, deuce take it," said Kovalyov. "Hi, cab! Drive straight to the police-master's."

Kovalyov got into a cab and shouted to the driver: "Drive like a house on fire!"

"Is the police-master at home?" he cried, going into the entry.

"No," answered the porter, "he has only just gone out."

"Well, I declare!"

"Yes," added the porter, "and he has not been gone so long; if you had come but a tiny minute earlier you might have found him."

Kovalyov, still keeping the handkerchief over his face, got into the cab and shouted in a voice of despair: "Drive on."

"Where?" asked the cabman.

"Drive straight on!"

"How straight on? Here's the turning, is it to the right or to the left?"

This question pulled Kovalyov up and forced him to think again. In his position he ought first of all to address himself to the department of law and order, not because it had any direct connection with the police but because the intervention of the latter might be far more rapid than any help he could get in other departments. To see satisfaction from the higher officials of the department in which the nose had announced himself as serving would have been injudicious, since from the nose's own answers he had been able to perceive that nothing was sacred to that man and that he might tell lies in this case too, just as he had lied in declaring that he had never seen him before. And so Kovalyov was on the point of telling the cabman to drive to the Department of Law and Order, when again the idea occurred to him that this rogue and scoundrel who had at their first meeting behaved in such a shameless way might seize the opportunity and slip out of the town—and then all his searches would be in vain, or might be prolonged, which God forbid, for a whole month. At last it seemed that Heaven itself directed him. He decided to go straight to a newspaper office and without loss of time to publish a circumstantial description of the nose, so that anyone meeting it might at once present it to him or at least let him know where it was. And so, deciding upon this course, he told the cabman to drive to the newspaper office, and all the way never ceased pommelling him with his fist on the back, saying, as he did so, "Quicker, you rascal; make haste, you knave!"

"Ugh, sir!" said the cabman, shaking his head and flicking with the reins at the horse, whose coat was as long as a lapdog's. At last the cab stopped and Kovalyov ran panting into a little reception-room where a grey-headed clerk in spectacles, wearing an old tail-coat, was sitting at a table, and with a pen between his teeth was counting over some coppers he had before him.

"Who receives enquiries here?" cried Kovalyov. "Ah, good day!"

"I wish you good day," said the grey-headed clerk, raising his eyes for a moment and then dropping them again on the money lying in heaps on the table.

"I want to insert an advertisement…"

"Allow me to ask you to wait a minute," the clerk pronounced, with one hand noting a figure on the paper and with the finger of his left hand moving two beads on the reckoning board. A flunkey with braid on his livery and a rather clean appearance, which betrayed that he had at some time served in an aristocratic family, was standing at the table with a written paper in his hand and thought fit to display his social abilities: "Would you believe it, sir, that the little cur is not worth eighty kopecks; in fact I wouldn't give eight for it, but the countess is fond of it—my goodness, she is fond of it—and here she will give a hundred roubles to anyone who finds it! To speak politely, as you and I are speaking now, people's tastes are quite incompatible. When a man's a sportsman, then he'll keep a setter or a poodle; he won't mind giving five hundred or a thousand so long as it is a good dog."

The worthy clerk listened to this with a significant air, and at the same time was reckoning the number of letters in the advertisement. Along the sides of the room stood a number of old women, shop-boys and house-porters who had brought advertisements. In one it was announced that a coachman of sober habits was looking for a situation; in the next a second-hand carriage brought from Paris in 1814 was offered for sale; next a maid-servant, aged nineteen, experienced in laundry work and also competent to do other work, was looking for a situation; a strong droshky with only one spring broken was for sale; a spirited, young, dappled grey horse, only seventeen years old, for sale; a new consignment of turnip and radish seed from London; a summer villa with all conveniences, stabling for two horses and a piece of land that might well be planted with fine birches and pine trees; there was also an appeal to those wishing to purchase old boot-soles, inviting such to come for the same every day between eight o'clock in the morning and three o'clock in the afternoon. The room in which all this company was assembled was a small one and the air in it was extremely thick, but the collegiate assessor Kovalyov was incapable of noticing the smell both because he kept his handkerchief over his face and because his nose was goodness knows where.

"Dear sir, allow me to ask you…my case is very urgent," he said at last impatiently.

"In a minute, in a minute!… Two roubles, forty-three kopecks!… This minute! One rouble and sixty-four kopecks!" said the grey-headed gentleman, flinging the old women and house-porters the various documents they had brought. "What can I do for you?" he said at last, turning to Kovalyov.

"I want to ask…" said Kovalyov. "Some robbery or trickery has occurred; I cannot make it out at all. I only want you to advertise that anyone who brings me the scoundrel will receive a handsome reward."

"Allow me to ask what is your surname?"

"No, why put my surname? I cannot give it to you! I have a large circle of acquaintances: Madame Tchehtarev, wife of a civil councillor, Pelageya Grigoryevna Podtatchin, widow of an officer…they will find out. God forbid! You can simply put 'a collegiate assessor,' or better still, 'a person of major's rank.'"

"Is the runaway your house-serf then?"

"A house-serf indeed! That would not be so great a piece of knavery! It's…my nose has run away from me…my own nose."

"Hm, what a strange surname! And is it a very large sum that Mr Nosov has robbed you of?"

"Nosov!… you are on the wrong tack. It is my nose, my own nose that has disappeared, I don't know where. The devil wanted to have a joke at my expense."

"But in what way did it disappear? There is something I can't quite understand."

"And indeed, I can't tell you how it happened—the point is that now it is driving about the town, calling itself a civil councillor. And so I beg you to announce that anyone who catches him must bring him at once to me as quickly as possible. Only think, really, how can I get on without such a conspicuous part of my person. It's not like a little toe, the loss of which I could hide in my boot and no one could say whether it was there or not. I go on Thursdays to Madame Tchehtarev's; Pelageya Grigoryevna Podtatchin, an officer's widow, and her very pretty daughter are great friends of mine; and you can judge for yourself what a fix I am in now…I can't possibly show myself now…"

The clerk pondered, a fact which was manifest from the way he compressed his lips.

"No, I can't put an advertisement like that in the paper," he said at last, after a long silence.

"What? Why not?"

"Well. The newspaper might lose its reputation. If everyone is going to write that his nose has run away, why…As it is, they say we print lots of absurd things and false reports."

"But what is there absurd about this? I don't see anything absurd in it."

"You fancy there is nothing absurd in it? But last week, now, this was what happened. A government clerk came to me just as you have; he brought an advertisement, it came to two roubles seventy-three kopecks, and all the advertisement amounted to was that a poodle with a black coat had strayed. You wouldn't think that there was anything in that, would you? But it turned out to be a lampoon on someone: the poodle was the cashier of some department, I don't remember which."

"But I am not asking you to advertise about poodles but about my own nose; that is almost the same as about myself."

"No, such an advertisement I cannot insert."

"But since my nose really is lost!"

"If it is lost, that is a matter for the doctor. They say there are people who can fit you with a nose of any shape you like. But I observe you must be a gentleman of merry disposition and are fond of having your joke."

"I swear as God is holy! If you like, since it has come to that, I will show you."

"I don't want to trouble you," said the clerk, taking a pinch of snuff. "However, if it is no trouble," he added, moved by curiosity, "it might be desirable to have a look."

The collegiate assessor took the handkerchief from his face.

"It really is extremely strange," said the clerk. "The place is perfectly flat, like a freshly fried pancake. Yes, it's incredibly smooth."

"Will you dispute it now? You see for yourself I must advertise. I shall be particularly grateful to you and very glad this incident has given me the pleasure of your acquaintance."

The major, as may be seen, made up on this occasion to resort to a little flattery.

"To print such an advertisement is, of course, not such a very great matter," said the clerk. "But I do not foresee any advantage to you from it. If you do want to, put it in the hands of someone with a skilful pen, describe it as a rare freak of nature, and publish the little article in the *Northern Bee*—" at this point he once more took a pinch of snuff—"for the benefit of youth—" at this moment he wiped his nose—"or anyway as a matter of general interest."

The collegiate assessor felt quite hopeless. He dropped his eyes and looked at the bottom of the paper where there was an announcement of an entertainment; his face was ready to break into a smile as he saw the name of a pretty actress, and his hand went to his pocket to feel whether he had a five-rouble note there, for an officer of his rank ought, in Kovalyov's opinion, to have a seat in the stalls; but the thought of his nose spoiled it all.

Even the clerk seemed touched by Kovalyov's difficult position. Desirous of relieving his distress in some way, he thought it befitting to express his sympathy in a few words: "I am really very much grieved that such an incident should have occurred to you. Wouldn't you like a pinch of snuff? It relieves headache and dissipates depression; even in intestinal trouble it is of use.' Saying this, the clerk offered Kovalyov his snuffbox, rather neatly opening the lid with a portrait of a lady in a hat on it.

This unpremeditated action drove Kovalyov out of all patience.

"I can't understand how you can think to make a joke of it," he said angrily. "Don't you see that I am without just what I need for sniffing! The devil take your snuff! I can't bear the sight of it now, not merely your miserable Berezina snuff but even if you were to offer me rappee itself!" Saying this, he walked out of the newspaper office, deeply mortified, and went in the direction of the local police superintendent, a fanatic lover of sugar. At his home, the whole of his front room, which was also the dining-room, was filled with sugar loaves, delivered to him in friendship by sugar traders. At that point, the cook was removing the superintendent's regulation boots; his sword and other military accoutrements were already calmly hanging in the corners, and his terrible three-cornered hat had already been grabbed by his three-year old son; and he, after a military life of combat, was ready to taste the pleasure of peace.

Kovalyov walked in at the very moment when he was stretching and clearing his throat and saying: "Ah, I should enjoy a couple of hours' nap!" So it might be foreseen that the collegiate assessor's visit was not very opportune, and I do not know whether he would have been received too warmly even had he brought several pounds of tea or cloth. The police superintendent was a great patron of all arts and manufactures; but the paper note he preferred to everything. "That is a thing," he used to say, "there is nothing better than that thing; it does not ask for food, it takes up little space, there is always room for it in the pocket, and if you drop it, it does not break."

The police superintendent received Kovalyov rather coldly and said that after dinner was not the time to make an enquiry, that nature itself had ordained that man should rest a little after eating (the collegiate assessor could see from this that the sayings of the ancient sages were not unfamiliar to the local superintendent) that a respectable man does not have his nose pulled off and that there are many majors in the world who do not even own underclothes that are in proper condition, as they drag themselves around to all kinds of obscene places.

This was adding insult to injury. It must be said that Kovalyov was very easily offended. He could forgive anything whatever said about himself, but could never forgive insult to his rank or his calling. He was even of the opinion that any reference to officers of the higher ranks might be allowed to pass in stage plays, but that no attack ought to be made on those of a lower grade. The reception given him by the local superintendent so disconcerted him that he tossed his head and said with an air of dignity and a slight gesticulation of surprise: "I must observe that after observations so insulting on your part I can add nothing more…" and went out.

He went home hardly conscious of the ground under his feet. By now it was dusk. His lodgings seemed to him melancholy, or rather utterly disgusting, after all these unsuccessful efforts. Going into his entry-hall he saw his valet, Ivan, lying on his dirty leather sofa; he was spitting on the ceiling and rather successfully aiming at the same spot. The nonchalance of his servant enraged him; he hit him on the forehead with his hat, saying: "You pig, you are always doing something stupid.' Ivan leaped up and rushed headlong to help him off with his cloak.

Going into his room, weary and dejected, the major threw himself into an easy chair, and, at last, after several sighs, said: "My God, my God! Why has this misfortune befallen me? if I had lost an arm or a leg—anyway it would have been better; but without a nose a man is goodness knows what: neither fish nor fowl nor human being, good for nothing but to fling out of the window! And if only it had been cut off in battle or in a duel, or if I had been the cause of it myself, but, as it is, it is lost for no cause of reason, it is lost for nothing, absolutely nothing! But no, it cannot be," he added after a moment's thought. "It's incredible that a nose should be lost. It must be a dream or an illusion. Perhaps by some mistake I drank instead of water the vodka I use to rub my chin after shaving. Ivan, the fool, did not remove it and very likely I took it." To convince himself that he was not drunk, the major pinched himself so painfully that he shrieked. The pain completely convinced him that he was living and acting in real life. He slowly approached the looking-glass and at first screwed up his eyes with the idea that maybe his nose would appear in its proper place; but at the same minute sprang back, saying: "What a caricature!"

It really was incomprehensible; if a button had been lost or a silver spoon or a watch or anything similar—but to have lost this, and in one's own flat too!... Thinking over all the circumstances, Major Kovalyov reached the supposition that what might be nearest the truth was that the person responsible for this could be no other than Madam Podtatchin, who wanted him to marry her daughter. He himself liked flirting with her, but avoided a definite engagement. When the mother had informed him directly that she wished for the marriage, he had slyly put her off with his compliments, saying that he was still too young, that he must serve for four years so as to be exactly forty-two. And that Madame Podtatchin had therefore made up her mind, probably out of revenge, to ruin him, and had hired for the purpose some peasant witches, because it was impossible to suppose that the nose had been cut off in any way; no one had come into his room; the barber Ivan Yakovlevitch had shaved him on Wednesday, and all Wednesday, and even all Thursday, his nose had been all right—that he remembered and was quite certain about; besides, he would have felt pain, and there could have been no doubt that the wound could not have healed so soon and been as flat as a pancake. He formed various plans in his mind: either to summon Madame Podtatchin formally before the court or to go to her himself and tax her with it. These reflections were interrupted by a light which gleamed through all the cracks of the door and let him know that a candle had been lit in the entry by Ivan. Soon Ivan himself appeared, holding it before him and lighting up the whole room. Kovalyov's first movement was to snatch up his handkerchief and cover the place where yesterday his nose had been, that his really stupid servant might not gape at the sight of anything so peculiar in his master.

Ivan had hardly time to retreat to his lair when there was the sound of an unfamiliar voice in the entry, pronouncing the words: "Does the collegiate assessor Kovalyov live here?"

"Come in, Major Kovalyov is here," said Kovalyov, jumping up hurriedly and opening the door.

There walked in a police officer of handsome appearance, with whiskers neither too fair nor too dark, and rather fat cheeks, the very one who at the beginning of our story was standing at the end of St Isaac's Bridge.

"You, if you please, have lost your nose, sir?"

"That is so."

"It is now found."

"What are you saying?" cried Major Kovalyov. He could not speak for joy. He gazed open-eyed at the police officer standing before him, on whose full lips and cheeks the flickering light of the candle was brightly reflected. "How?"

"By a strange chance: he was caught almost on the road. He had already taken his seat in the diligence and was intending to go to Riga, and had already taken a passport in the name of a government clerk. And the strange thing is that I myself took him for a gentleman at first, but fortunately I had my spectacles with me and I soon saw that it was a nose. You know I am short-sighted. And if you stand before me I only see that you have a face, but I don't notice your nose or your beard or anything. My mother-in-law, that is my wife's mother, doesn't see anything either."

Kovalyov was beside himself with joy. "Where? Where? I'll run at once."

"Don't disturb yourself. Knowing that you were in need of it, I brought it along with me. And the strange thing is that the man who has had the most to do with the affair is a rascal of a barber in Voznesensky Street, who is now in custody. I have long suspected him of drunkenness and thieving, and only the day before yesterday he carried off a strip of buttons from one shop. Your nose is exactly as it was." With this the police officer put his hand in his pocket and drew out the nose, which was wrapped in paper.

"That's it!" Kovalyov cried. "That's certainly it. You must have a cup of tea with me this evening."

"I should look upon it as a great pleasure, but I can't possibly manage it: I have to go from here to the penitentiary...How the prices of all provisions are going up!... At home I have my mother-in-law, that is my wife's mother, and my children, the eldest particularly gives signs of great promise, he is a very intelligent child; but we have absolutely no means for his education..."

Kovalyov understood him perfectly and grabbed a red banknote from the table and put it in the hands of the officer, who shuffled about and then walked out, and at almost the same minute, Kovalyov heard his voice on the street, where he was knocking the teeth from a stupid *muzhik* who had driven his cart right on to the boulevard.

For some time after the policeman's departure the collegiate assessor remained in a state of bewilderment, and it was only a few minutes later that he was capable of feeling and understanding again: he was reduced to such stupefaction by this unexpected good fortune. He took the recovered nose carefully in his two hands, holding them together like a cup, and once more examined it attentively.

"Yes, that's it, it's certainly it," said Major Kovalyov. "There's the pimple that came out on the left side yesterday." The major almost laughed aloud with joy.

But nothing in this world is of long duration, and so his joy was not so great the next moment; and the moment after, it was still less, and in the end he passed imperceptibly into his ordinary frame of mind, just as a circle on the water caused by a falling stone gradually passes away into the unbroken smoothness of the surface. Kovalyov began to think, and reflected that the business was not finished yet; the nose was found, but it had to be put on, fixed in its proper place.

"And what if it won't stick?" Asking himself this question, the major turned pale.

With a feeling of irrepressible terror he rushed to the table and moved the looking-glass forward that he might not put the nose on crooked. His hands trembled. Cautiously and circumspectly he replaced it in its former position. Oh, horror, the nose would not stick on!... He put it to his lips, slightly warmed it with his breath, and again applied it to the flat space between his two cheeks; but nothing would make the nose keep on.

"Come, come, stick on, you fool!" he said to it; but the nose seemed made of wood and fell on the table with a strange sound as thought it were a cork. The major's face worked convulsively.

"Is it possible that it won't grow on again?" he kept saying in distress. But, however often he applied it to the proper place, the attempt was as unsuccessful as before.

He called Ivan and sent him for a doctor who tenanted the best flat on the first storey of the same house. The doctor was a handsome man, he had magnificent pitch-black whiskers, a fresh and healthy wife, ate fresh apples in the morning and kept his mouth extraordinarily clean, rinsing it out for nearly three-quarters of an hour every morning and cleaning his teeth with five different sorts of brushes. The doctor appeared immediately. Asking how long ago the trouble had occurred, he took Major Kovalyov by the chin and with his thumb gave him a flip on the spot where the nose had been, making the major jerk back his head so abruptly that he knocked the back of it against the wall. The doctor said that that did not matter, and, advising him to move a little away from the wall, he told him to bend his head round first to the right, and feeling the place where the nose had been, said, "Hm!" Then he told him to turn his head round to the left side and again said, "Hm!" And in conclusion he gave him again a flip with his thumb, so that Major Kovalyov threw up his head like a horse when his teeth are being looked at. After making this experiment the doctor shook his head and said: "No, it's impossible. You had better stay as you are, for it may be made much worse. Of course, it might be stuck on; I could stick it on for you at once, if you like; but I assure you it would be worse for you.'

"That's a nice thing to say! How can I stay without a nose?" said Kovalyov. "Things can't possibly be worse than now. It's simply beyond everything. Where can I show myself with such a caricature of a face? I have a good circle of acquaintants. Today, for instance, I ought to be at two evening parties. I know a great many people; Madame Tchehtarev, the wife of a civil councillor, Madame Podtatchin, an officer's widow…though after the way she has behaved, I'll have nothing more to do with her except through the police. Do me a favour," Kovalyov went on in a supplicating voice; "is there no means of sticking it on? Even if it were not neatly done, so long as it would keep on; I could even hold it up with my hand at critical moments. I don't dance, in any case, so there wouldn't be any rash movements could upset it. As for remuneration for your services, you may be assured that as far as my means allow…"

"Believe me," said the doctor, in a voice neither loud nor low but persuasive and magnetic, "that I never work from mercenary motives; that is opposed to my principles and my science. It is true that I accept a fee for my visits, but that is simply to avoid wounding my patients by refusing it. Of course I could replace your nose; but I assure you on my honour, since you do not believe my word, that it will be much worse for you. You had better wait for the action of nature itself. Wash it frequently with cold water, and I assure you that even without a nose you will be just as healthy as with one. And I advise you to put the nose in a bottle, in spirits or, better still, put two tablespoonfuls of sour vodka on it and heated vinegar—and then you might get quite a sum of money for it. I'd even take it myself, if you don't ask too much for it."

"No, no, I wouldn't sell it for anything," Major Kovalyov cried in despair. "I'd rather it were lost than that!"

"Excuse me!" said the doctor, bowing himself out, "I was trying to be of use to you…Well, there is nothing for it! Anyway, you see that I have done my best." Saying this, the doctor walked out of the room with a majestic air. Kovalyov did not notice his face, and, almost lost to consciousness, saw nothing but the cuffs of his clean and snow-white shirt peeping out from the sleeves of his black tail-coat.

Next day he decided, before lodging a complaint with the police, to write to Madame Podtatchin to see whether she would consent to return him what was needful without a struggle. The letter was as follows:

> Dear Madam Alexandra Grigoryevna—I cannot understand this strange conduct on your part. You may rest assured that you will gain nothing by what you have done, and you will not get a step nearer forcing me to marry your daughter. Believe me, that business in regard to my nose is no secret, no more than it is that you and no other are the person chiefly responsible. The sudden parting of the same from its natural position, its flight and masquerading, at one time in the form of a government clerk and finally in its own shape, is nothing else than the consequence of the sorceries practised by you or by those who are versed in the same honourable arts as you are. For my part I consider it my duty to warn you, if the above

mentioned nose is not in its proper place today, I shall be obliged to resort to the assistance and protection of the law.

I have, however, with complete respect to you, the honour to be

    Your respectful servant,

PLATON KOVALYOV

DEAR SIR, PLATON KUZMITCH!—Your letter greatly astonished me. I must frankly confess that I did not expect it, especially in regard to your unjust reproaches. I assure you I have never received the government clerk of whom you speak in my house, neither in masquerade nor in his own attire. It is true that Filipp Ivanovitch Potantchikov has been to see me, and although, indeed, he is asking me for my daughter's hand and is a well-conducted, sober man of great learning, I have never encouraged his hopes. You make some reference to your nose also. If you wish me to understand by that that you imagined that I meant to make a long nose at you, that is, to give you a formal refusal, I am surprised that you should speak of such a thing when, as you know perfectly well, I was quite of the opposite way of thinking, and if you are courting my daughter with a view to lawful matrimony I am ready to satisfy you immediately, seeing that has always been the object of my keenest desires, in the hope of which I remain always ready to be of service to you.

ALEXANDRA PODTATCHIN

"No," said Kovalyov to himself after reading the letter, "she really is not to blame. It's impossible. The letter is written as it could not be written by anyone guilty of a crime." The collegiate assessor was an expert on this subject, as he had been sent several times to the Caucasus to conduct investigations. "In what way, by what fate, has this happened? Only the devil could make it out!" he said at last, letting his hands fall to his sides.

Meanwhile, the rumours of this strange occurrence were spreading all over the town, and of course not without especial additions. Just at that time the minds of all were particularly interested in the marvellous: experiments in the influences of magnetism had been attracting public attention only recently. Moreover, the story of the dancing chairs in Konyushenny Street was still fresh, and so there is nothing to be surprised at in the fact that people were soon beginning to say that the nose of a collegiate asses-sor called Kovalyov was walking along Nevsky Prospect at exactly three in the afternoon. Numbers of inquisitive people flocked there every day. Somebody said that the nose was in Yunker's shop—and near Yunker's there was such a crowd and such a crush that the police were actually obliged to intervene. One speculator, a man of dignified appearance with whiskers, who used to sell all sorts of cakes and tarts at the doors of the theatres, made purposely some very strong wooden benches, which he offered to the curious to stand on, for eighty kopecks each. One very worthy colonel left home earlier on account of it, and with a great deal of trouble made his way through the crowd; but to his great indignation, instead of the nose, he saw in the shop-windows the usual woollen vest and a lithograph depicting a girl pulling up her stocking while a foppish young man, with a waistcoat with revers and a small beard, peeps at her from behind a tree; a picture which had been hanging in the same place for more than ten years. As he walked away he said with vexation: "How can people be led astray by such stupid and incredible stories!" Then rumour would have it that it was not on Nevsky Prospect but in the Tavritchesky Park that Major Kovalyov's nose took its walks abroad; that it had been there for ever so long; that, even when Hozrev-Mirza used to live there, he was greatly surprised at this strange freak of nature. Several students from the Academy of Surgery made their way to the park. One worthy lady of high rank wrote a letter to the superintendent of the park asking him to show her children this rare phenomenon with, if possible, an explanation that should be edifying and instructive for the young.

All the gentlemen who invariably attend social gatherings and like to amuse the ladies were extremely thankful for all these events, for their stock of anecdotes was completely exhausted. A small group of worthy and well-intentioned persons were greatly displeased. One gentleman said with indignation that he could not understand how in the present enlightened age people could spread abroad these absurd inventions, and that he was surprised that the government took no notice of it. This gentleman, as may be seen, belonged to the number of those who would like the government to meddle in everything, even in their daily quarrels with their wives. After this…but here again the whole adventure is lost in fog, and what happened afterwards is absolutely unknown.

III

WHAT IS UTTERLY nonsensical happens in the world. Sometimes there is not the slightest resemblance to truth about it: all at once, that very nose which had been driving about the place in the form of a civil councillor and had made such a store in the town, turned up again as though nothing had happened, in its proper place, that is, precisely between the two cheeks of Major Kovalyov. This took place on the seventh of April. Waking up and casually glancing into the looking-glass, he sees—his nose! He grabs it with his hands—it was actually his nose! "Aha!" said Kovalyov, and in his joy he almost danced a jig barefoot about his room; but the entrance of Ivan checked him. He ordered the latter to bring him water at once, and as he washed he glanced once more into the looking-glass—the nose! As he wiped himself with the towel he glanced again into the looking-glass—the nose!

"Look, Ivan, I fancy I have a pimple on my nose," he said, while he thought: "How dreadful if Ivan says, 'No, indeed, sir, there's no pimple and, indeed, there is no nose either!'"

But Ivan said: "There is nothing, there is no pimple: your nose is quite clear!"

"Good, dash it all!" the major said to himself, and he snapped his fingers.

At that moment Ivan Yakovlevitch the barber peeped in at the door, but as timidly as a cat who has just been beaten for stealing the bacon.

"Tell me first: are your hands clean?" Kovalyov shouted to him while he was still some way off.

"Yes."

"You are lying!"

"Upon my word, they are clean, sir."

"Well, mind now."

Kovalyov sat down, Ivan Yakovlevitch covered him up with a towel, and in one instant with the aid of his brushes had smothered the whole of his beard and part of his cheek in cream, like that which is served at merchants' name-day parties.

"My eye!" Ivan Yakovlevitch said to himself, glancing at the nose and then turning his customer's head on the other side and looking at it sideways. "There it is, sure enough. What can it mean?" He went on pondering, and for a long while he gazed at the nose. At last, lightly, with a cautiousness which may well be imagined, he raised two fingers to take it by the tip. Such was Ivan Yakovlevitch's system.

"Now, now, now, mind!" cried Kovalyov. Ivan Yakovlevitch let his hands drop, and was flustered and confused as he had never been confused before. At last he began circumspectly tickling him with the razor under his beard, and, although it was difficult and not at all handy for him to shave without holding on to the olfactory portion of the face, yet he did at last somehow, pressing his rough thumb into his cheek and lower jaw, overcome all difficulties, and finish shaving him.

When it was all over, Kovalyov at once made haste to dress, took a cab and drove to the confectioner's shop. Before he was inside the door he shouted, "Waiter, a cup of chocolate!" and at the same instant peeped at himself in the looking-glass. The nose was there. He turned round gaily and, with a satirical air, slightly screwing up his eyes, looked at two military men, one of whom had a nose hardly bigger than a waistcoat button. After that he set off for the office of the department, in which he was urging his claims to post as vice-governor or, failing that, the post of an executive clerk. After crossing the waiting-room he glanced at the mirror; the nose was there. Then he drove to see another collegiate assessor or major, who was much given to making fun of people, and to whom he often said in reply to various sharp observations: "There you are, I know you, you are as sharp as a pin!" On the way he thought: "If even the major does not split with laughter when he sees me, then it is a sure sign that everything is in its place." But the sarcastic collegiate assessor said nothing. "Good, good, dash it all!" Kovalyov thought to himself. On the way he met Madame Podtatchin with her daughter; he was profuse in his bows to them and was greeted with exclamations of delight—so there could be nothing amiss with him, he thought. He conversed with them for a long time and, taking out his snuffbox, purposely put a pinch to each nostril while he said to himself: "So much for you, you petticoats, you hens! But I am not going to marry your daughter all the same. Just simply *par amour*—I dare say!"

And from that time forth Major Kovalyov promenaded about, as though nothing had happened, on Nevsky Prospect, and at the theatres and everywhere. And the nose, too, as though nothing had happened, sat on his face without even a sign of coming off at the sides. And after this Major Kovalyov was always seen in a good humour, smiling, resolutely pursuing all the pretty ladies, and even on one occasion stopping before a shop in Gostiny Dvor and buying the ribbon of some order, I cannot say with what object, since he was not himself a cavalier of any order.

So this is the strange event that occurred in the Northern capital of our spacious empire! Only now, on thinking it all over, we perceive that there is a great deal that is improbable in it. Apart from the fact that it certainly is strange for a nose supernaturally to leave its place and to appear in various places in the guise of a civil councillor—how was it that Kovalyov did not grasp that he could not advertise about his nose in a newspaper office? I do not mean to say that I should think it too expensive to advertise: that is nonsense, and I am by no means a mercenary person: but it is unseemly, awkward, not nice! And again: how did the nose come into the loaf, and how about Ivan Yakovlevitch himself?... No, that I cannot understand, I am absolutely unable to understand it! But what is stranger, what is more incomprehensible than anything, is that authors can choose such subjects. I confess that is quite beyond my grasp, it really is...No, no! I cannot understand it at all. In the first place, it is absolutely without profit to the fatherland; in the second place...but in the second, too, there is no profit. I really do not know what to say of it...

And yet, with all that, though of course one may admit the first point, the second and the third...may even...but there, are there not inconsequences everywhere?—and yet, when you think it over, there really is something in it. Whatever anyone may say, such things do happen—not often, but they do happen.

THE OVERCOAT

IN THE DEPARTMENT of...but I had better not mention in what department. There is nothing in the world more readily moved to wrath than a department, a regiment, a government office, and in fact any sort of official body. Nowadays every private individual considers all society insulted in his person. I have been told that very lately a petition was handed in from a police captain of what town I don't recollect, and that in this petition he set forth clearly that the institutions of the State were in danger and that its sacred name was being taken in vain; and, in proof thereof, he appended to his petition an enormously long volume of some work of romance in which a police captain appeared on every tenth page, occasionally, indeed, in an intoxicated condition. And so, to avoid any unpleasantness, we had better call the department of which we are speaking a certain department.

And so, in a certain department there was a government clerk; a clerk of whom it cannot be said that he was very remarkable; he was short, somewhat pockmarked, with rather reddish hair and rather dim, bleary eyes, with a small bald patch on the top of his head, with wrinkles on both sides of his cheeks and the sort of complexion which is usually associated with haemorrhoids...no help for that, it is the Petersburg climate. As for his grade in the service (for among us the grade is what must be put first), he was what is called a perpetual titular councillor, a class at which, as we all know, various writers who indulge in the praiseworthy habit of attacking those who cannot defend themselves jeer and jibe to their hearts' content. This clerk's surname was Bashmatchkin. From the very name it is clear that it must have been derived from a shoe *(bashmak)*; but when and under what circumstances it was derived from a shoe, it is impossible to say. Both his father and his grandfather and even his brother-in-law, and all the Bashmatchkins without exception wore boots, which they simply resoled two or three times a year. His name was Akaky Akakyevitch. Perhaps it may strike the reader as a rather strange and far-fetched name, but I can assure him that it was not far-fetched at all, that the circumstances were such that it was quite out of the question to give him any other name. Akaky Akakyevitch was born towards nightfall, if my memory does not deceive me, on the twenty-third of March. His mother, the wife of a government clerk, a very good woman, made arrangements in due course to christen the child. She was still lying in bed, facing the door, while on her right hand stood the godfather, an excellent man called Ivan Ivanovitch Yeroshkin, one of the head clerks in the Senate, and the godmother, the wife of a police official, and a woman of rare qualities, Arina Semyonovna Byelobryushkov.

Three names were offered to the happy mother for selection—Moky, Sossy or the name of the martyr Hozdazat. "No," thought the poor lady, "they are all such names!" To satisfy her, they opened the calendar at another place, and the names which turned up were: Trifily, Dula, Varahasy. "What an infliction!" said the mother. "What names they all are! I really never heard such names. Varadat or Varuh would be bad enough, but Trifily and Varahasy!" They turned over another page and the names were: Pavsikahy and Vahtisy. "Well, I see," said the mother, "it is clear that it is his fate. Since that is how it is, he had better be called after his father, his father is Akaky, let the son be Akaky, too." This was how he came to be Akaky Akakyevitch. The baby was christened, and cried, and made wry faces during the ceremony, as though he foresaw that he would be a titular councillor. So that was how it all came to pass. We have recalled it here so that the reader may see for himself that it happened quite inevitably and that to give him any other name was out of the question. No one has been able to remember when and how long ago he entered the department, nor who gave him the job.

However many directors and higher officials of all sorts came and went, he was always seen in the same place, in the same position and at the very same duty, precisely the same copying clerk, so that they used to declare that he must have been born a copying clerk, in uniform all complete and with a bald patch on his head. No respect at all was shown him in the department.

The porters, far from getting up from their seats when he came in, took no more notice of him than if a simple fly had flown across the vestibule. His superiors treated him with a sort of domineering chilliness. The head clerk's assistant used to thrust papers under his nose without even saying,

"Copy this," or, "Here is an interesting, nice little case," or some agreeable remark of the sort, as is usually done in well-behaved offices. And he would take it, gazing only at the paper without looking to see who had put it there and whether he had the right to do so; he would take it and at once set to work to copy it. The young clerks jeered and made jokes at him to the best of their clerkly wit, and told before his face all sorts of stories of their own invention about him; they would say of his landlady, an old woman of seventy, that she beat him, would enquire when the wedding was to take place, and would scatter bits of paper on his head, calling them snow. Akaky Akakyevitch never answered a word, however, but behaved as though there were no one there. It had no influence on his work, even; in the midst of all this teasing, he never made a single mistake in his copying. Only when the jokes were too unbearable, when they jolted his arm and prevented him from going on with his work, he would bring out "Leave me alone! Why do you insult me?" and there was something strange in the words and in the voice in which they were uttered. There was a note in it of something that aroused compassion, so that one young man, new to the office, who, following the example of the rest, had allowed himself to mock at him, suddenly stopped as though cut to the heart, and from that time forth, everything was, as it were, changed and appeared in a different light to him. Some unnatural force seemed to push him away from the companions with whom he had become acquainted, accepting them as well-bred, polished people. And long afterwards, at moments of the greatest gaiety, the figure of the humble little clerk with a bald patch on his head rose before him with his heart-rending words, "Leave me alone! Why do you insult me?" and in those heart-rending words he heard others: "I am your brother." And the poor young man hid his face in his hands, and many times afterwards in his life he shuddered, seeing how much inhumanity there is in man, how much savage brutality lies hidden under refined, cultured politeness, and—my God!—even in a man whom the world accepts as a gentleman and a man of honour...

It would be hard to find a man who lived in his work as did Akaky Akakyevitch. To say that he was zealous in his work is not enough; no, he loved his work. In it, in that copying, he found a varied and agreeable world of his own. There was a look of enjoyment on his face; certain letters were favourites with him, and when he came to them he was delighted; he chuckled to himself and winked and moved his lips, so that it seemed as though every letter his pen was forming could be read in his face. If rewards had been given according to the measure of zeal in the service, he might to his amazement have even found himself a civil councillor; but all he gained in the service, as the wits, his fellow clerks, expressed it, was a buckle in his buttonhole and a pain in his back. It cannot be said, however, that no notice had ever been taken of him. One director, being a good-natured man and anxious to reward him for his long service, sent him something a little more important than his ordinary copying; he was instructed from a finished document to make some sort of report for another office; the work consisted only of altering the headings and in places changing the first person into the third. This cost him such an effort that it threw him into a regular perspiration: he mopped his brow and said at last, "No, better let me copy something." From that time forth they left him to go on copying forever. It seemed as though nothing in the world existed for him outside his copying. He gave no thought at all to his clothes; his uniform was—well, not green but some sort of rusty, muddy colour. His collar was very short and narrow, so that, although his neck was not particularly long, yet, standing out of the collar, it looked as immensely long as those of the plaster kittens that wag their heads and are carried about on trays by the dozen on the heads of foreign traders. And there were always things sticking to his uniform, either bits of hay or threads; moreover, he had a special art of passing under a window at the very moment when various rubbish was being flung out into the street, and so was continually carrying off bits of melon rind and similar litter on his hat. He had never once in his life noticed what was being done and going on in the streets, all those things at which, as we all know, his colleagues, the young clerks, always stare, carrying their sharp sight so far even as to notice anyone on the other side of the pavement with a trouser strap hanging loose—a detail which always calls forth a sly grin.

Whatever Akaky Akakyevitch looked at, he saw nothing anywhere but his clear, evenly written lines, and only perhaps when a horse's head suddenly appeared from nowhere just on his shoulder, and its nostrils blew a perfect gale upon his cheek, did he notice that he was not in the middle of his writing, but rather in the middle of the street.

On reaching home, he would sit down at once to the table, hurriedly sup his cabbage soup and eat a piece of beef with an onion; he did not notice the taste at all, but ate it all up together with the flies and anything else that Providence chanced to send him. When he felt that his stomach was beginning to stick out, he would rise up from the table, get out a bottle of ink and set to copying the papers he had brought home with him. When he had none to do, he would make a copy expressly for his own pleasure, particularly if the document were remarkable not for the beauty of its style but for the fact of its being addressed to some new or important personage.

Even at those hours when the grey Petersburg sky is completely overcast and the whole population of clerks have dined and eaten their fill, each as best he can, according to the salary he receives and his personal tastes; when they are all resting after the scratching of pens and bustle of the office, their own necessary work and other people's, and all the tasks that an over-zealous man voluntarily sets himself even beyond what is necessary; when the clerks are hastening to devote what is left of their time to pleasure; some more enterprising are flying to the theatre, others to the street to spend their leisure, staring at women's hats, some to spend the evening at a party paying compliments to some attractive girl, the star of a little official circle, while some—and this is the most frequent of all—go simply to a fellow clerk's flat on the third or fourth storey, two little rooms with an entry hall or a kitchen, with some pretensions to style, with a lamp or some such article that has cost many sacrifices of dinners and excursions—at the time when all the clerks are scattered about the little flats of their friends, playing a tempestuous game of whist, sipping tea out of glasses to the accompaniment of biscuits, sucking in smoke from long pipes, telling, as the cards are dealt, some scandal that has floated down from higher circles, a pleasure which the Russian can never by any possibility deny himself, or, when there is nothing better to talk about, repeating the everlasting anecdote of the commanding officer who was told that the tail had been cut off the horse on the Falconet monument—in short, even when everyone was eagerly seeking entertainment, Akaky Akakyevitch did not give himself up to any amusement. No one could say that they had ever seen him at an evening party. After working to his heart's content, he would go to bed, smiling at the thought of the next day and wondering what God would send him to copy.

So flowed on the peaceful life of a man who knew how to be content with his fate on a salary of four hundred roubles, and so perhaps it would have flowed on to extreme old age, had it not been for the various calamities that bestrew the path through life, not only of titular, but even of privy, actual court, and all other councillors, even those who neither give counsel to others nor accept it themselves.

There is in Petersburg a mighty foe for all who receive a salary of four hundred roubles or about that sum. That foe is none other than our northern frost, although it is said to be very good for the health. Between eight and nine in the morning, precisely at the hour when the streets are full of clerks going to their departments, the frost begins giving such sharp and stinging flips at all their noses indiscriminately that the poor fellows don't know how to hide them. At that time, when even those in the higher grade have a pain in their brows and tears in their eyes from the frost, the poor titular councillors are sometimes almost defenceless. Their only protection lies in running as fast as they can through five or six streets in a wretched, thin little overcoat and then stomping their feet thoroughly in the porter's room to warm them, till all their faculties and qualifications for their various duties thaw again after being frozen on the way. Akaky Akakyevitch had for some time been feeling that his back and shoulders were particularly nipped by the cold, although he did try to run the regular distance as fast as he could. He wondered at last whether there were any defects in his overcoat. After examining it thoroughly in the privacy of his home, he discovered that in two or three places, to wit on the back and the shoulders, it had become a regular sieve; the cloth was so worn that you could see through it and the lining was coming out. I must observe that Akaky Akakyevitch's overcoat had also served as a butt for the jibes of the clerks. It had even been deprived of the honourable name of overcoat and had been referred to as the "dressing-jacket." It was indeed of rather a strange cut. Its collar had been growing smaller year by year as it served to patch the other parts. The patches were not good specimens of the tailor's art, and they certainly looked clumsy and unappealing. On seeing what was wrong, Akaky Akakyevitch decided that he would have to take the overcoat to Petrovitch, a tailor who lived on a fourth storey up a back staircase, and, in spite of having only one eye and being pockmarked all over his face, was rather successful in repairing the trousers and coats of clerks and others—that is, when he was sober, be it understood, and had no other enterprise in his mind.

Of this tailor I ought not, of course, to say much, but since it is now the rule that the character of every person in a novel must be completely drawn, well, there is no help for it, here is Petrovitch too. At first he was called simply Grigory, and was a serf belonging to some gentleman or other. He began to be called Petrovitch from the time that he got his freedom and began to drink rather heavily on every holiday, at first only on the chief holidays, but afterwards on all church holidays indiscriminately, wherever there is a cross in the calendar. On that side he was true to the customs of his forefathers, and when he quarreled with his wife used to call her "a worldly woman and a German." Since we have now mentioned the wife, it will be necessary to say a few words about her too, but unfortunately not much is known about her, except indeed that Petrovitch had a wife and that she wore a cap and not a kerchief, but apparently she could not boast of beauty; anyway, none but soldiers of the Guards peeped under her cap when they met her, and they twitched their moustaches and gave vent to a rather peculiar sound.

As he climbed the stairs, leading to Petrovitch's—which, to do them justice, were all soaked with water and slops and saturated through and through with that smell of spirits which makes the eye smart, and is, as we all know, inseparable from the back stairs of Petersburg houses—Akaky Akakyevitch was already wondering how much Petrovitch would ask for the job, and inwardly resolving not to give more than two roubles. The door was open, for Petrovitch's wife was frying some fish and had so filled the kitchen with smoke that you could not even see the cockroaches. Akaky Akakyevitch crossed the kitchen unnoticed by the good woman, and walked at last into a room where he saw Petrovitch sitting on a big, wooden, unpainted table with his legs tucked under him like a Turkish pasha. The feet, as is usual with tailors when they sit at work, were bare; and the first object that caught Akaky Akakyevitch's eye was the big toe, with which he was already familiar, with a misshapen nail as thick and strong as the shell of a tortoise. Round Petrovitch's neck hung a skein of silk and another of thread and on his knees was a rag of some sort. He had for the last three minutes been trying to thread his needle, but could not get the thread into the eye and so was very angry with the darkness and indeed with the thread itself, muttering in an undertone "It won't go in, the savage! You wear me out, you rascal." Akaky Akakyevitch was vexed that he had come just at the minute when Petrovitch was in a bad humour; he liked to give him an order when he was a little "elevated," or, as his wife expressed it, "had fortified himself with home-brew, the one-eyed devil."

In such circumstances Petrovitch was as a rule very ready to give way and agree, and invariably bowed and thanked. Afterwards, it is true, his wife would come wailing that her husband had been drunk and so had asked too little, but adding a single ten-kopeck piece would settle that. But on this occasion Petrovitch was apparently sober and consequently curt, unwilling to bargain, and the devil knows what price he would be ready to lay on. Akaky Akakyevitch perceived this, and was, as the saying is, beating a retreat, but things had gone too far, for Petrovitch was screwing up his solitary eye very attentively at him and Akaky Akakyevitch involuntarily brought out: "Good day, Petrovitch!"

"I wish you a good day, sir," said Petrovitch, and squinted at Akaky Akakyevitch's hands, trying to discover what sort of goods he had brought. "Here I have come to you, Petrovitch, do you see…!"

It must be noticed that Akaky Akakyevitch for the most part explained himself by prepositions, adverbs and lexical items which have absolutely no significance whatsoever. If the subject were a very difficult one, it was his habit indeed to leave his sentences quite unfinished, so that very often after a sentence had begun with the words, "It really is, don't you know…" nothing at all would follow and he himself would be quite oblivious, supposing he had said all that was necessary.

"What is it?" said Petrovitch, and at the same time with his solitary eye he scrutinised the man's whole uniform from the collar to the sleeves, the back, the skirts, the buttonholes—with all of which he was very familiar as they were all his own work. Such scrutiny is habitual with tailors, it is the first thing they do on meeting one.

"It's like this, Petrovitch…the overcoat, the broadcloth…you see everywhere else it is quite strong; it's a little dusty and looks as though it were old, but it is new and it is only in one place just a little…on the back, and just a little worn on one shoulder and on this shoulder, too, a little…do you see? That's all, and it's not much work…" Petrovitch took the "dressing-jacket," first spread it out over the table, examined it for a long time, shook his head and put his hand out to the window for a round snuffbox with a portrait on the lid of some general—which precisely I can't say, for a finger had been thrust through the spot where a face should have been, and the hole had been pasted up with a square bit of paper.

After taking a pinch of snuff, Petrovitch held the "dressing-jacket" up in his hands and looked at it against the light, and again he shook his head; then he turned it with the lining upwards and once more shook his head; again he took off the lid with the general pasted up with paper and stuffed a pinch into his nose, shut the box, put it away and at last said: "No, it can't be repaired; a wretched garment!"

Akaky Akakyevitch's heart skipped a beat with these words.

"Why can't it, Petrovitch?" he said, almost in the imploring voice of a child. "Why, the only thing is it is a bit worn on the shoulders; why—you have got some little pieces…"

"Yes, the pieces will be found all right," said Petrovitch, "but it can't be patched, the stuff is quite rotten; if you put a needle in it, it would give way."

"Let it give way, but you just put a patch on it."

"There is nothing to put a patch on. There is nothing for it to hold on to; there is a great strain on it, it is not worth calling broadcloth, it would fly away at a breath of wind."

"Well, then, underpin it with something—upon my word, really, this is…!"

"No," said Petrovitch resolutely, "there is nothing to be done, the thing is no good at all. You had far better, when the cold winter weather comes, make yourself leg wrappings out of it, for there is no warmth in stockings, the Germans invented them just to make money." (Petrovitch was fond of a dig at the Germans occasionally.) "And as for the overcoat, it is clear that you will have to have a new one."

At the word "new" there was a mist before Akaky Akakyevitch's eyes, and everything in the room seemed muddled. He could see nothing clearly but the general with the piece of paper over his face on the lid of Petrovitch's snuffbox.

"A new one?" he said, still feeling as though he were in a dream. "Why, I haven't the money for it."

"Yes, a new one," Petrovitch repeated with barbarous composure.

"Well, and if I did have a new one, how much would it…"

"You mean what will it cost?"

"Yes."

"Well, three fifty-rouble notes or more," said Petrovitch, and he compressed his lips significantly. He was very fond of making an effect; he was fond of suddenly disconcerting a man completely and then squinting sideways to see what sort of a face he made.

"A hundred and fifty roubles for an overcoat," screamed poor Akaky Akakyevitch—it was perhaps the first time he had screamed in his life, for he was always distinguished by the softness of his voice.

"Yes," said Petrovitch, "and even then it's according to the coat. If I were to put marten on the collar, and add a hood with silk linings, it would come to two hundred."

"Petrovitch, please," said Akaky Akakyevitch in an imploring voice, not hearing and not trying to hear what Petrovitch said, and missing all his effects, "do repair it somehow, so that it will serve a little longer."

"No, that would be wasting work and spending money for nothing," said Petrovitch, and after that Akaky Akakyevitch went away completely crushed, and when he had gone, Petrovitch remained standing for a long time with his lips pursed up significantly before he took up his work again, feeling pleased that he had not demeaned himself nor lowered the dignity of the tailor's art.

When he got into the street, Akaky Akakyevitch was as though in a dream. "So that is how it is," he said to himself. "So the thing is, this is the thing…" And then after a pause he added, "So that's it! So, in the end, that's how it is! And I really could never have supposed it would have been so." There followed another long silence, after which he brought out: "So there it is! Well, it really is, exactly, utterly unexpected, that…it couldn't have… What a circumstance…"

Saying this, instead of going home he walked off in quite the opposite direction without suspecting what he was doing. On the way a clumsy sweep brushed the whole of his sooty side against him and blackened all his shoulder; a regular hatful of plaster scattered upon him from the top of a house that was being built. He noticed nothing of this, and only after he had jostled against a sentry who had set his halberd down beside him and was shaking some snuff out of his horn into his rough fist, he came to himself a little and then only because the sentry said, "Why are you poking yourself right in one's face, haven't you got the pavement to your-self?" This made him look round and turn homeward; only there did he begin to collect his thoughts, to see his position in a clear and true light and began talking to himself no longer incoherently but reasonably and openly as with a sensible friend with whom one can discuss the most intimate and vital matters. "No, indeed," said Akaky Akakyevitch, "it is no use talking to Petrovitch now; just now he really is…His wife must have been giving it to him. I had better go to him on Sunday morning; after the Saturday evening he will be squinting and sleepy, so he'll want a little drink to carry it off and his wife won't give him a penny. I'll slip ten kopecks into his hand and then he will be more accommodating and maybe take the overcoat…"

So reasoning with himself, Akaky Akakyevitch cheered up and waited until the next Sunday; then, seeing from a distance Petrovitch's wife leaving the house, he went straight in. Petrovitch was certainly squinting vigorously after the Saturday. He could hardly hold his head up and was very drowsy: but, for all that, as soon as he heard what he was speaking about, it seemed as though the devil had nudged him. "I can't," he said, "you must kindly order a new one." Akaky Akakyevitch at once slipped a ten-kopeck piece into his hand. "I thank you, sir, I will have just a drop to your health, but don't trouble yourself about the overcoat; it is not a bit of good for anything. I'll make you a fine new coat, you can trust me for that."

Akaky Akakyevitch would have said more about repairs, but Petrovitch, without listening, said: "A new one now I'll make you without fail; you can rely upon that, I'll do my best. It could even be like the fashion that has come in with the collar to button with silver claws under appliqué."

Then Akaky Akakyevitch saw that there was no escape from a new overcoat and he was utterly depressed. How indeed, for what, with what money could he get it? Of course, he could to some extent rely on the bonus for the coming holiday, but that money had long ago been appropriated and its use determined beforehand. It was needed for new trousers and to pay the cobbler an old debt for putting some new tops to some old boot-legs, and he had to order three shirts from a seamstress as well as two specimens of an undergarment which it is improper to mention in print; in short, all that money absolutely must be spent, and even if the director were to be so gracious as to assign him a gratuity of forty-five or even fifty, instead of forty roubles, there would be still left a mere trifle, which would be but as a drop in the ocean beside the fortune needed for an overcoat. Though, of course, he knew that Petrovitch had a strange craze for suddenly putting on the devil knows what enormous price, so that at times his own wife could not help crying out "Why, you are out of your wits, you idiot! Another time he'll undertake a job for nothing, and here the devil has bewitched him to ask more than he is worth himself!"—though, of course, he knew that Petrovitch would undertake to make it for eighty roubles; still, where would he get those eighty roubles? He might manage half of that sum; half of it could be found, perhaps even a little more; but where could he get the other half?... But, first of all, the reader ought to know where that first half was to be found. Akaky Akakyevitch had the habit every time he spent a rouble of putting aside two kopecks in a little locked-up box with a slit in the lid for slipping the money in.

At the end of every half-year he would inspect the pile of coppers there and change them for small silver. He had done this for a long time, and in the course of many years the sum had mounted up to forty roubles and so he had half the money in his hands, but where was he to get the other half—where was he to get another forty roubles? Akaky Akakyevitch pondered and pondered, and decided at last that he would have to diminish his ordinary expenses, at least for a year: chase away his need for tea in the evenings, give up burning candles in the evening, and if he had to do anything he must go into the landlady's room and work by her candle; that as he walked along the streets he must walk as lightly and carefully as possible, almost on tiptoe, on the cobbles and flagstones, so that his soles might last a little longer than usual; that he must send his linen to the wash less frequently, and that, to preserve it from being worn, he must take it off every day when he came home and sit in a thin cotton-shoddy dressing-gown, a very ancient garment which Time itself had spared. To tell the truth, he found it at first rather hard to get used to these privations, but after a while it became a habit and went smoothly enough—he even became quite accustomed to being hungry in the evening; on the other hand, he had spiritual nourishment, for he carried ever in his thoughts the idea of his future overcoat. His whole existence had in a sense become fuller, as though he had married, as though some other person was present with him, as though he were no longer alone, but an agreeable companion had consented to walk the path of life hand in hand with him, and that companion was no other than the new overcoat with its thick wadding and its strong, durable lining. He became, as it were, more animated, even more assertive, like a man who has set before himself a definite aim. Uncertainty, indecision, in fact all the hesitating and vague characteristics vanished from his face and his manners. At times there was a gleam in his eyes; indeed, the most bold and audacious ideas flashed through his mind. Why not really have marten on the collar? Meditation on the subject always made him absent-minded, On one occasion when he was copying a document, he very nearly made a mistake, so that he almost cried out "Ough!" aloud and crossed himself. At least once every month he went to Petrovitch to talk about the overcoat, where it would be best to buy the broadcloth, and what colour it should be, and what price, and, though he returned home a little anxious, he was always pleased at the thought that at last the time was at hand when everything would be bought and the overcoat would be made. Things moved even faster than he had anticipated.

Contrary to all expectations, the director bestowed on Akaky Akakyevitch a gratuity of no less than sixty roubles. Whether it was that he had an inkling that Akaky Akakyevitch needed a greatcoat, or whether it happened so by chance, owing to this he found he had twenty roubles extra. This circumstance hastened the course of affairs. Another two or three months of partial fasting and Akaky Akakyevitch had actually saved up nearly eighty roubles. His heart, as a rule very tranquil, began to throb. The very first day he set off in company with Petrovitch to the shops. They bought some very good broadcloth, and no wonder, since they had been thinking of it for more than six months before, and scarcely a month had passed without their going to the shop to compare prices; now Petrovitch himself declared that there was no better cloth to be had. For the lining they chose calico, but of a stout quality, which in Petrovitch's words was even better than silk, and actually as strong and handsome to look at. Marten they did not buy, because it certainly was dear, but instead they chose cat fur, the best to be found in the shop—cat which in the distance might almost be taken for marten. Petrovitch was busy over the coat for a whole fortnight, because there were a great many stitches needed, otherwise it would have been ready sooner. Petrovitch asked twelve roubles for the work; less than that it hardly could have been, everything was sewn with silk, with fine double seams, and Petrovitch went over every seam afterwards with his own teeth imprinting various figures with them. It was…it is hard to say precisely on what day, but probably on the most triumphant day of the life of Akaky Akakyevitch that Petrovitch at last brought the overcoat.

He brought it in the morning, just before it was time to set off for the department. The overcoat could not have arrived more in the nick of time, for rather sharp frosts were just beginning and seemed threatening to be even more severe. Petrovitch brought the greatcoat himself as a good tailor should. There was an expression of importance on his face, such as Akaky Akakyevitch had never seen there before. He seemed fully conscious of having completed a work of no little moment and of having shown in his own person the gulf that separates tailors who only put in linings and do repairs from those who make up new garments. He took the greatcoat out of the napkin in which he had brought it (the napkin had just come home from the wash); he then folded it up and put it in his pocket for future use. After taking out the overcoat, he looked at it with much pride and, holding it in both hands, threw it very deftly over Akaky Akakyevitch's shoulders, then pulled it down and smoothed it out behind with his hands; then draped it about Akaky Akakyevitch with somewhat jaunty carelessness.

The latter, as a man advanced in years, wished to try it with his arms in the sleeves. Petrovitch helped him to put it on, and it appeared that it looked splendid, too, with his arms in the sleeves. In fact it turned out that the overcoat was exactly a perfect fit. Petrovitch did not let slip the occasion for observing that it was only because he lived in a small street and had no signboard, and because he had known Akaky Akakyevitch so long, that he had done it so cheaply, but on Nevsky Prospect they would have asked him seventy-five roubles for the work alone. Akaky Akakyevitch had no inclination to discuss this with Petrovitch; besides, he was frightened of the big sums that Petrovitch was fond of flinging airily about in conversation. He paid him, thanked him and went off on the spot, with his new overcoat on, to the department. Petrovitch followed him out and stopped in the street, staring for a good time at the coat from a distance, and then purposely turned off and, taking a short cut by a side alley, ran into the street and got another view of the coat from the other side, that is, from the front.

Meanwhile Akaky Akakyevitch walked along with every emotion in its most holiday mood. He felt every second that he had a new overcoat on his shoulders, and several times he actually smirked from inward satisfaction. Indeed, it had two advantages: one that it was warm, and the other that it was good. He did not notice the way at all and found himself all at once at the department; in the porter's room he took off the overcoat, looked it over and put it in the porter's special care. I cannot tell how it happened, but all at once everyone in the department learned that Akaky Akakyevitch had a new overcoat and that the "dressing-jacket" no longer existed. They all ran out at once into the porter's room to look at Akaky Akakyevitch's new overcoat; they began welcoming him and congratulating him so that at first he could do nothing but smile and afterwards felt positively abashed. When, coming up to him, they all began saying that he must christen the new overcoat and that he ought at least to stand them all a supper, Akaky Akakyevitch lost his head completely and did not know what to do, how to get out of it, nor what to answer. A few minutes later, flushing crimson, he even began assuring them with great simplicity that it was not a new overcoat at all, that it was just nothing, that it was an old overcoat. At last one of the clerks—indeed, the assistant of the head clerk of the room—probably in order to show that he was not proud and was able to get on with those beneath him, said, "So be it, I'll give a party instead of Akaky Akakyevitch and invite you all to tea with me this evening; as luck would have it, it is my name-day." The clerks naturally congratulated the assistant of the head clerk and eagerly accepted the invitation. Akaky Akakyevitch was beginning to make excuses, but they all declared that it was uncivil of him, that it was simply a shame and a disgrace and that he could not possibly refuse. However, he felt pleased about it afterwards when he remembered that through this he would have the opportunity of going out in the evening, too, in his new overcoat.

That whole day was, for Akaky Akakyevitch, the most triumphant and festive day in his life. He returned home in the happiest frame of mind, took off the overcoat and hung it carefully on the wall, admiring the cloth and lining once more, and then pulled out his old "dressing-jacket," now completely coming to pieces, on purpose to compare them. He glanced at it and positively laughed, the difference was so immense! And long afterwards he went on laughing at dinner, as he recalled the position in which the "dressing-jacket" was placed. He dined in excellent spirits and after dinner wrote nothing, no papers at all, but just took his ease for a little while on his bed, till it got dark, then, without putting things off, he dressed, put on his overcoat, and went out into the street. Where precisely the clerk who had invited him lived we regret to say that we cannot tell; our memory is beginning to fail sadly, and everything there in Petersburg, all the streets and houses, are so blurred and muddled in our head that it is a very difficult business to put anything in orderly fashion. However that may have been, there is no doubt that the clerk lived in the better part of the town and consequently a very long distance from Akaky Akakyevitch. At first, the latter had to walk through deserted streets, scantily lit, but as he approached his destination the streets became more lively, more full of people, and more brightly lit; passers-by began to be more frequent; ladies began to appear, here and there, beautifully dressed; beaver collars were to be seen on the men. Cabmen with wooden trelliswork sledges, studded with gilt nails, were less frequently to be met; on the other hand, jaunty drivers in raspberry-coloured velvet caps with varnished sledges and bearskin rugs appeared, and carriages with decorated boxes dashed along the streets, their wheels crunching through the snow. Akaky Akakyevitch looked at all this as a novelty; for several years he had not gone out into the streets in the evening. He stopped with curiosity before a lit shop-window to look at a picture in which a beautiful woman was represented in the act of taking off her shoe and displaying as she did so the whole of a very shapely leg, while behind her back a gentleman with whiskers and a handsome imperial on his chin was putting his head in at the door. Akaky Akakyevitch shook his head and smiled, and then went on his way. Why did he smile? Was it because he had come across something quite unfamiliar to him, though every man retains some instinctive feeling on the subject, or was it that he reflected, like many other clerks, as follows: "Well, upon my soul, those Frenchmen! It's beyond anything! If they try anything of the sort, it really is…!" Though possibly he did not even think that; there is no creeping into a man's soul and finding out all that he thinks.

At last he reached the house in which the assistant of the head clerk lived in fine style; there was a lamp burning on the stairs, and the flat was on the second floor. As he went into the entry, Akaky Akakyevitch saw whole rows of galoshes. Amongst them in the middle of the room stood a samovar hissing and letting off clouds of steam. On the walls hung coats and cloaks, among which some actually had beaver collars or velvet revers. The other side of the wall there was noise and talk, which suddenly became clear and loud when the door opened and the footman came out with a tray full of empty glasses, a jug of cream and a basket of biscuits. It was evident that the clerks had arrived long before and had already drunk their first glass of tea. Akaky Akakyevitch, after hanging up his coat with his own hands, went into the room, and at the same moment there flashed before his eyes a vision of candles, clerks, pipes and card tables, together with the confused sounds of conversation rising up on all sides and the noise of moving chairs. He stopped very awkwardly in the middle of the room, looking about and trying to think what to do, but he was observed and received with a shout, and they all went at once into the entry and again took a look at his overcoat. Though Akaky Akakyevitch was somewhat embarrassed, yet, being a simple-hearted man, he could not help being pleased at seeing how they all admired his coat. Then of course they all abandoned him and his coat, and turned their attention as usual to the tables set for whist. All this—the noise, the talk, and the crowd of people—was strange to Akaky Akakyevitch. He simply did not know how to behave, what to do with his arms and legs and his whole figure; at last he sat down beside the players, looked at the cards, stared first at one and then at another of the faces, and in a little while began to yawn and felt that he was bored—especially as it was long past the time at which he usually went to bed. He tried to take leave of his hosts, but they would not let him go, saying that he absolutely must have a glass of champagne in honour of the new coat. An hour later supper was served, consisting of salad, cold veal, pasties, pies and tarts from the confectioner's, and champagne. They made Akaky Akakyevitch drink two glasses, after which he felt that things were much more cheerful, though he could not forget that it was twelve o'clock and that he ought to have been home long ago. That his host might not take it into his head to detain him, he slipped out of the room, hunted in the entry for his greatcoat, which he found, not without regret, lying on the floor, shook it, removed every last bit of fluff from it, put it on and went down the stairs into the street.

It was still light in the streets. Some little general shops, those perpetual clubs for house-serfs and all sorts of people, were open; others which were closed showed, however, a long streak of light at every crack of the door, proving that they were not yet deserted, and probably maids and menservants were still finishing their conversation and discussion, driving their masters to utter perplexity as to their whereabouts. Akaky Akakyevitch walked along in a cheerful state of mind; he was even on the point of running, goodness knows why, after a lady of some sort who passed by like lightning with every part of her frame in violent motion. He checked himself at once, however, and again walked along very gently, feeling positively surprised, himself, at the inexplicable impulse that had seized him. Soon the deserted streets, which are not particularly cheerful by day and even less so in the evening, stretched before him.

Now they were still more dead and deserted; the street lamps were scantier, the oil was evidently running low; then came wooden houses and fences; not a soul anywhere; only the snow gleamed on the streets and the low-pitched slumbering hovels looked black and gloomy with their closed shutters. He approached the spot where the street was intersected by an endless square, which looked like a fearful desert with houses scarcely visible on the further side. In the distance, goodness knows where, there was a gleam of light from some sentry-box which seemed to be standing at the end of the world. Akaky Akakyevitch's light-heartedness grew somehow sensibly less at this place. He stepped into the square, not without an involuntary uneasiness—as though his heart had a foreboding of evil. He looked behind him and to both sides—it was as though the sea were all round him. "No, better not look," he thought, and walked on, shutting his eyes, and when he opened them to see whether the end of the square were near, he suddenly saw standing before him, almost under his very nose, some men with moustaches; just what they were like he could not even distinguish. There was a mist before his eyes and a throbbing in his chest. "I say the overcoat is mine!" said one of them in a voice like a clap of thunder, seizing him by the collar. Akaky Akakyevitch was on the point of shouting "Help!" when another put a fist the size of a clerk's head against his very lips, saying, "You just shout now." Akaky Akakyevitch felt only that they took the overcoat off, and gave him a kick with their knees, and he fell on his face in the snow and was conscious of nothing more. A few minutes later he came to himself and got to his feet, but there was no one there. He felt that it was cold on the ground and that he had no overcoat, and began screaming, but it seemed as though his voice could not carry to the end of the square.

Overwhelmed with despair and continuing to scream, he ran across the square straight to the sentry-box, beside which stood a sentry leaning on his halberd and, so it seemed, looking with curiosity to see who the devil the man was who was screaming and running towards him from the distance. As Akaky Akakyevitch reached him, he began breathlessly shouting that he was asleep and not looking after his duty not to see that a man was being robbed. The sentry answered that he had seen nothing, that he had only seen him stopped in the middle of the square by two men, and supposed that they were his friends, and that, instead of abusing him for nothing, he had better go the next day to the superintendent and that he would find out who had taken the overcoat. Akaky Akakyevitch ran home in a terrible state: his hair, which was still comparatively abundant on his temples and the back of his head, was completely dishevelled; his sides and chest and his trousers were all covered with snow. When his old landlady heard a fearful knock at the door she jumped hurriedly out of bed and, with only one slipper on, ran to open it, modestly holding her shift across her bosom; but when she opened it she stepped back, seeing what a state Akaky Akakyevitch was in. When he told her what had happened, she clasped her hands in horror and said that he must go straight to the superintendent, that the police constable of the quarter would deceive him, make promises and lead him a dance; that it would be best of all to go to the superintendent, and that she knew him indeed, because Anna the Finnish girl who was once her cook was now in service as a nurse at the superintendent's, and that she often saw him himself when he passed by their house, and that he used to be every Sunday at church too, saying his prayers and at the same time looking good-humouredly at everyone, and that therefore by every token he must be a kind-hearted man. After listening to this advice, Akaky Akakyevitch made his way very gloomily to his room, and how he spent that night I leave to the imagination of those who are in the least able to picture the position of others. Early in the morning he set off to the police superintendent's, but was told that he was asleep. He came at ten o'clock, he was told again that he was asleep; he came at eleven and was told that the superintendent was not at home; he came at dinner-time, but the clerks in the anteroom would not let him in, and insisted on knowing what was the matter and what business had brought him and exactly what had happened; so that at last Akaky Akakyevitch for the first time in his life tried to show the strength of his character and said curtly that he must see the superintendent himself, that they dare not refuse to admit him, that he had come from the department on government business, and that if he made complaint of them they would see. The clerks dared say nothing to this, and one of them went to summon the superintendent. The latter received his story of being robbed of his overcoat in an extremely strange way.

Instead of attending to the main point, he began asking Akaky Akakyevitch questions. Why had he been coming home so late? Wasn't he going, or hadn't he been, to some house of ill-fame? Akaky Akakyevitch was overwhelmed with confusion, and went away without knowing whether or not the proper measures would be taken in regard to his overcoat. He was absent from the office all that day (the only time that it had happened in his life). Next day he appeared with a pale face, wearing his old "dressing-jacket," which had become a still more pitiful sight. The tidings of the theft of the overcoat—though there were clerks who did not let even this chance slip of jeering at Akaky Akakyevitch—touched many of them. They decided on the spot to get up a subscription for him, but collected only a very trifling sum, because the clerks had already spent a good deal on subscribing to the director's portrait and on the purchase of a book, at the suggestion of the head of their department, who was a friend of the author, and so the total realised was very insignificant. One of the clerks, moved by compassion, ventured at any rate to assist Akaky Akakyevitch with good advice, telling him not to go to the district police inspector, because, though it might happen that the latter might be sufficiently zealous of gaining the approval of his superiors to succeed in finding the overcoat, it would remain in the possession of the police unless he presented legal proofs that it belonged to him; he urged that far the best thing would be to appeal to a Person of Consequence; that the Person of Consequence, by writing and getting into communication with the proper authorities, could push the matter through more successfully. There was nothing else for it. Akaky Akakyevitch made up his mind to go to the Person of Consequence. What precisely was the nature of the functions of the Person of Consequence has remained a matter of uncertainty. It must be noted that this Person of Consequence had only lately become a person of consequence, and until recently had been a person of no consequence. Though, indeed, his position even now was not reckoned of consequence in comparison with others of still greater consequence. But there is always to be found a circle of persons to whom a person of little consequence in the eyes of others is a person of consequence. It is true that he did his utmost to increase the consequence of his position in various ways, for instance by insisting that his subordinates should come out on to the stairs to meet him when he arrived at his office; that no one should venture to approach him directly but all proceedings should be by the strictest order of precedence, that a collegiate registration clerk should report the matter to the provincial secretary, and the provincial secretary to the titular councillor or whomsoever it might be, and that business should only reach him by this channel. Everyone in Holy Russia has a craze for imitation, everyone apes and mimics his superiors.

I have actually been told that a titular councillor who was put in charge of a small separate office, immediately partitioned off a special room for himself, calling it the head office, and set special porters at the door with red collars and gold braid, who took hold of the handle of the door and opened it for everyone who went in, though the "head office" was so tiny that it was with difficulty that an ordinary writing-table could be squeezed into it. The manners and habits of the Person of Consequence were dignified and majestic, but not complex. The chief foundation of his system was strictness, "strictness, strictness, and—strictness!" he used to say, and at the last word he would look very significantly at the person he was addressing, though, indeed, he had no reason to do so, for the dozen clerks who made the whole administrative mechanism of his office stood in befitting awe of him; any clerk who saw him in the distance would leave his work and remain standing at attention till his superior had left the room. His conversation with his subordinates was usually marked by severity and almost confined to three phrases: "How dare you?"; "Do you know to whom you are speaking?"; "Do you understand who I am?" He was, however, at heart a good-natured man, pleasant and obliging with his colleagues; but the rank of general had completely turned his head. When he received it, he was perplexed, thrown off his balance, and quite at a loss how to behave. If he chanced to be with his equals, he was still quite a decent man, a very gentlemanly man, in fact, and in many ways even an intelligent man, but as soon as he was in company with men who were even one grade below him, there was simply no doing anything with him: he sat silent and his position excited compassion, the more so as he himself felt that he might have been spending his time to incomparably more advantage. At times there could be seen in his eyes an intense desire to join in some interesting conversation, but he was restrained by the doubt whether it would not be too much on his part, whether it would not be too great a familiarity and lowering of his dignity, and in consequence of these reflections he remained everlastingly in the same mute condition, only uttering from time to time monosyllabic sounds, and in this way he gained the reputation of being a very tiresome man.

So this was the Person of Consequence to whom our friend Akaky Akakyevitch appealed, and he appealed to him at a most unpropitious moment, very unfortunate for himself, though fortunate, indeed, for the Person of Consequence. The latter happened to be in his study, talking in the very best of spirits with an old friend of his childhood who had only just arrived and whom he had not seen for several years. It was at this moment that he was informed that a man called Bashmatchkin was asking to see him. He asked abruptly, "What sort of man is he?" and received the answer, "A government clerk."

"Ah! He can wait, I haven't time now," said the Person of Consequence. Here I must observe that this was a complete lie on the part of the Person of Consequence: he had time; his friend and he had long ago said all they had to say to each other, and their conversation had begun to be broken by very long pauses during which they merely slapped each other on the knee, saying, "So that's how things are, Ivan Abramovitch!"—"There it is, Stepan Varlamovitch!" but, for all that, he told the clerk to wait in order to show his friend, who had left the service years before and was living at home in the country, how long clerks had to wait in his anteroom. At last, after they had talked, or rather been silent to their hearts' content, and had smoked a cigar in very comfortable armchairs with sloping backs, he seemed suddenly to recollect, and said to the secretary, who was standing at the door with papers for his signature, "Oh, by the way, there is a clerk waiting, isn't there? Tell him he can come in." When he saw Akaky Akakyevitch's meek appearance and old uniform, he turned to him at once and said, "What do you want?" in a firm and abrupt voice, which he had purposely practised in his own room in solitude before the looking-glass for a week before receiving his present post and the rank of general. Akaky Akakyevitch, who was overwhelmed with befitting awe beforehand, was somewhat confused and, as far as his tongue would allow him, explained to the best of his powers, with even more frequent 'ers' than usual, that he had had a perfectly new overcoat and now he had been robbed of it in the most inhuman way, and that now he had come to beg him by his intervention either to correspond with his Honour the Head Police-Master or anybody else, and find the overcoat. This mode of proceeding struck the general for some reason as taking a great liberty. "What next, sir?" he went on as abruptly. "Don't you know the way to proceed? To whom are you addressing yourself? Don't you know how things are done? You ought first to have handed in a petition to the office; it would have gone to the head clerk of the room, and to the head clerk of the section, then it would have been handed to the secretary and the secretary would have brought it to me..."

"But, your Excellency," said Akaky Akakyevitch, trying to collect all the small allowance of presence of mind he possessed and feeling at the same time that he was getting into a terrible perspiration, "I ventured, your Excellency, to trouble you because secretaries...er...are people you can't depend on..."

"What? what? what?" said the Person of Consequence. "Where did you get hold of that spirit? Where did you pick up such ideas? What insubordination is spreading among young men against their superiors and betters!"

The Person of Consequence did not apparently observe that Akaky Akakyevitch was well over fifty, and therefore if he could have been called a young man it would only have been in comparison with a man of seventy. "Do you know to whom you are speaking? Do you understand who I am? Do you understand that, I ask you?" At this point he stamped, and raised his voice to such a powerful note that Akaky Akakyevitch would not have been alone in being terrified. Akaky Akakyevitch was positively petrified; he staggered, trembling all over, and could not stand; if the porters had not run up to support him, he would have flopped upon the floor; he was carried out almost unconscious. The Person of Consequence, pleased that the effect had surpassed his expectations and enchanted at the idea that his words could even deprive a man of consciousness, stole a sideways glance at his friend to see how he was taking it, and perceived not without satisfaction that his friend was feeling very uncertain and even beginning to be a little terrified himself. How he got downstairs, how he went out into the street—of all that Akaky Akakyevitch remembered nothing, he had no feeling in his arms or his legs. In all his life he had never been so severely reprimanded by a general, and this was by one of another department, too. He went out into the snowstorm, that was whistling through the streets, with his mouth open, and as he went he stumbled off the pavement; the wind, as its way is in Petersburg, blew upon him from all points of the compass and from every side street. In an instant it had blown a quinsy into his throat, and when he got home he was not able to utter a word; with a swollen face and throat he went to bed. So violent is sometimes the effect of a suitable reprimand!

Next day he was in a high fever. Thanks to the gracious assistance of the Petersburg climate, the disease made more rapid progress than could have been expected, and when the doctor came, after feeling his pulse he could find nothing to do but prescribe a fomentation, and that simply that the patient may not be left without the benefit of medical assistance; however, at the same time, he said that within two days the patient would be kaput, after which he turned to the landlady and said: "And you had better lose no time, my good woman, but order him now a pine coffin—an oak one will be too dear for him." Whether Akaky Akakyevitch heard these fateful words or not, whether they produced a shattering effect upon him, and whether he regretted his pitiful life, no one can tell, for he was all the time in delirium and fever.

Apparitions, each stranger than the one before, were continually haunting him: first, he saw Petrovitch and was ordering him to make a greatcoat trimmed with some sort of traps for robbers, who were, he fancied, continually under the bed, and he was calling his landlady every minute to pull out a thief who had even got under the quilt; then he kept asking why his old "dressing-jacket" was hanging before him when he had a new overcoat, then he fancied he was standing before the general listening to the appropriate reprimand and saying, "I am sorry, your Excellency," then finally he became abusive, uttering the most awful language, so that his old landlady positively crossed herself, having never heard anything of the kind from him before, and the more horrified because these dreadful words followed immediately upon the phrase "your Excellency." Later on, his talk was a mere medley of nonsense, so that it was quite unintelligible; all that could be seen was that his incoherent words and thoughts were concerned with nothing but the overcoat. At last poor Akaky Akakyevitch gave up the ghost. No seal was put upon his room nor upon his things, because, in the first place, he had no heirs and, in the second, the property left was very small, to wit: a bundle of goose-feathers, a quire of white government paper, three pairs of socks, two or three buttons that had come off his trousers, and the "dressing-jacket" with which the reader is already familiar. Who came into all this wealth God only knows; even I who tell the tale must own that I have not troubled to enquire. And Petersburg remained without Akaky Akakyevitch, as though, indeed, he had never been in the city. A creature had vanished and departed whose cause no one had championed, who was dear to no one, of interest to no one, who never even attracted the attention of the student of natural history, though the latter does not disdain to fix a common fly upon a pin and look at him under the microscope—a creature who bore patiently the jeers of the office and for no particular reason went to his grave, though even he at the very end of his life was visited by a gleam of brightness in the form of an overcoat that for one instant brought colour into his poor life—a creature on whom calamity broke as insufferably as it breaks upon the heads of the mighty ones of this world…! Several days after his death, the porter from the department was sent to his lodgings with instructions that he should go at once to the office, for his chief was asking for him; but the porter was obliged to return without him, explaining that he could not come, and to the enquiry "Why?" he added, "Well, you see: the fact is he is dead, he was buried three days ago." This was how they learned at the office of the death of Akaky Akakyevitch, and the next day there was sitting in his seat a new clerk who was very much taller and who wrote not in the same upright hand but made his letters more slanting and crooked.

But who could have imagined that this was not all there was to tell about Akaky Akakyevitch, that he was destined for a few days to make a noise in the world after his death, as though to make up for his life having been unnoticed by anyone? But so it happened, and our poor story unexpectedly finishes with a fantastic ending. Rumours were suddenly floating about Petersburg that in the neighbourhood of Kalinkin Bridge and for a little distance beyond, a corpse had taken to appearing at night in the form of a clerk looking for a stolen overcoat, and stripping from the shoulders of all passers-by, regardless of rank and calling, overcoats of all descriptions—trimmed with cat fur or beaver, or wadded, lined with raccoon, fox and bear—made, in fact, of all sorts of skin which men have adapted for the covering of their own. One of the clerks of the department saw the corpse with his own eyes and at once recognised it as Akaky Akakyevitch; but it excited in him such terror, however, that he ran away as fast as his legs could carry him and so could not get a very clear view of him, and only saw him hold up his finger threateningly in the distance. From all sides complaints were continually coming that backs and shoulders, not of mere titular councillors, but even of upper-court councillors, had been exposed to taking chills, owing to being stripped of their greatcoats. Orders were given to the police to catch the corpse regardless of trouble or expense, alive or dead, and to punish him in the cruellest way, as an example to others, and, indeed, they very nearly succeeded in doing so. The sentry of one district police station in Kiryushkin Place snatched a corpse by the collar on the spot of the crime in the very act of attempting to snatch a frieze overcoat from a retired musician, who used in his day to play the flute. Having caught him by the collar, he shouted until he had brought two other comrades, whom he charged to hold him while he felt just a minute in his boot to get out a snuffbox in order to revive his nose which had six times in his life been frostbitten, but the snuff was probably so strong that not even a dead man could stand it. The sentry had hardly had time to put his finger over his right nostril and draw up some snuff in the left when the corpse sneezed violently right into the eyes of all three. While they were putting their fists up to wipe them, the corpse completely vanished, so that they were not even sure whether he had actually been in their hands. From that time forward, the sentries conceived such a horror of the dead that they were even afraid to seize the living and confined themselves to shouting from the distance, "Hey, you there, be off!" and the dead clerk began to appear even on the other side of Kalinkin Bridge, rousing no little terror in all timid people. We have, however, quite deserted the Person of Consequence, who may in reality almost be said to be the cause of the fantastic ending of this perfectly true story.

To begin with, my duty requires me to do justice to the Person of Consequence by recording that soon after poor Akaky Akakyevitch had gone away crushed to powder, he felt something not unlike regret. Sympathy was a feeling not unknown to him; his heart was open to many kindly impulses, although his exalted grade very often prevented them from being shown. As soon as his friend had gone out of his study, he even began brooding over poor Akaky Akakyevitch, and from that time forward, he was almost every day haunted by the image of the poor clerk who had succumbed so completely to the befitting reprimand. The thought of the man so worried him that a week later he actually decided to send a clerk to find out how he was and whether he really could help him in any way. And when they brought him word that Akaky Akakyevitch had died suddenly in delirium and fever, it made a great impression on him, his conscience reproached him and he was in a bad mood all day. Anxious to distract his mind and to forget the unpleasant impression, he went to spend the evening with one of his friends, where he found a genteel company and, what was best of all, almost everyone was of the same grade so that he was able to be quite free from restraint. This had a wonderful effect on his spirits; he expanded, became affable and genial—in short, spent a very agreeable evening. At supper he drank a couple of glasses of champagne—a proceeding which we all know has a happy effect in inducing good humour. The champagne made him inclined to do something unusual, and he decided not to go home yet but to visit a lady of his acquaintance, one Karolina Ivanovna—a lady apparently of German extraction, for whom he entertained extremely friendly feelings. It must be noted that the Person of Consequence was a man no longer young, an excellent husband, and the respectable father of a family. He had two sons, one already serving in his office, and a nice-looking daughter of sixteen with a rather turned-up, pretty little nose, who used to come every morning to kiss his hand, saying: *"Bonjour,* Papa." His wife, who was still blooming and decidedly good-looking, indeed, used first to give him her hand to kiss and then would kiss his hand, turning it the other side upwards. But though the Person of Consequence was perfectly satisfied with the kind amenities of his domestic life, he thought it proper to have a lady friend in another quarter of the town. This lady friend was not a bit better looking nor younger than his wife, but these mysterious facts exist in the world and it is not our business to criticise them.

And so the Person of Consequence went downstairs, got into his sledge, and said to his coachman, "To Karolina Ivanovna," while, luxuriously wrapped in his warm fur coat, he remained in that agreeable frame of mind sweeter to a Russian than anything that could be invented; that is, when one thinks of nothing while thoughts come into the mind of themselves, one pleasanter than the other, without the labour of following them or looking for them. Full of satisfaction, he recalled all the amusing moments of the evening he had spent, all the phrases that had set the little circle laughing; many of them he repeated in an undertone and found them as amusing as before, and so, very naturally, chuckled very heartily at them again. From time to time, however, he was disturbed by a gust of wind which, blowing suddenly, God knows whence and wherefore, cut him in the face, pelting him with flakes of snow, puffing out his coat collar like a sack, or suddenly flinging it with unnatural force over his head and giving him endless trouble to extricate himself from it. All at once, the Person of Consequence felt that someone had clutched him very tightly by the collar. Turning round, he saw a short man in a shabby old uniform, and not without horror recognised him as Akaky Akakyevitch. The clerk's face was white as snow and looked like that of a corpse, but the horror of the Person of Consequence was beyond all bounds when he saw the mouth of the corpse distorted into speech and, breathing upon him the chill of the grave, it uttered the following words: "Ah, so here you are at last! At last I've…er… caught you by the collar. It's your overcoat I want, you refused to help me and abused me into the bargain! So now give me yours!" The poor Person of Consequence very nearly died. Resolute and determined as he was in his office and before subordinates in general, and though anyone looking at his manly air and figure would have said, "Oh, what a man of character!" yet in this plight he felt, like very many persons of athletic appearance, such terror that not without reason he began to be afraid he would have some sort of fit. He actually flung his overcoat off his shoulders as fast as he could and shouted to his coachman in a voice unlike his own, "Drive home and make haste!" The coachman, hearing the tone which he had only heard in critical moments and then accompanied by something even more rousing, hunched his shoulders up to his ears in case of worse following, swung his whip and flew on like an arrow. In a little over six minutes the Person of Consequence was at the entrance of his own house. Pale, panic-stricken, and without his overcoat, he arrived home, instead of at Karolina Ivanovna's, dragged himself to his own room and spent the night in great perturbation, so that next morning his daughter said to him at breakfast, "You look quite pale today, Papa," but her papa remained mute and said not a word to anyone of what had happened to him, where he had been, and where he had been going.

The incident made a great impression upon him. Indeed, it happened far more rarely that he said to his subordinates, "How dare you? Do you understand who I am?" and he never uttered those words at all until he had first heard all the rights of the case.

What was even more remarkable is that from that time the apparition of the dead clerk ceased entirely. Apparently the general's overcoat had fitted him perfectly; anyway, nothing more was heard of overcoats being snatched from anyone. Many restless and anxious people refused, however, to be pacified, and still maintained that in remote parts of the town the ghost of the dead clerk went on appearing. One sentry in Kolomna, for instance, saw with his own eyes a ghost appear from behind a house; but, being by natural constitution somewhat feeble—so much so that on one occasion an ordinary, mature piglet, making a sudden dash out of some building, knocked him off his feet to the vast entertainment of the cabmen standing round, from whom he exacted two kopecks each for snuff for such rudeness—he did not dare to stop it, and so followed it in the dark until the ghost suddenly looked round and, stopping, asked him, "What do you want?" displaying a fist such as you never see even among the living. The sentry said, "Nothing," and turned back on the spot. This ghost, however, was considerably taller and adorned with immense moustaches, and, directing its steps apparently towards Obuhov Bridge, vanished into the darkness of the night.

NIKOLAI GOGOL AND THE SCOURGE OF
NATIONAL IDENTITY
by Patrick Maxwell

Russian literature, like any great culture, is aware of its very greatness. Inside its grand pantheon lie a selection of the titans, the monoliths of
a golden age long past but fully enmeshed in the canon. Tolstoy, Dostoevsky,
Chekhov: our conceptions of them are defined, bound, by their inseparable
attachment to nationality. They are "the great Russians," the best chron-
iclers of the huge Empire in its decadent, fading magnitude and variety.

Nikolai Gogol has long been appropriated as the father of these towering
writers. When the Golden Age writers grew up, it was Gogol they learnt
from, Gogol's mix of the early surrealist and the socially realist that they
took to such lengths and depths in such works as *The Brothers Karamazov*
and *War and Peace*. Fierce reactionaries like Dostoevsky or the high-flown
aristocrats like Tolstoy described their country in such searching, all-en-
compassing terms because of what they had learnt from Gogol. For the
Russian radicals and proto revolutionaries who stalked the backstreets of
St. Petersburg, Gogol's turn to a beleaguered conservatism was a betrayal,
just as it was to Vissarion Belinsky when he wrote his epochal *Letter to
Gogol* in 1847. When he died at the age of forty-two five years later, having
burnt the second part of his most famous work and starved himself out
of existence with a beguilingly mysterious private life and eclectic corpus,
Gogol somehow secured his mythic status. Here was a crazed Russian
writer, preparing the way for his crazed successors.

But Gogol was Ukrainian, not Russian, and his descriptions of the great
Imperial power were written from Rome. His expropriation into that canon
of Russian greatness was a symptom of that very Imperial might, an aspect

of the canonization and acceptance that Gogol wanted in his own life, but which distorts the truth. Gogol was among the first to describe the Russian peasantry with sympathy, and to delve into the grisly realities of life for the Russian masses. Yet what Gogol was talking about—the places, the people, the culture—was not the same as Dostoevsky or Tolstoy. He often took his inspiration from Ukrainian culture—the culture of outposts and far-flung transport stations, lowly civil servants and town officials. The lives of the ordinary middle classes would be taken up by Gogol's successors, but their situations, their mindsets, were different. Dostoevsky went to the underground world of the cities for his tales, whereas Gogol speaks of the traveling merchants and upstart gentleman, unaware of their standing in society and yearning to establish themselves; very like Gogol himself.

When asked about his nationality, Gogol was evasive. He seemed happy to look at himself as a Ukrainian-Russian; gloriously hyphenated and contentedly cosmopolitan. Some of his first published stories, which made his name in the early 1830s, described small town life in Ukraine. Yet his greatest work—*Dead Souls*—catapulted him to the status of a prophet of Russian liberation, as if he was foretelling the 1861 liberation of the serfs. But then this was followed by his rift with Belinsky, fermented by a now-forgotten book in which Gogol defended Tsardom, autocracy, and the Orthodox Church. Anyone, it seems, could place Gogol anywhere that they liked.

"Gogol was a strange creature," wrote Vladimir Nabokov, "but then genius is always strange." If Nabokov became the late twentieth-century's spokesman for Russian literature in the West—which he probably was— then we should lend credence to such a description. Nabokov certainly strikes closer to the core of what Gogol meant to do and say than any nationalist appropriations: he was a "strange genius," for whom nationalism and political affiliation were but passing fits of intrigue. We would get a lot more out of Gogol's life and intentions to look at his work as purely literary before judging him on any nationalistic grounds.

Russia invaded Ukraine on 24 February 2022. President Vladimir Putin's troops pillaged and ravaged the very places that Gogol described with such humour, poignancy and horror almost two hundred years ago. It would be clichéd to say that the invasion was just as surreal as one of Gogol's stories. Yet in the face of murderous aggression, Russian culture of all forms became suspect. Orchestras cancelled performances of Tchaikovsky and visiting tours from Russia were cancelled. More reasonably, artists too close to the regime were ostracised. The infantile stupidity of brandishing all Russian culture under the same label only played into the hands of the tyrannical Putin, but also did a grave disservice to our conceptions of Russian culture. The damage done by the grotesque war will be felt in the West in our bookshelves and our reading choices, just as much as in the paintings we see and the music we now hear. What is "appropriate" is ready for sharp debate.

Gogol's debated nationality comes under greater scrutiny as the map changes and continent reacts. Here is a writer who displays the very same anxiety and weakness in the face of the same imperial strength. Here is someone whose greatest work was banned by the Russian censors before being later hailed as a masterwork of social realism. Here is someone who luxuriated in the nineteenth-century European Romantic movement while setting the groundwork for literary modernism in its starkest twentieth-century incarnation. Here is a writer who gloried in Pushkin's very Russian glory, but died young as well, having never been fully accepted, in the end, in literary circles. Our only serious way to read him now is to take a troubled genius at his word. Two centuries of readings on Gogol cannot obscure the authors' own perverse idiosyncrasy. Attempts to put him in a straitjacket will be as illusory as "The Overcoat," his greatest and most famous short story.

Yet Gogol was still a writer of his time, and an endlessly mysterious time it was too. After the fallout of the Napoleonic Wars, Russia was an imperial titan, able to stretch its muscle from Europe to the Pacific, and as far south as the British in India. Successive Tsars attempted reform and reaction with varied success, but generally maintained the strict religious autocracy and industrial malaise which had kept Russian stubbornly behind the rest of Europe for centuries. With this new power, the nation needed literature to herald the success. Dependence on translations of the great European works was a well-worn practice: the birth of the novel in Western Europe, which had occurred there a hundred years earlier, was bearing incipient fruit in the East. In the words of scholar Robert A. Maguire, "Russians had come to view literature…as a measure of national virility." In order to ensure that life was breathed into it, they needed writers who could be recognized as fitting into this new national mould. Since his first success, Gogol has struggled with that uncomfortable accommodation.

Yet his identity belies the truth of Gogol's reading public. In the decades after his death, the Russian reading public increased hugely. Rather than just the landed aristocracy with too much time on their hands (as described in *Dead Souls*), it was the middle-classes and peasantry who became aware of the great flowering in literature. The momentous works of the canon, it must be remembered, were published in segments, gradually sating the desire of the nationwide public before being shipped abroad in full. Peasant readers of Gogol in the 1880s and onwards came across his Ukrainian stories first—engaging tales such as "The Fair at Sorochinsti" and "A Terrible Vengeance." When *Dead Souls* was first released, some critics put Gogol's strange language techniques down to his Ukrainian heritage, or a lack of Russian understanding in language or custom. Stories like *"The Tale of How Ivan Ivanovich Quarreled with Ivan Nikiforovich"* and "The Viy" were equally popular with newer readers—cheaply available at market places for a few kopeks. *Dead Souls* was far too pricey; the only two of his more "canonic" works to reach the masses were "The Nose" and "The Overcoat." It is little surprise, then, that those two are the most well-known examples of Gogol's storytelling. *Dead Souls*, his greatest work, has been the property of Westerners and intellectuals to play with.

The only enduring truth to be learnt of Gogol, then, is that he cannot be categorised. Taxonomic expropriations do nothing as close to the truth as an honest reading of his greatest stories in their full, highly original surrealism and complexity. It is that—rather than the guns or fire of troops, the voices of the censor, and the distorting lens of nationalism—that does real service to his writer of unmistakable depth, genius, and brilliant mystery.

BIOGRAPHICAL TIMELINE

1809   Nikolai Vasilyevich Gogol is born on March 31, near Poltava, Ukraine, to Vasily Gogol-Yanovsky, a descendant of Ukrainian Cossacks of lower nobility. In his lifetime Gogol's father authors a number of theater pieces in Russian and in Ukrainian that are successfully staged by the famous theatre patron Dmitry Troshchinsky. Gogol's mother, Maria Ivanovna Gogol, is descended from Leonty Kosyarovsky, an officer of the Lubny Regiment of 1710. Her strict devotion to the Orthodox Church influences Gogol throughout his life.

1820–28 Attends high school in Nezhin and begins to write. Father dies in 1825.

        After finishing school in 1928, moves to St. Petersburg in hopes of entering the civil service. In an effort to earn money and to achieve fame as a poet, he funds the publication of a Romantic poem of German idyllic life, "Hans Küchelgarten." The poem is rejected by all the magazines to which he submits it. He vows never to write poetry again. He burns all remaining copies and considers emigrating to the United States. Instead, he uses money his mother sent for payment of the mortgage on her farm to tour Germany. After running out of money, returns to St. Petersburg and obtains a low-paying government post.

1831   The first volume of Gogol's Ukrainian stories, *Evenings on a Farm near Dikanka)* is published with immediate success and he becomes famous overnight. His writing earns the praise and attention of writers Aleksander Pushkin and Vasily Zhukovsky and the influential literary critic Vissarion Belinsky.

1832	The second volume of *Evenings on a Farm near Dikanka* is published.

1834   Gogol is made Professor of Medieval History at the University of St. Petersburg, in spite of his lack of qualifications for the position. He is completely unable to perform the job.

1835   Resigns his chair at the University of St. Petersburg.

Mirgorod, a two-volume collection of short stories and *Arabesques*, also a collection of short stories, are published. Important Russian editors and critics regard him as a regional Ukrainian writer whose works illustrate Ukrainian national character.

1836   By order of the emperor, Nicholas I, his comedy, *The Government Inspector*, is performed at the St. Petersburg State Theatre on April 19. (Gogol believes in a divinely inspired mission for both the House of Romanov and the Russian Orthodox Church.) The play, which lampoons bureaucratic corruption, is a triumph but also triggers fierce criticism from the reactionary press and officialdom. Russian critics reverse their views, reclassifying Gogol from a Ukrainian to a Russian writer.

For the next twelve years Gogol lives abroad, traveling through Germany and Switzerland and spending the winter of 1836–37 in Paris, among Russian ex-patriots and Polish exiles. He eventually settles in Rome where he studies art, Italian literature, and develops a passion for opera.

1842   *Dead Souls* is published in Moscow under the title imposed by censorship, *The Adventures of Chichikov*. The book cements his reputation as one of the greatest prose writers of the language. By this time, Vissarion Belinsky recognizes Gogol as the first Russian-language realist writer and head of the Natural School, a literary movement that includes the works of Ivan Turgenev and Fyodor Dostoevsky.

An edition of Gogol's collected works is published, which includes his most famous short story, "The Overcoat."

1847   Gogol comes under attack from Vissarion Belinsky for his defense of autocracy, serfdom and the Orthodox Church.

1848	Gogol returns to Russia after a pilgrimage to Jerusalem and visits the country's capitals and various Russian and Ukrainian friends. He increases his prayers and ascetic practices and comes under the influence of a fanatical Russian Orthodox priest, Father Matvey Konstantinovsky, who launches Gogol into a schedule of ritual torture, branded as "atonement."
1852	On the night of February 24, at the direction Father Matvey Konstantinovsky, Gogol burns some of his manuscripts, including the second part of *Dead Souls*. (Gogol intends *Dead Souls* to be a modern-day counterpart to Dante's *Divine Comedy*, which is composed of three parts: *Inferno*, *Purgatorio*, and *Paradiso*.) He then undertakes an extreme religious fast. Within days, his health broken, he dies on March 4. He is buried at the Danilov Monastery.
1931	Moscow authorities demolish Danilov Monastery and transfer Gogol's remains to Novodevichy Cemetery. His body is discovered lying face down, giving rise to the story that Gogol had been buried alive.

www.ingramcontent.com/pod-product-compliance
Lightning Source LLC
Chambersburg PA
CBHW020121180626
46812CB00006B/2690